# THE MILLS OF GOD

*Recent Titles by Deryn Lake from Severn House*

*The Apothecary John Rawlings Mysteries*

DEATH AND THE BLACK PYRAMID

# THE MILLS OF GOD

## Deryn Lake

This first world edition published 2010
in Great Britain and in the USA by
SEVERN HOUSE PUBLISHERS LTD of
9–15 High Street, Sutton, Surrey, England, SM1 1DF.
Trade paperback edition published
in Great Britain and the USA 2010 by
SEVERN HOUSE PUBLISHERS LTD

British Library Cataloguing in Publication Data

Lake, Deryn.
  The Mills of God.
  1. Police – England – Sussex – Fiction. 2. Vicars,
  Parochial – England – Sussex – Fiction. 3. Serial murder
  investigation – Fiction. 4. Detective and mystery stories.
  I. Title
  823.9'14-dc22

ISBN-13: 978-0-7278-6834-3    (cased)
ISBN-13: 978-1-84751-243-7    (trade paper)

*All Severn House titles are printed on acid-free paper.*

Severn House Publishers support The Forest Stewardship Council [FSC],
the leading international forest certification organisation. All our titles that
are printed on Greenpeace-approved FSC-certified paper carry the FSC logo.

**Mixed Sources**
Product group from well-managed
forests and other controlled sources
www.fsc.org  Cert no. SA-COC-1565
© 1996 Forest Stewardship Council

Typeset by Palimpsest Book Production Ltd.,
Grangemouth, Stirlingshire, Scotland.
Printed and bound in Great Britain by
MPG Books Ltd., Bodmin, Cornwall.

*For N.C.C. who was there when I desperately needed him*

# ACKNOWLEDGEMENTS

My grateful thanks are due to Inspector Paul Cave for all his help over police procedure. The mistakes are entirely mine!

And to Dr Wojciech Kasztura who somehow transformed into Dr Kasper Rudniski.

# ONE

I t was, thought Nick, peering through the windscreen of his somewhat battered red Peugeot, a very oddly shaped village. A High Street ran down the middle from which sprawled off, rather like the tributaries of a river, streets and alleyways going in all directions. To the north stood massively built Victorian houses, the former country homes of merchants and shop owners, now mostly divided into flats, though one or two still remained in the hands of the wealthy. There were a dozen or so of those and then the High Street proper began. Truly ancient houses lined it, all, Nick supposed, with a fascinating history. One in particular caught his eye, a massive Tudor building, heavily beamed on the exterior, now turned into a pub and called The Great House according to the sign which swung to and fro outside. Visions of a brimming pint flashed through Nick's mind which he firmly put away until later.

Opposite The Great House stood the beautiful church, lying back from the High Street, a few steps leading up to the path which went to its massive oak door. Much as he would have loved to have ventured inside, seeing it for the first time as *his* church, the place of which he had become the incumbent, Nick shelved the idea along with the pint. Ahead of him rumbled the removal van, driven all the way from Manchester this very day with himself following gamely behind. He had risen at five that morning and had been on the motorway more or less non-stop ever since. To Nick it felt as if his whole life had changed dramatically when he had finally pulled away from the run-down working-class parish where he had been acting as curate. Born in the south of England, he was now – at the age of twenty-eight – returning; returning to take up a new parish in Sussex, in the quaint and historic village of Lakehurst. With a smile which threatened to break into a broad grin, the Reverend Nicholas Lawrence headed for the vicarage.

The removal van had pulled up outside already and the team of four men had got out and were surreptitiously having a fag before the work of unloading began.

'All right, Reverend?' said the foreman, hiding his cigarette behind his back.

'Fine, thanks,' Nick answered. 'We made good time, didn't we.'

'Early start, Guv. It always pays. Now, have you got the keys?'

Nick looked stricken. 'No, but the churchwardens should be here any minute. I phoned Mrs Cox on my mobile when we stopped at Clacketts Lane.'

But even as he said the words the stick-thin figure of the lady in question, complete with an unbecoming felt hat, appeared and hurried up to Nick.

'Oh, Reverend Lawrence, I'm ever so sorry to be late. I just had to pop in on old Mrs Meadows and she does keep one talking so.' She smiled gaily at the removal men, who had hastily put out their fags and were now standing somewhat ill at ease. 'I'm sure you're all looking forward to a nice cup of tea. I've even brought the kettle.'

She rootled in the shopping basket she had over one arm and produced a bunch of keys, selected one, and opened the vicarage door.

'Welcome to your new home, Vicar,' she said, as Nick stepped forward into a house redolent with age, with charm, and with a sweet warm smell about it.

But he hardly had time to take it in because Mrs Cox was heading purposefully for the kitchen, pulling an electric kettle from her basket and saying, 'Who's for tea then?'

Nick, who only had tea without milk and preferred Lapsang Souchong, muttered a half-hearted sound of agreement and went through the house and out into the garden. It was beautiful. Roses tumbled everywhere, climbing the ancient brick wall and growing, richly and profusely, in the borders. There were other flowers too, fuchsias and dahlias adding their colour to the loveliness of late summer. Nick, with a sigh, realized that he was going to have to take up the spade to help keep the place looking as appealing as it did at the moment.

'Tea's ready,' called Mrs Cox from the kitchen and the vicar reluctantly went indoors.

Members of the gang who had been hauling furniture from the van and taking it into the rooms for which it had been labelled appeared and helped themselves to copious amounts of sugar. Nick was handed a milky cup of brown liquid with a pallid biscuit languishing in the saucer beside it. He thanked Mavis Cox politely and bit into the biscuit which had a sweet almondy taste that did not appeal to him.

'Are you a keen gardener, Vicar?' said Mavis gushingly.

'Well, I haven't been but I can see that I'm going to have to make a start.'

'Mrs Simpkins did a lot herself but I think Bert came in once a week to help her.'

'Oh, that would be useful. Would you mention me to him?'

'Of course I will. So you're not thinking of getting married, then? No young lady tucked away in the background?'

'So far, no.'

'Well, you might wed a nice village girl and please everybody.'

Nick went a little pale at the thought but continued to smile politely. He had lived with a cellist from the Manchester Philharmonic but she had left him after four years and gone off with a trumpeter. After that he had been ordained, had another girlfriend who had proposed to him before they had split up, and then, still single, he had been noticed by Bishop Claude and been granted his first parish. It was a great honour at the age of twenty-eight. And it had been a some-what unusual choice. And for Nick himself it was the turning point of his life.

He took a mouthful of the cold tea, forced himself to swallow, then while Mavis's back was turned emptied the contents out of the window.

She turned on him a gleaming smile. 'Another cuppa? My old mum always used to say it was a life-saver. In fact she had just finished a cup when she passed away, bless her.'

Nick thought this remark rather contradictory but giving another of his extremely appealing smiles he shook his head.

'Thank you, but no. I really have had enough.'

'You're sure?' She looked round the room but the four

removal men were already getting back to work. Nick was just going to give them a hand with the chests when a modulated voice called clearly from the hallway.

'Anyone at home?'

The vicar made his way to the front door to see a vision of yesteryear. A matinee idol, circa 1950, stood there. Dark hair swept back immaculately, very bright and twinkling blue eyes, a thin and small moustache, a dazzling smile, all combined to leave a lasting impression on whoever he was meeting.

'How very nice to see you again, sir,' Nick said, holding out his hand. The other shook it firmly and warmly.

'So glad you made the journey without disaster,' Richard Culpepper said. 'Let us hope that this is the start of a long and satisfactory relationship. Both for myself and Lakehurst.'

'Well yes, indeed,' Nick answered, somewhat surprised.

'I would have called earlier,' Culpepper continued, 'but I have just returned from the studios.'

'Ah,' replied the vicar, thinking it sounded very Hollywood.

'Yes, I was filming a commercial.' Culpepper pulled a face. 'Frightful stuff really but it does help to keep the money rolling in.'

'Oh yes, I'm sure it does.'

'I started my career in the West End of London, you know, but things are so hard these days that I try to get work where and when I can.' He gave a vivacious laugh.

Nick smiled sympathetically.

Culpepper went on. 'What I basically need is a part in a soap. Something to brighten the old bank balance. That would suit me down to the ground.'

The actor opened his mouth to continue but at that moment Mavis Cox reappeared.

'Now is there anything else I can help you with, Vicar?'

'No, thank you, really. I'll be perfectly all right.'

'Well, I'll be on my way.' She gave Culpepper a smile that was merely a twitch of the lower part of her face.

'As I was explaining to the Reverend . . .'

Nick interrupted. 'Please call me Nick.'

'I don't think that would be quite suitable,' said Mavis, putting on a pious face. 'I must address you in some correct way.'

'How about Father Nick?' This from Culpepper.

'Sounds good to me,' said the vicar.

Culpepper cleared his throat. 'Very well. I shall put the word about amongst the parishioners.'

'Give my regards to Mrs Culpepper,' said Mavis waspishly.

'Of course I will. She'll be delighted.'

'Goodbye Father Nick. Just ring if you need me.'

Mavis turned and spied a neighbour across the road who glanced very curiously at the new vicar. Nick hastily bade farewell to Richard Culpepper and going into the vicarage, firmly shut the door.

The atmosphere of the beautiful old house overwhelmed him. It had about it a feeling of centuries of care, of generations of children born and brought up in it, of many people professing their simple faith, that God was good and kind and all was well with the world. On top of all this it had a superb smell; of ancient furniture polish, of flowers, of lovely and well-loved wood.

Reluctantly Nick ended his reverie and proceeded to help the men with the boxes.

Three hours later it was all done. The vicar's simple furniture – other than for those precious antiques that his mother had left him – had been unloaded and placed in the right rooms. The bed had been made, a piece of maternal advice which Nick had always obeyed, the boxes – though still packed – stood in the right rooms. It was time, Nick thought, to have that pint.

He left the vicarage, locking the door behind him, and felt a strange sense of pride that the place was his. Directly across the road stood the church and even though he had seen it before on his several visits to Lakehurst, he now longed to have a brief look round. Shelving the idea of the pint for another thirty minutes, he climbed the steps and made his way up the path to the great oak door.

Inside it was shadowy. The time was now seven p.m. and the month late September. A rather unpleasant statue of St Catherine looking extremely pious stood on a shelf staring sightlessly at the crowds arriving in church. Hopefully! Nick pushed the door to behind him and stood gazing at the east window in awe. A magnificent portrayal of Christ seated in

heaven surrounded by various angels and mortals dominated
the scene. Slowly Nick made his way up the aisle towards
it. And then he stopped. Somebody not far away was whispering prayers rather loudly. Slightly embarrassed, the vicar
stood still, waiting for them to stop. Which they did, quite
suddenly and shockingly.

The person praying, realizing they were not alone, suddenly
scrambled to their feet and made off down one of the side
aisles, threw open the oak door and crashed out into the
night. Somewhat startled Nick knelt before the great altar
wondering who on earth it could have been. Eventually,
having looked round, his visit somewhat spoiled by the
strange behaviour he had just witnessed, he went out the
same way, this time carefully locking the church door behind
him, and crossed the road.

The Great House entirely lived up to its name, being as
heavily beamed within as it was out. A huge oak bar stood
in the heart of it and Nick, aware of several pairs of eyes
following his every move, made his way towards it.

'What can I get you?' asked a dark young man, without
smiling.

Nick, very aware that he was still wearing jeans and a
tee-shirt and had still not put on his dog collar, said, 'A pint
of Harvey's please.'

'That will be . . .'

But a voice with a strong Sussex burr said, 'No, I'll get
that if you've no objection.'

Nick looked round into a craggy face with a pair of sky
blue eyes crowned by an aureole of brilliant red hair.

'Well thank you very much,' he said.

'It will be my pleasure, Vicar.'

Wondering how on earth the man knew, dressed as he was
in jeans and casual shirt, Nick raised his glass.

'Well, thank you very much, Mr . . .?'

'Fielding. Giles Fielding. Nice to meet you, Vicar.'

'How did you know? That I'm a vicar, I mean.'

Giles laughed, an amusing sound. 'Truth to tell, Mr
Lawrence . . .'

'Call me Nick.'

'Right you are. Well, you see, in this village of Lakehurst

everyone knows what you're doing before you've even done it.'

'A hotbed of gossip, is it?'

'I'd say. Old Mrs Weaver in the post office is queen bee. People used to write messages for her on postcards because they knew she'd read 'em.'

Nick laughed. 'I get the picture. I see I shall have to watch my step.'

'You'll be meat and drink to them. Unmarried, young. They'll have you courting every spinster in the parish – including the old ones.'

The vicar lowered his voice. 'Tell me about the people in here. Are they regulars?'

'Most of 'em.'

'Who's that chap sitting in the corner with his back to us, avidly studying the *Daily Telegraph*?'

'That be Jack Boggis. He's parish clerk. Bit of an old misery but his heart's in the right place – at least I think it is.'

'Does he go to church?'

'Never sets foot in the place.'

Nick sighed. 'Oh dear.'

Giles looked sad. 'No more do I. I'm sorry, Father Nick. I've too much to do looking after the animals.'

'I take it you farm.'

'Yes, I do. Up at Speckled Wood. Sheep mostly. You must come up and have a look.'

'Thank you. Yes, I'd like to. And who's that younger man holding forth rather noisily.'

'That's Phil Webster. He's the local solicitor. Bit of a card but they say he be mighty powerful in court.'

'And the chap with the hook nose and the thin face?'

'Oh that's old Gerrard Riddell. I think he's bent.'

'Do you mean he's a crook?'

'No, bent, a pouffe. He's very artistic, so he keeps telling us all. Lives alone in one of the little cottages down West Street. Has friends for the weekend.'

Giles said this last with such an amazing amount of expression that Nick found himself grinning broadly.

'Now, he will go to church,' the farmer continued. 'Every Sunday, regular as clockwork. Stands near the front and sings the hymns very loudly. He's under the impression that he's got a good voice and nobody has the heart to tell him that it's buggered to bits.'

Nick chortled aloud. He liked Giles Fielding, thought him down to earth and straight-talking. 'Let me get you a pint,' he said.

'Don't mind if I do,' the farmer answered cheerfully.

It was a pleasant evening. The pub was outstanding because of its historic past and the vicar had enjoyed sitting at the bar and chatting with somebody friendly. During the time he was there he had been spoken to by Jack Boggis who had said, 'Good evening. I'm the parish clerk,' in a broad Yorkshire accent.

'Good evening to you. As you probably know I am the new vicar.'

Jack had supped his ale even while he was paying for it.

'Yes, I had heard. Well, I hope you'll be happy here.'

'Thank you very much. I hope so too.'

Jack had nodded, somewhat tersely, and gone back to his solitary chair where he had picked up the *Daily Telegraph* and buried his nose in it.

Nick had looked at Giles. 'Well, my friend, I think I must be getting back. It's been a great pleasure to meet you.'

'Likewise, Father Nick. Come up and inspect the farm some time.'

'I certainly will when I've settled down.'

He strolled back to the vicarage and felt a moment's thrill when he let himself in with the front door key. Inside the house was still and dark, but friendly and welcoming. Nick climbed the stairs and as he reached the half landing thought for a second that he saw the outline of a man standing at the top.

'Who's there?' he called.

But there was only silence and Nick was glad to go into his room and get into bed, leaving his window open so that the smells of the flowers filled the air.

# TWO

The next morning Nick rose punctually at seven and spent two hours unpacking boxes, then feeling like some fresh air, he put on a pair of respectable trousers, a shirt and jacket and his dog collar, and stepped out of the front door.

He decided to visit the church last of all, his grand finale, but making up his mind to walk on the sunny side he crossed the road. He was aware of a woman in the window of the post office, a large pair of pink-rimmed glasses beaming like searchlights in his direction, and then the door flew open and what could only be old Mrs Weaver bore down on him.

'Oh, Vicar, it's nice to meet you. I'm Mabel Weaver. I work here.'

All this was said in a breathless whisper and Nick hazarded a guess that she had been hanging round the window for the last two hours, longing to get a glimpse of him. He held out his hand.

'How do you do, Mrs Weaver.'

She took it and he felt a large, moist palm.

'Such a thrill to get someone young in the parish. The last vicar – dear old man, we were all so sorry to see him go – was quite withdrawn, you know. Not from his duties, you understand, but socially. He had his own circle of friends and that was it. He came to see everything, of course, but never joined in.'

Wise man, thought Nick, but did not say anything.

'I hear that there is no Mrs Lawrence,' Mabel continued. 'But Lakehurst has a reputation for courting couples, you know.' She laughed loudly and archly and wagged a finger at him.

Nick inwardly shuddered but kept smiling bravely.

'Well, it's been a pleasure to meet you,' he said.

'Likewise, Vicar, likewise. I shall see you on Sunday no doubt.'

'No doubt.' He gave her a small, courtly bow and continued on his way.

The village, though of the most peculiar shape, was for all that attractive. The High Street ended in two roads, one sweeping away towards the nearest town, the other going steeply downhill. Here lay the truly ancient cottages. On either side of the road they clustered, their small front gardens rich with roses and creepers. One of them clearly had a hidden cellar and Nick wondered at once about the history of smuggling in this area. Admittedly the village lay inland but that did not necessarily preclude it from having been involved. Another was shaped like a ship, heavily weatherboarded on the outside and leaning very slightly. Despite himself Nick paused to have a better look. The front door flew open.

'Cooee,' called a voice. 'I say, Vicar, cooee.'

A woman was advancing down the path, a woman who could have stepped straight out of the fifties. She wore a dirndl skirt and sandals and had on a strange white blouse covered with a hand-crocheted shawl.

She stopped. 'You are the new vicar, aren't you? I haven't made an utter idiot of myself?'

'No, no. You're quite right. I'm Nicholas Lawrence. I arrived yesterday.'

She clasped her hands together ecstatically. 'I'm so pleased. I'm always mistaking people for other people, you know. Silly habit of mine. Passing of the years I daresay. Do come in and have a cup of tea – or coffee if you prefer. Or I have some elderflower wine. I went gathering in at harvest time.'

Nick stood irresolutely, changing his weight from foot to foot. 'Well, I . . . er. I'm not officially on parish visits yet.'

'Oh dear. And there was me hoping for a little company.'

Eyes like great saucers looked melancholy behind their heavy horn rims and the vicar's better nature won.

'I can spare a quarter of an hour,' he said.

'Oh goody.' Both sandalled feet left the ground as she jumped in the air and clapped her hands. 'How nice. Now enter, do.'

The house inside could have been lovely but instead was an altar to tweeness. Little framed poems hung on the walls, together with pressed flowers and cut-outs of rather malicious-looking children in jolly seaside romping gear. His hostess, watching the direction of the vicar's eyes, said, 'Ah, you like poetry I see. Now, what will it be to drink?'

'I think just a small black coffee, please.'

'Of course, of course. Now forgive me for a moment or two.'

She bustled off through a door with a porcelain plaque on it saying 'Kitchen' where she could be heard banging about. Nick peered at the poems and saw that other than the usual things like 'Don't Give Up' and 'If' there were several with titles such as 'Picking Blackberries in Late Summer with Adrian' and 'Missing Train at Mdina Once More.'

His hostess popped her head round the kitchen door. 'Sugar, Vicar?'

'No, thank you. Do you write poetry yourself?'

She pulled a face. 'Ah, my secret is out. Yes, I am a poet.'

'Really? Have you had a lot published?'

'Oh yes. Several collections.

'Who are your publishers?'

She looked a little vague. 'A very nice firm in Eastbourne.'

She disappeared again and came back with a tray which depicted a cat playing with several kittens and a ball of wool. Balanced on this were two mugs of coffee and the same pallid biscuits that Mavis Cox had brought to the vicarage. Wondering if they were a sweetmeat beloved of the citizens of Lakehurst, Nick balanced on the edge of a chair, declined the biscuit and took the mug proffered him. He jumped as his hostess leapt in the air once more.

'Oh please, whatever will you think of me, Vicar? I haven't introduced myself. I am Ceinwen Carruthers.'

Nick, who had a mug of coffee half way to his mouth, put it down again.

'How do you do. As I've already said, I am Nick Lawrence.'

Ceinwen sat down again in a whirl of dirndl skirt which revealed hairy legs shaped like inverted milk bottles.

'And how are you liking the vicarage?'

'It's a lovely house, really old and comfortable. At least I think it will be when I can get all my boxes unpacked.'

Ceinwen neighed a laugh. 'Oh, those dreadful things. Everyone's nightmare. If I can help you . . .'

'No,' Nick answered hastily, 'really, I can manage. I've set myself a target of so many a day.' He sipped his coffee.

'I went to the vicarage once. Mrs Simpkins asked me to tea. She was interested in my poetry.'

'As am I,' the vicar answered gallantly.

Ceinwen simpered a little. 'I've had three collections published and many, many poems published in poetry magazines. I am what you might call moderately successful.'

'How interesting. Did you write these?'

He indicated the framed odes on the wall. Ceinwen looked modest.

'They are some of mine, yes. You see I take inspiration from nature, from places I visit, from flora and fauna and forestry. I have founded a local group, here, in Lakehurst. We call ourselves the Pixie Poets.'

'What an unusual name.'

'Yes, but some of us believe in the wee folk. But enough of that. I hope that you will live long and prosper – as they say on *Star Trek* – in our village.' Ceinwen suddenly glanced at her watch – an old fashioned little gold one – and said, 'Oh my, is that the time. I'm afraid I must fly. I'm meeting someone –' she blushed – 'in ten minutes.'

Realizing he was dismissed Nick put down his mug and stood up. 'Well, thank you so much for inviting me in, Miss Carruthers. It has been most interesting.'

'Anytime, my dear Vicar. Please call again.'

'Thank you.'

He gave her his odd little courtly bow and proceeded down the path.

Arrow Street bent round to the left, its junction marked by an ancient pub called The White Hart which was just opening its doors. Nick popped inside to answer a call from nature and then ordered an orange juice, having made a promise to himself not to drink till after six except in exceptional circumstances. The place was empty but there was a bored-looking barmaid with very long red finger-nails and a short black skirt.

She plonked the glass down on the bar and said, 'One pound, twenty-five, please,' in a pronounced south-east accent.

Nick fished in his pocket and produced the right change.

The girl checked it in her hand. 'Thank you,' she said, and banged it into the till.

'A nice day,' ventured Nick.

'Yeah.'

'Can you tell me where this road leads to?'

'It goes off to Speckled Wood.'

'And the one ahead? Where does that go?'

The girl gave him a curious glance from kohl-ringed eyes. 'You're the new vicar, aren't you?'

'Yes. How did you know?'

'Me gran told me you had arrived. Yesterday, wasn't it? And me brother saw you last night in The Great House.'

'Gracious, I didn't realize I was so famous.'

The girl gave a sly grin and said, 'Everybody knows everything that goes on in Lakehurst.'

'I see. Well I'm just walking round the parish now so where does the road in front go?'

'It's South Street. But off it on the right is the posh place.'

'What do you mean?'

'It's called The Maze. That's where all the rich people hang out. It's full of private houses. My gran calls it Nob's Row.'

Nick was just about to ask another question when a voice from the back bellowed, 'Kylie, you're wanted,' and the barmaid vanished without another word.

Finishing his juice, Nick went outside and breathed in the morning. The air was quite literally scented by the many roses which bloomed in the tiny front gardens of South Street. And the view itself was crystal clear; he felt he could see a leaf drop a mile away. Deciding that to visit Nob's Row at this stage would take up too much of the morning, Nick turned around, crossed the road, and started the steep climb back to the vicarage.

The phone was ringing as he came through the front door. He hastily picked it up. It was a woman's voice that spoke.

'Hello, is that the Reverend Lawrence?'

'Speaking.'

'Oh hello. My name is Olivia Beauchamp. I wondered if I could pop in and see you. It's about the recital.'

'Of course you can come but I'm afraid you've lost me. I don't know anything about a recital.'

She laughed quietly, a warm and pleasing sound. 'No, of course you don't. That's what I wanted to explain. I made a promise to the old vicar that I would play for him for charity and at last I've got a free slot. I'll explain when I see you. How's your diary?'

Nick laughed. 'Blissfully free, till I get bogged down with parish affairs. When do you want to come?'

'How about six o'clock? We can meet in The Great House if you're still in a mess. Or don't you go to places like that?'

'I'm a modern vicar. I'll go anywhere.'

Olivia laughed again. 'Six o'clock then. Goodbye.'

Nick put the phone down and wondered who the owner of such a delightful laugh could possibly be. He decided to tackle another box after snatching a sandwich and a cup of coffee and, in fact, was halfway through it when there was a ring at the front door. He opened it to find Mavis Cox standing there balancing a large cake on a plate.

'Oh Father Nick, so glad to have caught you in. I've come to help.'

'Thank you, but . . .'

But she had marched past him straight into the kitchen.

'I've brought you a cake for your tea. Shall we get this room sorted out? I always think the kitchen is the worst job of all.'

And she had her coat off and her arms in a box before Nick could utter a word. He had to admit, though, that she was a terrific worker. Drawers were being opened and kitchen implements placed within them and what tins he had brought were put in a cupboard over the cooker.

He smiled at her. 'Shall we not talk parish business until tomorrow?'

'Not if you don't wish it, Father Nick.'

'I'd rather you told me something about the village. About the people who live here.'

'Well, I don't like to gossip but they're a very mixed bunch as you can imagine. They're the old villagers, the people born and bred here, though they're not so many of them left.'

'I suppose commuters have taken their place.'

'And you'd suppose right, Vicar. There are masses of those here – the gin and tonic set I call them.'

Her small eyes had a malicious gleam in them momentarily.

'And who else do we have?'

'The arty crowd and the horsey crowd. Like to live in the heart of the country, or at least be seen to do so.'

'So who's in the horsey crowd?'

'Oh, several of them. There's a livery stable out towards Speckled Wood. Owned by one Cheryl Hamilton-Harty. She rides up and down the High Street on a huge great stallion.' Mavis muttered something like, 'Looking for one I shouldn't wonder.'

Nick thought this extremely naughty from one of his churchwardens but pretended he hadn't heard it and continued to unpack his box.

'And tell me about the arty crowd.'

'Well, you've already met one, my other half – in the churchwarden sense only. I lost my husband some while ago.'

Mavis looked downcast and Nick felt obliged to say, 'I'm sorry.'

She sniffed a bit but answered bravely, 'But life goes on. He's gone to a better place is how I look at it.'

'Yes, indeed.'

'Well I was saying, Richard Culpepper calls himself an actor but gets precious little work. He teaches drama at evening classes and has one or two private pupils to make ends meet. But it's his wife who's the moneyed one, believe me.'

'And what does she do?'

'Retired now. But used to be in films, I believe.'

'Roseanna, isn't it?'

'Yes. Then there's Gerrard Riddell. He's a costume designer and is awfully handy with his needle.'

She gave Nick a sly glance and he couldn't help but grin.

'And Miss Olivia Beauchamp, of course.'

Nick knew at once by the tone of Mavis Cox's voice that she was jealous of the lady in question.

'Tell me about her,' he said from deep within a box.

'She lives in London a lot of the time. She's a violinist – professional, I mean. Anway, she has a weekend cottage here which used to belong to her parents. The village doesn't like weekenders but she's forgiven because she was brought up here.'

'I see. And what about Ceinwen Carruthers?'

Mavis gave an audible snort. 'That amateur and her fairy folklore. She pays to have her books published. Makes out that is genuine publishing but I know different. My Alf's brother was a printer so I do know what's what in that line.'

The vicar murmured something suitable like, 'Quite so.'

'Anyway, that's that box finished. What would you like me to do next, Father Nick?'

'How about making a cup of tea and telling me something of the history of the vicarage.'

They sat down on the kitchen chairs while the kettle boiled and Mavis said, 'Well, it's a Tudor house, like a lot of the others in Lakehurst.'

'I knew it was very old.'

'And it has belonged to the village vicar since the fifteen hundreds.'

'Has it got a ghost?' Nick asked.

Mavis looked disapproving. 'Surely you don't believe in such things.'

'I like to keep an open mind.'

'Well, there are rumours about it but I put those down to all the tales that people like that Carruthers woman spin.'

'What are they?'

'There's some old Elizabethan servant called William supposed to haunt the place. The story goes that he was so happy working here that he could never leave. Stuff and nonsense. I've never seen anything in the many times I've visited the vicarage.'

She stopped for breath and suddenly a chill little breeze swept through the kitchen making the unpacked mugs rattle on their newly screwed-in hooks.

'William?' said the vicar, only half joking.

And from upstairs came the sound of a door banging shut.

# THREE

T he Great House had lit the first log fire of the autumn season. It roared redly up the huge chimney and threw a comforting glow on the many people who sat at tables close to it. Nick, who hadn't realized quite how cold it had got, thought of warming the vicarage and wondered about ordering logs and finding out about the central heating. He looked round the room and saw that Jack Boggis was sitting in his usual seat, back turned, hiding behind the *Daily Telegraph*, but that there was nobody else there that he recognized.

A very handsome man sat alone, puzzling over a cross-word and totally ignoring the group of four young women – all uncannily alike, Nick thought – who sat near him, giggling and talking loudly. Other than for Jack Boggis there was nobody that the vicar had seen before. Despite that several rural types said, 'Evening, Vicar,' and one even asked him how he was getting on in the vicarage.

'Still unpacking,' Nick answered cheerfully. 'But it's a wonderful house.'

'It is that. Provided old William leaves you in peace.'

'The ghost? What do you know about him?'

The man looked surprised. 'I didn't even think he was real. I thought it was just a story.'

'It probably is,' Nick answered enigmatically as he ordered himself a pint.

Somebody came up behind him and said, 'Reverend Lawrence?'

He turned and gazed into a pair of eyes that were full of fun and could only belong to the owner of that lovely laugh.

'Miss Beauchamp?' he responded.

'Call me Olivia,' she said and held out her hand.

Nick took it and could hardly speak as he felt its warmth.

'Call me Nick,' he managed, then recovered himself. 'Shall

we sit over there?' He motioned towards a table for two. 'And what would you like to drink?'

'I'll have a glass of rosé, please.'

'You go and sit down and I'll bring it over.'

'Whatever you say, Vicar.'

She was absolutely stunning, Nick thought, with her great tumbling mass of curling black hair, light green eyes and smiling mouth. In fact he was so knocked out by her presence that it took a great effort of self control to maintain his dignity and carry the glasses over to the table.

'Well now, Olivia, it's nice to meet you.'

Her eyes crinkled at the corners. 'And you, Nick. How are you getting on with the move?'

He winced. 'Slowly, I think is the right answer.'

'But do you like the vicarage?'

'I love it. I'm very lucky to get such a delightful parish.'

He was longing to say with such delightful people in it but thought he would sound too smooth if he said any such thing. Instead he asked, 'Now what about this recital?'

'You know that I am a violinist?'

'Yes, the churchwarden mentioned something.'

'Well, the Reverend Simpkins was always asking when I would give a concert in aid of the steeple fund. And, as I told you on the phone, at last I've got a free slot. Do you still want me to go ahead?'

'Of course. How kind of you. Where would you play?'

'We thought in the church.'

'I see. I believe it is used a great deal for that sort of thing?'

'Yes, a great deal.' She laughed her captivating laugh. 'Why, don't you approve?'

'One doesn't have to pray to worship,' Nick answered solemnly. 'One can do so in a million different ways.'

'So you've no objection to the music festival taking place?'

'None at all.'

Bishop Claude had mentioned to him at the time of his application that Lakehurst had a music festival that was quite famous and that some of the concerts were held in the church.

'Tell me about you,' said Nick, who couldn't stop staring at her. 'When did you start playing?'

'When I was four. I had a toy violin I used to scrape on

and then my parents bought me a miniature one for my fifth birthday. After that there was no holding me.'

'Who do you most admire of the current players?'

'I've got a bit of a thing for Joshua Bell,' Olivia answered, 'and Anne-Sophie Mutter.'

At that moment Nick became aware of someone standing at their table and looking up saw that the handsome man had left his place and was patiently waiting for a lull in their conversation in order to get a word in.

Olivia glanced in his direction.

'Oh hello, Kasper. How are you?'

'I am well, thank you.'

He had a foreign accent and the vicar, regarding him closely, decided that the brilliant looks could only belong to someone from central Europe.

'Nick, allow me to introduce Dr Kasper Rudniski, one of the village doctors. Kasper, this is the Reverend Nick Lawrence, the new vicar.'

'I am delighted to meet you, sir.'

Definitely European, Nick decided, his manners were far too good for him to be anything else.

'A pleasure, Doctor.'

'May I join you?'

'Of course,' said Nick, pulling a chair over from another table. 'Please sit down.'

He was very slightly annoyed that he would no longer have Olivia to himself but had to make the best of it.

'I'm afraid I am the least popular of the doctors, for my sins,' Kasper said with a sad smile.

'Oh, why's that?' asked Nick.

'Because I am a "bloody foreigner". I don't have many patients.'

'Oh surely it's building up by now,' put in Olivia.

'A little maybe. But in general they go to see Dr Macey or old Dr Haskell.'

'But he must be getting on for retirement.'

'He is staying to supervise my arrival.'

'So you are new to the village?' asked Nick.

Kasper gave the most eloquent shrug. 'If you can call six months new, then yes.'

The vicar changed the subject. 'What can I get you to drink, Doctor?'

'I'll have a glass of vodka, if you please.'

His speech was careful, almost punctilious, and Nick smiled as he stood at the bar. But turning his head he saw something that wiped the grin away. Dr Rudniski had placed one of his hands over one of Olivia's and was whispering close to her ear.

Damn, thought Nick. But then he thought that he wouldn't have a chance in a million with such a beautiful and talented girl as she was. He resignedly carried the drinks back to the table.

'I hear that Olivia is giving a concert in the church. I shall buy a ticket,' Kasper announced cheerfully.

'I hope that plenty of people will,' she answered, raising her glass to the vicar.

'Let's hope it is a sell out,' Nick said somewhat lamely.

'Well there goes one who won't be there,' said Olivia, glancing at the door.

Nick looked and saw Jack Boggis sweeping out clutching his paper.

'Doesn't he support local events?'

'Not he. He prefers to go home and watch television and drink beer from tins.'

'One day he will have trouble with his liver,' Kasper announced in sepulchral tones.

'Is he married?' asked Nick.

'She died of cancer a few years ago. Smoked herself to death I'm afraid.'

'Poor fellow.'

'Poor both of them.'

Kasper stood up. 'I must be getting back. Goodbye, Olivia, I'll see you soon no doubt.' He turned to Nick and held out his hand. 'Goodbye, Reverend, it has been a pleasure to meet you.'

'Goodbye, Doctor. I'll register with you as soon as I've settled in.'

'How kind. Goodnight.'

He went out and Nick said, 'Handsome fellow.'

'I think he's divine looking. Every girl in the village is after him. Even potty old Ceinwen.'

'You know her?'

'Not 'arf. She tried to get me to join her poetry group.'

'And did you?'

'No fear. I made an excuse about my busy career.'

'And is it? Are you very busy?'

'Completely and utterly. But I often come to Lakehurst at weekends.'

'Do you go to church?'

'Sometimes,' answered Olivia, and laughed her wonderful laugh.

'Well, I'll have to make do with that,' Nick answered boldly, then changed the subject.

He left The Great House half an hour later, Olivia having fixed the date of the recital with him and then saying she had to go. He had offered to walk her home but she told him she had her car in the car park.

'I live near Speckled Wood. It would take you ages to get there.'

'Well one day I'll drive out. When I'm doing my parish visits.'

'I look forward to that. Goodbye, Nick.' She held out her hand.

'Goodbye, Olivia.'

And she was gone in a flash of blue Vauxhall. The vicar, sighing a little, came out of the car park and turned right, going up the High Street to a small supermarket he had noticed on the corner. It was one of those open-all-hours affairs and purported to sell everything – at a price. Nick wandered round the somewhat cramped aisles and got himself some rather tired-looking pork chops and a listless cauliflower. He then added a packet of Lapsang Souchong teabags and a jar of instant coffee, some biscuits – chocolate, not the pallid shade so loved by Mrs Cox and Ceinwen – and one or two things that he felt were generally needed. He went to pay. A very round Pakistani man greeted him with a broad grin.

'Good evening, Vicar. It is a pleasure to meet you. My name is Ali and I will always be happy to serve you.'

'Good evening, Ali. I take it you are the owner?'

'Yes, indeed I am. We stock everything here as you may have noticed.'

'I was very impressed that you had china teas.'

'We stock those for Mr Riddell down West Street. He won't drink anything else.'

The vicar felt immediately that he was in rather odd company but merely smiled.

'I do hope you enjoy it here, good sir,' Ali continued. 'I personally am a Muslim but I applaud all men of religion. My wife does too. She is upstairs at the moment but I can fetch her down if it is your wish to meet her.'

'No, please don't disturb her on my account. I am sure she will be preparing your evening meal.'

'Oh yes indeed. Perhaps you will honour us with your presence one night. Do you like curry?'

'I'm afraid that it upsets my stomach. Very weak of me, I know.'

Ali pulled a face. 'One cannot help the way one is consti-tuted. But the invitation still is there. My wife can cook something else.'

'Thank you. I'll look in my diary.'

Ali placed his palms together and bowed. 'It will be our pleasure to await you.'

Even with his bags of shopping, Nick felt compelled to go into the church, realizing that it ought to be locked for the night, something he should have done earlier.

Yet again, switching on the lights that were situated behind the oak door, its beauty and calmness overwhelmed him though he still half expected that person to be present, muttering audible prayers in a sinister manner. Nick walked down the centre aisle staring into the pews. There was nobody there but he could hear a rustling sound coming from the stalls on the right hand side. Assuming an air of authority – an emotion he was very far from feeling – the vicar marched over and peered into them. A pair of emerald eyes met his and he realized that it was an animal of some kind. And then a large ginger cat stood up, arched its back, stretched, and sat down again.

'What are you doing in here?' Nick asked. 'Go on, out you go.'

The cat did not reply but it got up, minced down the side aisle and out through the oak door.

'Lakehurst is a truly strange place,' said Nick.

He went to the altar, knelt in prayer for a few minutes, then got up and checking that the church was truly empty, put out the lights and turned the key in the great lock.

He had hoped for a quiet night in, watching the television, but this was to be short-lived. No sooner had he sat down and switched on *Have I Got News For You*, than the front door bell rang loudly. A woman stood there, half hidden by the darkness of the street outside.

'Oh hello, Reverend Lawrence,' she said in highly refined tones. 'Excuse the lateness of the hour. I just called to see if you needed anything and if I could be of any assistance.'

'Come in,' Nick answered reluctantly.

She rolled past him in a hip-gyrating walk and settled herself in the living room.

'Oh, I watch this programme too,' she said. 'I think it's so funny. Of course I utterly adore Ian Hislop.'

Then why don't you watch him in your own house? Nick thought in a highly unchristian manner.

'But I'm disturbing you,' she added.

'Not at all,' he said, and switched the television off.

She smiled up at him archly and he observed that she had a heavily lined face and somewhat small eyes, that is what he could see of them beneath her layers of make-up.

'Allow me to introduce myself,' she said, 'I am Sonia Tate.'

'Just call me Father Nick,' Nick replied somewhat pompously.

'Oh.' Sonia looked slightly put out. 'Very well. Now Father Nick –' she emphasized the words as she said them – 'I expect you probably have heard things about me.'

He looked blank and shook his head.

'I'm afraid that in the past I fell out with Mrs Cox, your churchwarden, and I thought she might have mentioned something to you.'

'No. Not a word.'

'I'm relieved. It is not my habit to gossip so I'll say no more about it except that it involved Alfred.'

'Alfred?' the vicar repeated, nonplussed.

'Alfred Cox, Mavis's husband. The poor fellow fell madly in love with me. Went off his head with it. It was quite the most horrible situation.'

'What happened?' Nick asked, interested despite himself.

'I met someone else,' Sonia replied brightly. 'But for evermore the man gave me dirty looks when we passed in the street.' She smiled up at him, her eyes shining. 'But that's just silly old me. Always landing myself in scrapes.'

The vicar had a sinking feeling, fearing that she was going to tell him her life story. He stood up resolutely.

'It was very kind of you to call, Mrs Tate, but I really think I can manage quite well. If I feel desperate I shall announce it from the pulpit on Sunday.'

'I shall be there.' She too stood up. 'Well thank you for your hospitality,' she said rather pointedly.

Nick immediately worried that he had offered her nothing. 'I shall be giving a welcoming party as soon as I am organized,' he said. 'You must come to it.'

Her manner changed completely. 'I'd love to,' she gushed. 'It will be so lovely to see the old vicarage full of life once more.' She went out into the hall and turned to face him, extending her hand. For the briefest of seconds Nick wondered whether she intended him to kiss it. He shook it instead.

'Goodbye, Mrs Tate. So kind of you to call.'

'Anytime, Father Nick.' She gave him a dazzling smile. 'And I mean that.' Then, moving swiftly, she was through the door and out into the street.

'Whew,' Nick muttered, as he closed it again.

Suddenly tired, he cooked his meal quickly and had it on a tray in front of the television. Then he went upstairs.

It was quiet in the upper part of the vicarage and Nick felt more than ready for bed. He prayed very briefly that he would like Lakehurst and that the village – or at least the majority of it – would like him in return. Then he got into the very beautiful four-poster, left to him by his mother.

He woke in the middle of the night feeling a presence in the room, a presence which was warm and friendly and did not frighten him in the least.

'Is that you William?' he said.

There was no answer but he distinctly heard his bedroom door close very gently as something went out.

# FOUR

akehurst was really quite a large village, Nick decided, having taken a day off from parish duties and walked round the entire perimeter. To the east it had a large meadow which opened out into what must surely be one of the finest views in Europe, displaying distant hills and lovely lush fields on which cattle grazed in serene contentment. The ground, sloping gently downwards to a lively brook, rose again on the other side to a faraway ring of trees. Nick, shading his eyes as he looked at it, wondered if it had any magical associations.

Before him the view stretched on, behind him was a little path which led to the Remembrance Hall. He had thought as he walked past it what a particularly ugly building it was, but now the vicar made his way there. The doors were open and there was the sound of conversation from within. Boldly, he stepped inside.

A tall, gawky woman with a face like a parrot regarded him with an unfriendly stare. 'Can I help you?' she asked frostily.

Nick put on his most charming smile. 'Excuse me bursting in like this. I just wanted to have a look round.'

'Well, the place is booked for a private function. It's the WI meeting this afternoon.'

'Sorry. I didn't realize. I'm the new vicar and I'm just making an assessment of my parish.'

Her whole attitude changed. 'Ah, Vicar, how nice to meet you. I am Ivy Bagshot and I'm the Chairman of the Women's Institute.'

She came forward with hand extended and gave him a gushing smile displaying a brilliant set of false teeth. Her grasp was dry and slightly masculine, Nick thought.

'How kind of you to look in,' she continued, staring at him from behind thick pebble glasses which magnified her eyes to an enormous size. They were a nondescript shade of grey and had a tendency to meet in the middle, he noticed.

'I do hope I'm not interrupting anything.'

'Not at all, Vicar. Not at all. We're just getting the sandwiches out on to plates. Do come in and have a nose round.'

It truly was a depressing building with a stage at one end and a large empty space at the other. It had been erected in the late forties, Nick guessed, and had all the architectural genius of the period. In other words, none.

But Mrs Bagshot, in her role as unofficial guide, was ushering him within and explaining that the chairs which were stacked round the side were pulled out for performances and set in serried rows.

'So who appears here?' asked Nick, assuming an interested expression.

'Well, the WI do a pantomime every year. We're rehearsing *Cinderella* at the moment. You must come and see it. It will be part of your parochial duties.'

She waved a waggish finger at him. Nick gulped.

'Of course. I shall be delighted.'

'I am playing Principal Boy. I'm the only one with long enough legs, you see.'

'Ah,' Nick replied, uncertain of what else to say.

Two other women popped their heads out of the kitchen area. Ivy turned to them with a brilliant smile.

'May I introduce two of our other girls; Mrs Emms and Mrs Sargent. Ladies, this is the new vicar.'

'Ever so pleased to meet you,' said one, while the other murmured something incomprehensible.

Nick did his stuff, shaking hands and smiling pleasantly while his eye ran over the plates of somewhat dry-looking sandwiches and fancy fairy cakes.

'Quite a spread you have there,' he commented amiably.

'It's just an ordinary tea,' answered Mrs Emms, then after a moment added, 'Would you like a sandwich?'

'No, thank you all the same. I must get back to the vicarage. I've got a meeting at four o'clock.'

'Do hope you're settling in all right,' Ivy said, giving him a smile and thrusting her glasses close to his face.

'Perfectly, thank you. Well, ladies, I must be off. Hope to see you all in church.'

'I shall be there,' Ivy said loudly while the other two shuf-
fled their feet.

'Goodbye then,' Nick answered, gave his odd polite bow,
and departed somewhat speedily.

He hurried back to the vicarage and went quickly through
the front door, realizing he had ten minutes before Richard
Culpepper was due to arrive. The ginger cat he had found
in church was sitting waiting for him and advanced towards
him, arching its back as it stretched out of its sleeping position. Nick bent to stroke it.

'Hello Radetsky,' he said, a name he had given to the cat
after the famous march written by Johann Strauss the Elder.
The cat purred loudly by way of reply.

Enquiries in the village, including notices put up in the
supermarket and The Great House, had yielded no clues about
the animal's owner. In fact there had been no response at all.
So the vicar, quite gladly as it happened, had adopted the creature which had moved into the vicarage with alacrity.

It was an odd sort of set-up, Nick thought as he prepared
the tea things. One male, one neutered cat and one ghost all
sharing the same roof. In fact if anyone had told him three
months earlier that this was how he was going to end up he
would have laughed in their face. But in actuality he quite
enjoyed the unusual situation and was whistling cheerfully
to himself when the front door bell rang. Richard Culpepper,
wearing an Austrian jacket and looking as if he'd just stepped
out of a production of *The Sound of Music*, stood there.

'Do hope I'm not late,' he said. His breath had an undertone of alcohol.

'Not at all. Please come in. I'm just making some tea.'

He ushered Richard into the sitting room and went to the
kitchen where he retrieved a tray.

'Now, how do you like your tea?'

'Strong, please. And I think I'll take a dash of sugar today.
I need the energy.'

'Oh dear. Nothing wrong I hope?'

'No, no. Just one of those things.'

'How's the acting?' asked the vicar, sitting down and
sipping his Lapsang Souchong.

'Going quite well actually. I've been offered a role in a fringe theatre production.'

'Oh really. What's that?'

'It's the part of a forensics expert in a play about John Major.'

'What's it called? *The Man in Grey*?' asked Nick and fell about laughing at his own joke.

Richard looked very slightly huffy. 'The title has not yet been decided upon. No, the trouble is it will probably mean staying in London, which will annoy my wife of course.'

Nick pulled his features into a serious expression. 'I am sorry to hear that. How long will you be away?'

'Oh about six weeks I would imagine.'

'And you can't get back on a Sunday?'

'No, unfortunately we perform on that day too. Which brings me to my next point. I shall have to let you down as churchwarden for a short while. How do you feel about that?'

Nick thought. The service on his one and only Sunday in the parish had been conducted by the Reverend Mills, a dear old man who helped out when the vicar was ill or away, and who had acted as priest during the period between the departure of the Reverend Simpkins and Nick's arrival. He would be there at Nick's debut and introduce him to the congregation. Everything would be fine.

'I am sure we will be able to manage perfectly well. Mrs Cox will smooth out any wrinkles.'

Richard put on a pleased expression though his mouth hardened a little.

'Well, in that case I have no need to worry. I shall send my wife along to deputize for me, of course, and I am sure she will cope. Have you met her yet?'

'No. I look forward to doing so.'

'Her name is Roseanna. She used to be an actress, years ago. We met when we were both filming.'

Nick finished his tea and bit into a biscuit. 'Why did she stop?'

Richard looked a little vague. 'Well, she wanted a family but, alas, that did not happen. Then when she gave up on that idea and tried to make a comeback there just weren't the parts around for a woman of an *âge certain*.'

The vicar did not know quite how to react, so he just sat there, looking wise.

Richard finished his cup and stood up. 'Well, Father Nick,' he said cheerfully, 'as you've given one of your wayward parishioners leave of absence I think I had better go. I must be in town early tomorrow. We start rehearsals at ten o'clock. We are working with the author.'

'How nice. Who is he? Anyone I would know?'

'No, he's only a young chap but he won the St Pancras Award with a previous play.'

Nick mentally gave up. It was all getting way beyond him. He had never heard of the St Pancras Award and had a fated feeling that he might never do so again.

'Oh, well done,' was all he could think of saying as he bowed Richard Culpepper out of the front door.

Radetsky looked along the hall from the kitchen where he was busily digging into his feeding bowl. The vicar approached him.

'Well, Rad, what do you think?'

The cat stared at him solemnly from his enormous green eyes. Then gave a great yawn and went out through the cat flap which the vicar had had installed when nobody had replied to his advertisement. Nick could see him through the window washing his face thoroughly.

Very much as he had anticipated the church was packed to overflowing on the following Sunday. In fact while donning his vestments Nick had a decided feeling of panic. Already the line was starting to form up to march down the aisle towards the altar and he knew that he was going to be the object of a great deal of scrutiny. He swallowed hard and the Reverend Mills turned to him with a kindly expression.

'Nervous?'

'A little.'

'No need, dear boy, no need. God will see you through.'

And with that the vestry door was flung open and a young man carrying the gold cross high before him strode out. He was followed by two other assistants and then came Nick, Mills walking a step or two behind him, leading out the choir who, singing lustily, processed to the stalls in their long gowns. Reaching the altar the new vicar turned to face the congregation and said, 'May the Lord be with you.' And was greeted by a ringing, 'And also with you.'

Afterwards when he stood outside the church, greeting his new parishioners, the vicar felt a moment of great pride. Most of Lakehurst had been there to see him and Olivia had turned up to put the icing on the cake. He shook her hand with a certain amount of warmth.

'So you came then.'

'You know I did. You gave me communion.'

'I'm afraid things were a bit blurred. I didn't really notice.'

Her eyes sparkled. 'How very remiss of you. But despite that let me say welcome to Lakehurst, Father Nick.'

'Will you come to my party? It's a fortnight on Friday at the vicarage.'

'I will if I'm here. I'll go home and look in the diary.'

'Please do.' And with a final squeeze of her hand he reluctantly passed on to the next person.

It took Nick the best part of an hour to greet everyone and by the time he had bidden farewell to the last of the choir he suddenly found that he was standing alone, even kindly Reverend Mills having returned to his lunch of roast pork and vegetables cooked by his sister. Nick went back into the church and offered up a brief prayer of thanks before heading purposefully for The Great House.

Already he recognized several people. Giles Fielding was standing with a group of local lads, leaning up against the bar, his hair quite fiery red where it caught the early afternoon sun. Jack Boggis was sitting in his usual corner, back to the room, reading an item in the Sunday paper. Standing alone and downing neat vodka was Kasper Rudniski, looking soulful and extremely handsome. Nick was most relieved to see that Olivia was not with him. He went over.

'Hello, Kasper. How are you today?'

The doctor brightened. 'I am well, thank you. I have just come from the Catholic church. I support the opposition, you see.' He grinned disarmingly.

'There's only one God,' Nick answered briskly. 'What can I get you to drink?'

'Vodka, please. I drink it unadorned.'

'So I noticed. Don't you find it rather strong?'

'It is very warming to the stomach.'

'I see,' said Nick – though he didn't – and put in his order for the doctor and himself.

Giles came up to them and extended a work-worn hand. 'How you getting on then, Vicar?'

'Very well. I played to a full house this morning.'

'Glad to hear it.'

A voice spoke beside them. 'Oh Father Nick, I am so glad to catch up with you at last. I was in church this morning but arrived somewhat late, I fear, so I had to sit near the back. But I sang up lustily, I can tell you.'

Nick turned and looked into the face of Gerrard Riddell.

He was very much as he had been described, clearly homosexual with a high, somewhat irritating voice, and an old-womanish manner. He smiled at Nick displaying a row of formidably tiny teeth. The vicar held out his hand.

'How do you do? I'm sorry but I seemed to miss you when you left.'

'Oh, I hurried out. I remembered that I had left a candle burning in my house and had to dash back to put it out. Fortunately, nothing had gone amiss.'

'That's as well then,' put in Giles. 'You can have a lot of trouble with burning candles.' A foxy look came over his rugged face. 'Was it alight in front of your Buddha, Gerrard?'

Mr Riddell's face suffused to a purplish shade. 'I don't see that that is any of your business, Fielding.'

Giles laughed loudly. 'Oh, it's Fielding now, is it? Well, suit yourself, "Mr" Riddell. Bit of a change from when you wanted to buy a leg of lamb cheaply, as I recall.'

Mr Riddell said snappishly, 'You can recall anything you like, as far as I am concerned. Good day to you.' And he ostentatiously turned his back on the sheep farmer before he asked, 'You were saying, Vicar?'

Nick, who had been extremely uncomfortable during the previous exchange, replied, 'Nothing of any importance. Let me buy you a drink.'

'Thank you. I'll have a gin and Dubonnet, just like the late Queen Mother.' He let out a soprano laugh.

Kasper joined in. 'How are you feeling, Mr Riddell?'

'Quite well, thank you. Dr Haskell is very pleased with me.'

If this last were a dig at Dr Rudniski's place as the most junior doctor, Kasper let it pass him by. 'I am delighted to hear it,' he said serenely, and raised his glass.

There was a sudden burst of sound from the local lads, whom Giles had gone to rejoin. Nick turned to glance in their direction and momentarily had the oddest sensation of not being part of his surroundings, of merely being an observer. He saw everything as if he were looking through a telescope. He saw Jack Boggis rocking with silent laughter over something in the *Sunday Telegraph*, not a paper usually known for its hilarity. He noticed without jealousy that Kasper had film-star looks; that Gerrard Riddell had a waspish pinched expression, rather as if he were expecting a bad smell to erupt; that the fire needed another log on it. He also noticed that there was no sign of the beautiful Olivia anywhere.

With an effort Nick pulled himself together and, concentrating hard, applied himself to his role of sympathetic listener and reliable man who did not experience strange flights of fancy.

# FIVE

It was the night of Nick's welcoming party and the vicarage was a blaze of gentle light. Candles had been placed in the downstairs rooms and fires lit in the sitting and dining rooms. With Mavis Cox expressing disapproval in every way possible the vicar had switched all but the essential overhead lights off so that the old house had a charming and somewhat romantic atmosphere. Nick's one hope was that William would not make this an occasion for one of his noisier exhibitions.

Everyone connected with the church was present. Mavis, of course, even more disgruntled because the vicar had taken over the organization of the food. Instead of sausage rolls and vol-au-vents he had plumped for a ham, a large salmon and a side of beef, all of which he had cooked himself. He had then prepared several salads, though he had to admit to buying coleslaw and cheese. Truth to tell, Nick was extremely useful in the kitchen, a fact which had been carefully noted by his former girlfriends.

Along with Mavis came Sonia Tate, Ivy Bagshot, the woman from the post office, Ceinwen Carruthers – clutching a poem welcoming the new vicar – and various other assorted females all of whom looked terribly well meaning. And then the doorbell rang and there was Olivia, much to Nick's delight and relief.

'So you managed to get here,' he said as he let her in.

'It was clever of you to make it a Friday,' she answered, giving him a glance that sent him reeling. 'And to pick one of my nights off.'

'I looked in my crystal ball,' he replied lightly as he ushered her into the sitting room.

Already gathered there were the handsome doctor Kasper, Giles Fielding – who was playing it extremely cool with Gerrard Riddell – and, unbelievably, Jack Boggis, who had refused wine and was standing with a frothing pint of beer in his hand. As Olivia entered the room he brightened up

and Nick made a mental note that Jack still fancied his chance
with the ladies.

'Hello,' Boggis said in a broad Yorkshire accent, 'aren't
you the fiddle player?'

'Yes, that's right,' she answered.

Kasper intervened. 'Miss Beauchamp is one of the
country's leading performers, Mr Boggis.'

'Oh ah! I stand corrected. But they're all fiddle players to
me any road.'

He gave a contented smile and looked round the room and
it occurred to Nick that the man was playing the part of a
typical Northerner, 'where's there's muck there's brass, by
gum.' He wondered what actually lurked beneath.

There was a swell of laughter from the dining room, where
most of the women had foregathered in that peculiar way
the English have of automatically segregating the sexes at
social gatherings. Nick looked round.

'I must go and dig out the ladies if you'll excuse me.'

He wandered off.

Kasper rolled his glorious eyes in the vicar's direction. 'A
very pleasant man, that.'

'Very,' Olivia replied, and changed the subject. She went
forward with hand extended. 'How are you, Giles?'

'I'm very well, my dear,' he replied in his Sussex accent.

Kasper joined them. 'Of course, you two are neighbours.'

'Yes, we are. I'm in Skylark Farm and Olivia owns one
of the old cottages.'

But they got no further with this pleasant exchange for
with a loud shriek Ceinwen came into the room brandishing
her poem.

'The vicar says that I must read this aloud,' she announced
to the startled company.

'Well, go on then,' said Giles, grinning broadly.

'Must you?' muttered Boggis under his breath.

She cleared her throat importantly. 'Along the nave he
processed, his chin high but not yet mighty . . .'

'I thought I spied a dicky bird aflying up his nightie,'
whispered Boggis.

Kasper and Olivia exchanged a look but controlled themselves admirably.

'He has come to us to lead our prayers, to give us all communion. One body we, we bravely shout, as we feel the bonds of union. We welcome thee, oh Father Nick, long may you stay to heal us . . .'

'To what?' said Giles, cupping his ear as if he were deaf.

'Heal not feel,' Kasper whispered back.

'Oh.'

'May your sword be sharp, your munificence strong, may you walk for ever tall. Greetings to you, oh man of the cloth, from the villagers, one and all.'

There was a second or two's silence and then a smattering of polite applause.

Kasper frowned. 'I don't think that quite scanned – is that the right word?'

Olivia gave her beautiful smile. 'Yes, it is and no it didn't. Let's go and get something to eat.'

They found Father Nick in the dining room, cutting sides off the meat and salmon and passing them to his women guests, who had formed a giggling queue and were oohing and aahing over the salads. It was perfectly obvious that one or two of them had taken a fancy to him and were desperate to attract his attention. A primary mover amongst these was Sonia Tate, who, to add to the glamour of the occasion no doubt, had a sexy feather boa in a colour once known as shocking pink firmly attached to her neck. Nick seemed perfectly oblivious but brightened up when he saw Olivia.

'Hello, you two. What can I get you to eat?'

'I'll have some salmon please.'

'And for me,' said Kasper.

'Of course I rarely eat,' said Jack Boggis, who had followed them into the dining room. 'I don't get all that hungry.'

'It's the booze,' muttered the doctor.

'That doesn't surprise me,' said Gerrard Riddell, waspishly.

He had come to the buffet moving silently and the vicar couldn't help but have uncharitable thoughts about him. He was an unpleasant little man, both in his small pinched face and his equally shrivelled up view of others, to say nothing of his tiny teeth. Nick desperately tried to imagine him as the hub of gay weekend parties and somehow couldn't manage it at all.

Olivia turned to Kasper with a laugh. 'Surely that is a very unprofessional remark, Doctor.'

He looked stricken. 'I merely made an observation. I know nothing of the man medically.'

'Did you like your poem, Father Nick?' asked Giles, approaching and looking roguish.

'Er hum. Yes. It was very interesting.'

'Happen,' said Jack Boggis, coming upon them suddenly and taking the smallest fragment of ham and half a tomato on to his plate.

'Spoken like a true gentleman,' said Gerrard nastily, and wandered away to talk to Ivy Bagshot.

The evening wore on in its inevitable way. Boggis hit the beer and became slightly incoherent – which was just as well – while others began to drift homewards. In the end everyone had left with the exception of Kasper and Olivia, whom Nick had persuaded to stay on and have a nightcap. Frankly he could have done without the doctor but for the fact that Kasper was giving the violinist a lift home.

'I have drunk little, you see,' he said somewhat mournfully.

'Whereas I,' Olivia put in, 'have had more than my fair share.' She changed the subject. 'Tell me, Nick, is this house really haunted?'

'Yes, I think it is. Mind you, I haven't seen William – that's the ghost's name by the way – but I've certainly heard him.'

'This is very interesting,' said Kasper, leaning forward, reluctantly sipping a mineral water. 'I was brought up in a haunted house, you see. I personally saw nothing but my sister did. In fact she insisted on having another bedroom because an old lady used to come and stare at her in bed – or so she said.' He gave his handsome grin. 'It could have been because she wanted a larger room, however.'

'Clever girl,' said Olivia. She stood up and held out her hand to Nick. 'Thank you so much for a wonderful evening. It really has been good fun.'

'Must you go?' he asked, not meaning to say that.

'Yes, I must. I'm off to London tomorrow and I've an early start. Kasper, are you ready?'

'Of course. Goodbye, Father Nick. It has been a great pleasure.'

His English was excellent but had the slightly mannered tones of someone speaking a foreign tongue. He held out his hand, bowing slightly. Nick shook it.

'Goodbye, Doctor. I shall make a point of signing up with you tomorrow.'

'I look forward to that.'

The vicar gave his odd little bow as the couple disappeared through the front door. Radetsky came through the cat flap, purring happily now that he was certain everyone had gone. Nick stooped down to stroke him, gave him a slice of ham which the cat attacked with gusto, then went upstairs to bed, feeling tired and more than a little miserable. It seemed to him that Olivia and Kasper had a special something between them, that the handsome doctor was probably going to spend the night with her. But then, Nick thought, he was the inter-loper after all.

William, God be praised, was quiet tonight, presumably showing his approval of the party. Nick got into bed and fell asleep only to be awoken again by the sound of a siren, wailing its way through the night. He sat bolt upright, wondering what it meant. Then he put his head back on the pillow and was just dozing off again when another siren sounded. This time he identified it as a car rushing past. Wondering where the police could possibly be going at this hour, Nick hesitated about getting out of bed but thought better of it and promptly fell into a deep and peaceful sleep.

# SIX

He was awoken some hours later by a thunderous knocking at his front door. Glancing at the alarm clock which stood beside the bed he saw that it was nearly eight o'clock and that he should have risen an hour ago. With his hair standing on end and pulling a dressing gown on, Nick went downstairs to open it. Mavis Cox stood there.

'Oh, Vicar, Vicar,' she burst out hysterically. 'Something terrible has happened. I think you should come at once.'

He led her into the hallway.

'What is it? What's the matter?'

'It's the Patels. They've been murdered.'

'You mean the supermarket man?'

'Yes. The police have closed the shop so none of us can buy anything.'

'Oh, how terrible. I mean about the murder not the shop.'

Mavis looked pained. 'Quite. But actually it is a shocking thing for the village. I know they were foreigners and all that but they were very well liked.'

'I'll get some clothes on and go up there though I doubt I can be of any help.'

'Nevertheless, I think you should put in an appearance.'

Despite the terrible circumstances Nick could not resist a smile. It was perfectly obvious that Mavis was making a bid to rule the roost. He gave one of his jerky bows.

'I shall do as you say, ma'am.'

Ten minutes later, dressed but not shaven, Nick walked up the road to see a hive of activity round the supermarket. The police had cordoned it off with their official tape and there were several police cars parked outside. A clutch of people dressed from head to toe in white were going in and out about their business. In fact, the vicar thought grimly, Ali would have considered it a day of extremely good trading.

He came to a halt by the police barrier where a young constable addressed him.

'Excuse me, sir, would you mind moving on.'

'No, I don't mind at all. I just thought I might be of help. Talking to the relatives or something.'

The constable stared at him and saw Nick's dog collar. 'Oh sorry, Vicar. I didn't realize.'

'Don't worry. I'll get along.'

Nick turned to go but at that moment the barrier was lifted to allow a newcomer and his assistant in. They were both dressed in blue protective clothing and Nick guessed that they must be some high-ups from the Sussex police.

One of the men was saying, 'Sorry I'm late. Had a long rehearsal. Where are the bodies?'

'In the upstairs bedroom, sir.'

'Anyone else been on the scene?'

'Only the girl who found them.'

'Right.' The man made eye contact with the vicar and gave him a brief smile. 'Morning, Vicar.'

'Good morning.'

'I'll come and see you later. Get your view on things.'

'Certainly. Meanwhile is there anything I can do to help?'

'Why don't you pop along to the local church hall or community centre and administer kind words to the parishioners.'

'Thanks very much. I'll do that.'

The man turned away and went into the supermarket and Nick was left with a vivid impression of unusually bright green eyes which radiated intelligence.

Halfway down the High Street stood a Georgian house which was used as a general meeting place for the community. Nick made his way there and found Sonia Tate already ensconced, looking wide-eyed over a cup of tea.

'Oh, Father Nick,' she said, her voice husky, 'what a ghastly thing to happen. I'm so glad you're here to give support.'

'Who found the bodies, do you know?'

'It was the girl who works for them on the early shift. Apparently she had a pass key to the shop and went in and when they weren't down by six she started calling out. The rest I leave to your imagination.'

'Poor woman. What a horrible shock.'

'I wonder if you know her. Her name is Kylie Saunters.'

'Does she by any chance serve in The White Hart in Arrow Street?'

'Yes, she does. Common little thing but she's a hard worker for all that. There are no jobs in Lakehurst so she does any little bits she can to make ends meet.'

'Why doesn't she go to the nearest town for work?'

'She lives with her grandmother, who dotes on her of course. Her and her brother.'

'What happened to their parents?' asked Nick.

Sonia gave an elaborate shrug. 'Who knows?'

At this moment they were interrupted by the arrival of a woman that Nick did not recognize. She was tall and absolutely striking, with the beautiful heavy-lidded eyes of Greta Garbo and the same full drooping lips.

Sonia stood up and said, 'I must be going,' banged down her mug of tea and left without another word. Nick stared after her and the stranger gave him a sympathetic smile.

'Sorry to interrupt.' She held out her hand and said, 'Allow me to introduce myself. My name is Roseanna Culpepper.'

Nick thought as he shook hands that the name became her. She looked rather like a rose that is just beginning to lose its first radiant beauty. Indeed the more he stared into her face the more he could see evidence of just how lovely she must once have been. Her scent, too, spoke of another era. Sniffing it delicately Nick thought he could detect Mitsouko by Guerlain, a perfume beloved of his mother.

She was smiling at him, a delicate, questioning smile. 'What is all the fuss that is going on in the High Street?'

'You haven't heard?'

'No. My husband is away, doing a play in London. He usually brings me the news.'

'There's been a murder, I'm afraid. The Patels who ran the supermarket.'

'What? Both of them?'

'I believe so.'

'How dreadful!' Roseanna's hands were raised to her mouth and she looked at the vicar piteously. 'But who could have done such a terrible thing?'

He shook his head. 'I have no idea. It must have been a burglary that went wrong.'

But he didn't believe that. Surely no burglar, no matter how high he might have been on drink and drugs, could have taken the lives of two people in cold blood.

Roseanna shook her head. 'Well, I must be on my way. I have one or two bits to buy.' She turned her glorious eyes on him. 'But with the supermarket closed I'd better get the car out and go to town.'

Nick stood up. 'Goodbye, Mrs Culpepper. It's been so nice to meet you.'

'Goodbye.'

She wafted out, her dress catching in the autumn wind which forced her to hold her slouch hat to her head. Nick stared after her with a kind of fascination. Then turned and made himself a strong black coffee.

News that he was in Cheltenham House doling out cuppas must have spread amongst the onlookers at the scene of crime because a steady stream of parishioners made their way in and, as if speaking in one voice, asked him about the murder. And despite his protests that he knew as little as they there was an air about them that he was withholding information on the instructions of the police.

Eventually they dwindled away and Nick was on the point of leaving when footsteps in the hall told him that somebody else was coming in. He looked up and into the interesting face of the senior policeman, this time dressed in a formal suit and tie, devoid of his protective clothing.

He was not a notably tall man, of average height, about five foot eight or nine, and slim of build. But his features were most arresting. A mass of black hair, longish and inclined to be wavy, the man had a pixieish look about him, caused, Nick thought, by those great brilliant eyes of his, the colour of gooseberries in a sun-ripened garden.

The detective held out his hand. 'I've caught up with you at last, Vicar. Sorry to be so long. There was rather a lot to see to.'

'How do you do?' Nick answered, clearing his throat. 'Nick Lawrence, newly arrived in Lakehurst. Terrible business this. The villagers have taken it extremely badly.'

The quizzical eyes flashed in Nick's direction with an unreadable expression. 'I'm sure they have. Particularly with their local shop out of bounds. Now, tell me what you know about it.'

'Not much, really. As I said, I'm newly arrived.'

'Quite so. Did you manage to find anything out whilst chatting this morning?'

'Nothing that would interest you, I'm afraid. Everyone seemed very upset – genuinely so – at the deaths.'

The pixie-face pulled a wry expression. 'I see. I believe you gave a party last night which a great many of the church-goers attended.'

'Not only them. I asked everyone I had met locally.'

'I wonder if you'd be kind enough to let me have a list of those who attended.' The man beamed a sudden smile and said, 'But I haven't introduced myself. How remiss of me. My name is Dominic Tennant. Detective Inspector,' he added by way of an afterthought.

Nick shook hands solemnly.

'I can certainly give you a list. Is there anything more, Inspector?'

'Yes. Can you tell me what time the party ended?'

'About ten thirty. The last to leave were Olivia Beauchamp . . .'

'The concert violinist?' Tennant interrupted surprisingly.

'Yes. And Dr Rudniski – he's one of the local GPs.'

The inspector nodded. 'And can you tell me where you were at around midnight last night, Vicar?'

'At home in bed.'

'Alone?'

For some ridiculous reason Nick felt himself going red. 'Yes. I'm not married, Inspector.'

'No, I didn't think you were.'

Tennant grinned and after a moment so did the vicar.

'Is there anything else you want to ask me?'

'Not at this time. But I'll be in touch should anything arise. I take it you are living in the vicarage?'

'Yes. It's in the High Street. May I ask you a question?'

'Certainly.'

'How did the Patels die?'

'They were stabbed as they slept in their bed. Several times.'

Nick looked a little sick. 'How ghastly. Who could have done such a thing?'

'I don't know but I fully intend to find out,' Tennant answered. He looked at his watch. 'Well, I must be off. No doubt we shall meet again.'

'No doubt,' answered Nick, as the Inspector made a somewhat dramatic exit from the room, whirling his longish coat with a flourish.

An hour later the vicar was just finishing a late breakfast when the phone rang.

'Nick, it's Olivia. I just wanted to thank you for the party last night.'

'Oh hello. I'm so glad you enjoyed it.' He paused, then said, 'Did you leave early this morning?'

'Very. I caught the seven twenty-seven. Why?'

'Because there's been a murder in the village. The Patels were killed during the night.'

There was a shocked silence, then Olivia said, 'Both of them?'

'Yes. According to the police they were stabbed in their bed. Around midnight, I believe.'

'Oh God, how awful. Do they know who did it?'

'Well, not yet. There's a very on-the-ball inspector though. I'm sure he'll crack the case if anyone can.'

'Did you give him my name?'

'Well, yes, I had to. I told him that you and Kasper were the last to leave my party.'

Olivia suddenly gave an unexpected laugh. 'I said goodbye to the good doctor outside your front door. He walked home. I should have done but I risked driving. So I have no alibi.'

Nick suddenly felt immensely cheered. 'That makes two of us.'

There was a silence before Olivia said, 'Sorry, I've got to go. I'm being called for a rehearsal. Goodbye, Nick. Keep me posted about what's going on.'

'I don't know your mobile number,' he said before he realized that she'd ended the call. Replacing his receiver, the vicar slowly dialled 1471 to be informed that the caller had withheld their number.

# SEVEN

Inspector Tennant sat in his office at police headquarters in Lewes, moodily staring out of the window and slowly chewing a peppermint, a habit he had taken up when he stopped smoking some seven years ago. At that moment he was not thinking of the murders in Lakehurst but instead about his ex-wife, who had gone off with her leading man after playing Eliza Doolittle to his Professor Higgins in an amateur production of *My Fair Lady*. It still grieved Dominic that she had taken with her his highly prized collection of Staffordshire pottery and had then proceeded to sell the lot on. Mind you, he had managed to replace some of the pieces but the rarer figures – some of which had been left to him by his parents – were irreplaceable.

'Bitch,' he muttered under his breath.

He had had several associations with women since his marriage had ended three years earlier but none of them had been of any lasting nature. He supposed that he had become warier, more suspicious of the female sex. In other words when it came to the time when he should have made some kind of commitment, he had shied away. This had not always been easy, for Dominic Tennant was a keen amateur actor himself and so mixed with a fairly tight-knit bunch of people. He was keenly aware that amongst the women he was labelled as being bad news and as a result had thrown himself into his work as the only alternative. Reminding himself of this, he pulled the report of various interviews he had had with the inhabitants of Lakehurst towards him and started to study them.

They were a strange lot, Tennant reckoned. From the totally eccentric to the bad and scheming. In the first category he placed Ceinwen Carruthers, in the second Sonia Tate. However, their stories were almost identical. It seemed that almost the entire village had gone to the vicar's party in the evening and had left in a body at ten thirty or thereabouts.

All of them – and this included everyone with the exception of Dr Rudniski and Olivia Beauchamp, both of whom the inspector had yet to interview – had apparently gone home to their beds where they had snuggled down like good Christian souls.

Tennant looked at the list of names and pictured each one. Ceinwen Carruthers, dirndl skirt and glasses; Mavis Cox, picture of respectability; Ivy Bagshot, he couldn't see her stripping off to do a calendar; the woman in the post office, village gossip; Jack Boggis, dour Yorkshireman but fancied himself with the ladies. That left him with Giles Fielding, apparently likeable, and poor little Kylie who had discovered the bodies and been in a state of shock ever since. Left to track down were the Culpeppers, Kylie's brother Dwayne, together with the doctor, the violinist, Gerrard Riddell and Cheryl Hamilton-Harty. The inspector sighed and drew towards him something found at the scene of the crime.

The Patels had been discovered lying in a great sea of blood, the victims of a frenzied knife attack. The police doctor had counted fifteen stab wounds on Mrs Patel and about twenty on poor Ali. On the bed head, above where they lay, had been pinned a piece of paper. Tennant looked at it now, wrapped in its evidence bag. It said, 'The first of the ten. Be on your guard. The Acting Light of the World.'

It was obviously the work of a religious maniac – or someone trying to fool the police into thinking so. The frenzy of the attack would tie in with that but Tennant had come across these sorts of tricks before and deliberately kept a completely open mind. He turned the message over and noticed that it was scrawled in red ink on a standard piece of A4. It seemed to him to be a con but on the other hand it could just be genuine.

There was a knock on the door and his sergeant, Mark Potter, stuck his head round.

'Can I see you a minute, sir?'

'Of course. Come in.'

Potter walked in, shut the door softly behind him and took a seat on the other side of the desk. He was a neat young man, quiet of manner and tidy of appearance, and quite, in Tennant's opinion, unsuited to police work.

'What is it, Potter?'

'I have caught up with Roseanna Culpepper, sir.'

'Oh good. What did you think of her?'

'Hard to say. The general impression is that she's come from another era. She was a very well-known actress years ago but not any longer. She didn't go to the vicar's party even though she was invited. She told me she had a migraine and went to bed early. I think she's a bit strange.'

'I see. I'll have a word with her myself and see if I get the same reaction. What about the Hamilton-Harty woman?'

'I went out to Speckled Wood and interviewed her. What can I say? She's very slight, like all these women who ride – or most of 'em anyway. She's got jet black hair, dyed. She likes to give the impression that she's terribly young and frisky but when you look into her face you can see all her lines and wrinkles. She runs a riding stable for yuppies who come down to ride at the weekends and stable their horses with her during the week. She was one of the few who was not invited to the vicar's party as she does not go to church because it clashes with her riding lessons. I got very little else out of her.'

'Did you discover where she was on Friday night?'

'She was terribly arch about the whole thing but eventually admitted that she stayed in with a friend.'

'Male or female?'

'Male of course. I reckon it was one of the blokes who keeps his horse stabled with her.'

Tennant grinned. 'And not only his horse it would seem.'

'As you say, sir.'

'I'll go and see her tomorrow along with the others. By the way, have you made any progress with Olivia Beauchamp?'

'She's on tour with the Royal Philharmonic. She's playing in Birmingham in two days time.'

Tennant groaned. 'She would be. And I really want to speak to her.'

'Really, sir? said Potter with a grin.

He had been to Tennant's flat on more than one occasion and noticed amongst his collection of CDs several depicting a dishy looking girl clutching a violin and wearing extremely alluring evening dresses. The name beneath had been Olivia Beauchamp.

Tennant, glimpsing the smile, said severely, 'Yes, really.'

'Very good, sir,' Potter answered, and made a hasty exit.

Left alone, Tennant pulled the polythene bag containing the apparently lunatic message towards him. 'The first of the ten' he read. What the devil did that mean? Surely it wasn't threatening ten murders? He sighed aloud. At the moment he was rehearsing *The Corn is Green* by Emlyn Williams, playing the part of the vacuous Squire. If there were going to be any more victims in Lakehurst this would be yet another show that he would have to drop out of.

At very short notice, Nick Lawrence arranged a short service of prayer for the late Patels. He publicized it by telling Mavis Cox and Mabel Weaver, the woman who worked in the post office, and by putting up a notice outside the church and another in The Great House. To his immense surprise the church was two-thirds full and he noticed several tear-filled eyes as he said a few words about the newly dead and how, even though they were of a different faith, they were still two human souls who needed praying for. Even Kasper, the Roman Catholic, was there, and afterwards invited Nick for a drink in the pub. As they crossed the road they saw the huge mobile police headquarters, driven up from Lewes that very afternoon, and containing an interview room, a kitchen and the necessary set of lavatories. It was parked most obviously in the High Street, dominating all.

The usual crowd was in there – Jack Boggis looking taciturn in the seat which he seemed to have adopted as his own, back turned, newspaper well up; Giles Fielding propping up the bar and telling anyone who was listening that he had popped into the supermarket at eleven o'clock last night and had bought a packet of cigarettes off Ali; Gerrard Riddell, waspish and fretting because he had been in London most of the day and had missed all the drama. Nick and the doctor, after one look at them, took their drinks into a quiet corner.

'It is a terrible business, this,' Kasper said, staring into the depths of his vodka and looking moody.

'Who could have done it?' answered Nick, gulping his pint. 'I mean it has to be a homicidal maniac.'

'Not necessarily. It could be a revenge killing. Or some strange vendetta.'

'Yes, it could I suppose.'

'The police have released no details so we have no way of judging the case,' Kasper said solemnly, and downed his drink.

'Let me get you another.' Nick rose to his feet and made his way to the bar.

There he was buttonholed by Gerrard.

'Tell me, Father Nick, do you know anything further about these terrible killings.'

'I'm afraid I don't. All I can say is that forensics are going through the entire supermarket with a fine toothcomb.'

Gerrard pursed his thin lips. 'The whole thing is horribly upsetting. Especially for those of us who live alone.'

'I don't quite see the logic of that.'

'Well, we'll be afraid of our own shadows.'

'Surely that is up to us as individuals. After all the Patels were two people, a couple.'

'Oh yes, as you wish,' Gerrard answered irritably, and flounced off.

Nick rejoined Kasper, who looked after the retreating figure and remarked gloomily, 'That man is neurotic.'

'I'm beginning to think I am as well. Do you realize that I was staring at a congregation this evening any one of whom might have been the killer?'

'Well, I can assure you that I was not he,' Kasper answered in his quaint English.

'No, well that's two of us in the clear. It wasn't me either.' They clinked their glasses.

'What did you think of the policeman?' Nick asked.

'I have yet to meet him. What impression did you get?'

'Not your average copper. A very intelligent man, I would say.'

'Are you saying that all policemen are thick?' asked Kasper with a laugh.

'No, I'm not saying that at all,' Nick answered thoughtfully.

\*   \*   \*

He had left the church open in case anyone wanted to go in and pray privately for the lost Patels and now, shivering slightly, he did not know why, Nick climbed the few steps that led up to the great oak doors. The church was lit by slightly dimmed lights. There were no burning candles as there had been a fire in the Lady Chapel caused by this very thing some time before Nick's arrival. For a moment as he went in the vicar could see nothing. And then his heart plummeted. Kneeling in the front pew was a figure – very similar to the one he had seen on his first night in the parish – muttering audibly but yet not quite loud enough for Nick to catch the words. Plucking up his courage the vicar advanced down the aisle.

His feet rang out on the stone and the figure turned its head. Nick noticed that it had a hood pulled well down utterly concealing its features. And then, moving at the speed of lightning, it stood up and bolted down a side aisle and once again reached the vestry and vanished. Nick shot after it but found the vestry door wide open and a cold wind blowing in. The creature had disappeared into the darkness and, quite honestly, the vicar had no intention of going to look for it.

In bed that night, having made sure the vicarage was locked and bolted, it suddenly occurred to Nick that the vestry door had been locked that evening, as it always was except on Sunday morning. So the intruder must have had a key. The vicar sat bolt upright and it was then that he heard somebody coming up the stairs. Getting out of bed as quietly as possible, Nick seized a chair – the only thing resembling a weapon that he could find – and flung his bedroom door wide. There was nobody there except Radetsky who was sitting crouched, his tail swollen and his fur on end.

'William, is that you?' called Nick.

There was no answer but a slight sound from the landing told him that he was right.

'You're frightening the cat – let alone me,' he added. He bent down and stroked Radetsky's fur back to its usual state. 'Come on, Rad, you can spend the night with me,' he said, and closed the door firmly shut.

# EIGHT

The alarm went off at six and somewhat begrudgingly Dominic Tennant crawled out of bed and went straight to the kitchen where he made himself a large mug of black coffee. Slumped on a chair he considered his life and whether he was making the best of it. He loved his work, there could be no doubt of that. Enjoyed playing mind games with criminals and slowly tracking them down to the very heart of their ghastly crimes. He also loved acting and would far have preferred going to drama school to becoming an ordinary policeman on the beat. But the financial circumstances of his family had demanded that he get a job, a job with a definite wage, rather than take his chance in the extremely precarious world of the professional actor. So he had done the next best thing and had become an amateur one. An amateur with a great deal of talent but for all that still an amateur.

The other thing that was definitely in a mess was his love life. He had married Fiona – a fellow thespian – ten years earlier. She had stayed around for three, steadfastly refused to have children, and then run off with her leading man, one Terry Belper. What had annoyed Tennant most about this *liaison dangereuse* was the fact that he would have been cast as Higgins had it not been for a demanding case he had been on at the time. But, he supposed, his job did have certain compensations, the forthcoming interview with Olivia Beauchamp being one of them.

He had been a fan for years, ever since he had seen her as one of the five finalists in the Young Musician of the Year contest. She had not won but he had not agreed with the judges' decision – had even written a letter to that effect to the BBC – and had followed her career ever since. A couple of times he had heard her play at the Wigmore Hall and been quite knocked out by her charismatic personality and elegant good looks. In fact he had had a slight crush on her for years in a manner quite unsuitable to a man of his age.

Tennant poured himself another cup of coffee and thought to himself that the time had come for him to find a pleasant companion, someone who might actually love him and in whose company he could relax and be happy. Though there was a great deal to be said for the bachelor life it certainly had disadvantages as well.

He got up and put two pieces of bread into the toaster, waited two minutes, then spread them with generous helpings of butter and marmalade. He was just crunching into the second one when the phone rang. It was Potter.

'Hello, sir.'

'What time do you call this? I'm still asleep.'

'Then you'd better wake up sharpish, sir. There's been another murder.'

'Where?'

'In Lakehurst. The cleaning lady went in early to get his breakfast and found him lying at the bottom of the stairs.'

'Who, Potter? For heaven's sake who?'

'Oh, sorry sir. Gerrard Riddell, one of the people you were still going to interview.'

'Damn and blast,' said Tennant violently. 'All right, I'll meet you outside in fifteen minutes. Have the mobile unit been informed?'

'They're already at the scene.'

Five minutes later, showered, shaved and suited, and looking remarkably smart despite the time in which he had had to get ready, Tennant dived into the car which Potter had brought almost to his front door.

'How can you be sure it wasn't an accident?' was his first question.

'We can't, that's the devil of it,' Potter answered, 'but it's a helluva coincidence, wouldn't you agree, sir?'

'Odd, to say the least. Step on it, Potter. I'm anxious to get a look at this one.'

Pausing only briefly at the police mobile unit to get kitted up in the familiar protective clothing, Tennant and Potter made for West Street. Turning into it from the High Street, the inspector grimaced, seeing before him a narrow road and a lot of parked cars, presumably belonging to the people who lived in cottages and houses on the raised embankment which bordered it. He promptly sent two uniformed men to either end to turn motorists away. He looked up at the raised dwellings and turned to his sergeant.

'Which house is it?'

'That one there. April Cottage. It's deceiving because it's larger than it looks.'

Tennant nodded and climbed the flight of stone steps that led to the residences above. The familiar tape was up and even though it was not yet eight o'clock a small crowd had already gathered beyond it. The inspector looked round for the vicar but thought that it must be a bit early for him.

The front door, guarded outside by a constable, led directly into a living room with french doors which opened on to a neatly kept garden, still bright with autumn flowers. Tennant stepped outside and breathed in the sharp morning air. Running his eye over the plot which was quite large, going down to newly mown lawns, he noticed a gate in the fence at the bottom.

'Where does that go to?' he asked Potter, who was hovering at his elbow.

'I'm not quite sure, sir, but I'll get one of the boys to have a look.'

'Yes, please do so.'

He turned back into the house and walked from the living room to an extremely chi-chi dining room, with silver candlesticks everywhere and masses of mirrors, many of which looked Georgian to Tennant's fairly knowledgeable eye.

Across a narrow passageway lay the kitchen and there, lying in a heap at the bottom of a spiral staircase, was the body. Tennant knelt down beside it and peered closely.

There was a huge blow to the back of the head but whether this had been caused by falling or whether by some blunt instrument it was hard to say.

'What do you think, sir?'

'Um. I don't know. Could have been an accident but somehow I don't think so.'

'Shall we take a look upstairs?'

'Is there another way up?'

Tennant, peering upwards, could see two forensic experts painstakingly going over the staircase, step by spiralling step.

'I don't think so, sir.'

'Odd, having the only access to the bedrooms from the kitchen.'

'That's old cottages for you,' Potter answered brightly.

Fifteen minutes later the police surgeon arrived to examine the body. He crouched down beside it and looked at the head, turned to the right partially revealing the expression on the late Gerrard Riddell's face.

'Looks a sour old puss, doesn't he?'

'So would you if you'd just taken a tumble down a spiral staircase,' Tennant answered drily.

'Ah, but did he fall or was he pushed,' the surgeon replied, fingering the corpse's skull with incredible delicacy.

'That's up to you to say.'

'Well, I won't know until after the post-mortem but my guess is that he received a clobbering before he descended.'

'So he had an assignation in his bedroom?'

'Now, now, Dominic. Don't go jumping to any conclusions.'

'When I can get upstairs I'll have a better idea.'

'You can do that in a minute, sir,' called a female voice and Tennant saw that one of the forensics specialists was a woman, who had reached the penultimate step.

'Anything up there?' he asked her.

'Plenty,' she said, 'but I won't spoil the surprise.'

'You found a weapon?'

'If you can call a great big statue of Buddha a weapon, yes.'

'Good God,' said Tennant.

'Plus a note attached to the wall.'

'Well, that clinches it. We're dealing with another murder, Potter.'

'I thought so all along, sir,' answered the sergeant somewhat smugly.

'Come on. Let's go and see for ourselves.'

They climbed the spiral with care, making sure to miss the blood which bespattered the stairs profusely. Forensics watched them with a smile.

'Careful where you put your feet, sir.'

Tennant merely growled.

They reached the top to find that it opened on to a small

landing which had been turned into a shrine. Yet again there
was a profusion of candles, some still lit, obviously having
burned all night.

Lying on the floor, fallen to one side in a grotesque parody
of the corpse that lay below, was a golden Buddha, drenched
in a great splatter of red around its head. Somewhere, right in
the back of Tennant's mind, a memory stirred but – elusive
as a dream – it was gone before he could catch it.

The Buddha was about three feet tall – Tennant had never
taught himself to think in metres – and probably nearly as
wide.

'Pop downstairs and get me an outsize evidence bag, will
you.'

Potter obeyed. Tennant stood quite still, running his eyes
over the crime scene and absorbing every detail. On the wall,
in the niche where the Buddha had once stood, was pinned
a piece of A4 paper. On it, scrawled in red were the words,
'Second of the ten. Where next? The Acting Light of the
World.' Tennant took it off the wall with his disposable gloves
and placed it in an evidence bag. Potter returned, breathing
hard.

'Here we are, sir. This should be alright.'

The Buddha was heavy but they managed to get it into
the bag.

'Do you think a woman could have done this?' asked
Tennant, catching his breath.

'If she was strong, yes I do.'

'Take a look at this.' And the inspector produced the piece
of paper in its bag.

'It's some religious nutter, I'm sure of it.'

Tennant shook his head. 'We can't be certain. Maybe that's
a deliberate bluff.'

'Well, if it is, he – or she – is carrying it off pretty well.'

'Do you think the wording means they intend to commit
ten murders?'

'Sounds like it, sir.'

They reached the bottom of the stairs, carrying the Buddha
between them, and thankfully handed it over to the forensic
team. The inspector removed his disposable gloves and his
protective gear.

'Now then, where's the cleaning lady? The one who found the body.'

'She's gone home, inspector, in the company of a WPC. Poor old soul was weeping and carrying on about getting her grandson out of bed to go to the job centre. In the circs we thought it was best to let her go.'

'Quite. What's the address?'

They told him the number in Love Lane.

'That runs parallel to this one, doesn't it?'

'Yes sir. We'll get the car out.'

'Don't bother. Potter and I will walk.'

Instead of going out of the front door the inspector made his way down the garden and through the gate in the fence at the bottom.

'Love Lane,' he said triumphantly. 'She doesn't have far to come to work then.'

'No, sir. Now what number was it?'

They found the cottage halfway up on the right. A peculiar shape, it almost seemed to go round a corner. As they approached the front door both men could hear the sound of raised voices. A particularly nasal youth was shouting, 'I can't help no bleeding murder. I ain't gettin' out of bed. Sod it.'

A quavering female answered something inaudible to which the youth responded. 'Bugger off and leave me alone.'

Tennant turned to Potter. 'Sounds as if we have a right little jerk to deal with.'

'The grandson?' mouthed the sergeant as he raised the knocker and gave it a hearty bash.

It was opened almost at once by the policewoman who was wearing a particularly strained expression.

'Trouble?' Tennant asked quietly.

'It's the grandchildren,' she whispered back. 'Poor old dear lives with them and it seems that the boy gives her hell, sir.'

'Um,' said the inspector and marched into the house looking profoundly grim.

The old lady was sitting in a chair sobbing silently into a handkerchief on which was embroidered the initial D in vivid emerald green. From upstairs came the sound of speakers blaring out garage music at absolute top volume.

'Excuse me, I'll just go and deal with this,' Tennant announced and marched upwards with Potter following close behind.

They entered a bedroom so indescribably untidy that it beggared belief. There were heaps of clothes everywhere, including several pairs of underpants in various stages of dishevelment. Dirty jeans abounded, topped by T-shirts with mucky necks. On the walls were large posters of various bands and singers, none of which Tennant recognized with the exception of one of the late Michael Jackson.

In the corner of the room was an unkempt bed with an even more unkempt individual lying in it, smoking a rolled-up fag. He looked round, moon-faced and startled at the sound of someone coming into his lair.

'Out!' said Tennant, and seizing the bedclothes pulled them off him.

''Ere,' answered the other, outraged.

'Police,' Potter stated maliciously. 'On your feet or I'll charge you.'

'Wot wiv?'

'Perverting the course of justice, that's what. Now stand up when you're being spoken to.'

Reluctantly the youth did as he was told, stubbing out his cigarette in an overflowing ashtray.

'Put some jeans on for God's sake,' Tennant said harshly. 'You ought to get out-of-doors more. You're white as a slug. And turn that music off while you're at it. I can hardly hear myself think.'

The grandson opened his mouth to make a snappy response but caught the look in Tennant's eye and rapidly shut it again.

'And now,' said Potter grandly, 'I would like your full name please.' He produced a notebook from a pocket and looked official.

'Dwayne Saunters,' the youth muttered inaudibly.

Beside him Potter was aware of the inspector's shoulders twitching. He compressed his lips tightly as he said, 'Middle name?'

'Jason.'

'And you live at this address.'

'Well, I ain't got nowhere else to bleedin' go, 'ave I?'

Potter remained silent as the inspector spoke.

'Are you prepared to answer questions here, Mr Saunters, or would you prefer to come down to the station?'

'I'll answer 'em 'ere. I don't want to go to no bloomin' station.'

'Right then. You'll put a shirt on and come downstairs. Stay with him, Potter.'

In the small front parlour, reserved for special occasions, Mrs Noakes, the grandmother, fortified by a brimming cup of tea provided by the WPC, sat controlling her tears as best she could. The inspector took a seat beside hers, waved away an offer of tea and said gently, 'Could you tell me how Mr Riddell's house was when you entered it, Mrs Saunters?'

She bristled very slightly.

'It's Mrs Noakes, sir. My daughter would insist on marrying Dick Saunters's son – and a bad lot he turned out to be. But, there, one mustn't speak ill of the dead, must one.'

'They were killed in a car crash, weren't they?'

'Always drove too fast, he did. A reckless fool. But my daughter – Wendy, her name was – she was attracted to uniforms, see.'

Tennant didn't, but decided not to be led down this path.

'Tell me, if you wouldn't mind, Mrs Noakes, everything you noticed about the deceased man's house this morning.'

The grandmother took a deep swig of tea, then put the cup down and launched into a story which, Tennant had the feeling, she would soon tell with relish to any passer-by who cared to listen.

'Well, as you know, I got up early and went across to get him his breakfast. I do that every morning except on Sundays when he has a lay in.'

'Do you have a key to the house?'

'To the garden door, yes. I go through the gate and across the garden and let myself in that way.'

'Quite so. Now tell me as clearly as you can what exactly you saw.'

'Well, nothing at first. I went into the kitchen and switched on the light and. . .'

'Before then. Did you notice any illumination coming from upstairs?'

'Yes, now you come to mention it, I did. There was a flickering light, like he'd left a candle burning in front of that Buddha of his, and there was a dull glow coming from his bedroom.'

'I see. So you switched on the kitchen light. What happened next?'

'I turned to put water in the kettle – and then I saw him. All huddled up at the bottom of his stairs, he was. There was blood – and stuff – oozing from his head.'

Tennant shook his head and made a sympathetic noise. 'Poor you. What a shock. So what did you do?'

'I ran out of the kitchen, still holding the kettle, and into the lounge. Then I come over all queer and had to sit down.'

'I see. Tell me something, Mrs Noakes, did you see anyone in the house or garden? Did anything at all arouse your suspicions?'

'No, sir, it didn't. I think the murderer – whoever he or she was – had been long gone.' She rolled a fearful eye in his direction. 'Is this connected with the killing of the Patels, do you think?'

'It's too early to say,' Tennant lied, thinking of the message signed The Acting Light of the World. 'I take it it was you who went to the mobile police station?'

'No, sir, tell the truth I was too afraid to stay in that house a moment longer. I run all the way round to the vicarage. I thought the vicar would know what to do.'

Tennant suppressed a smile. 'And did he?'

'Oh yes, sir. He was ever so good. He made me a cup of tea and went to the police pantech-thing straight away.'

'Was he dressed?'

Mrs Noakes shot him a peculiar look. 'Yes, he was. Why?'

'No reason,' the inspector answered vaguely.

The door opened and the unlovely Dwayne entered the room wearing a T-shirt with the logo 'None of Your Firkin Business' emblazoned across his chest.

'Get us a cuppa tea, Gran,' he ordered.

Tennant gave him a sweet smile. 'Your grandmother is answering a few questions at the moment, Mr Saunters. Perhaps you could go to the kitchen and make yourself a cup.'

The youth trembled on the brink of giving a rude reply

but was somewhat intimidated by the arrival of Potter who loomed behind him in a menacing manner. Giving the inspector a black look he turned on his heel and could be heard distantly trying to chat up the female police constable who was clearly having none of it.

'You must forgive my grandson, Inspector. He's a bit unruly.'

Tennant made a non-committal noise. 'Have you anything else to tell me, Mrs Noakes? Anything that struck you as out of the ordinary in any way?'

She paused, clearly thinking back. 'There was just one thing, sir.'

'Yes?'

'There were two glasses on the table in the lounge – and one of them had a lipstick smear on it.'

Tennant nodded. 'Thank you very much, Mrs Noakes. We'll leave you in peace now.' He stood up.

Potter muttered in his ear, 'What about the boy?'

'We'll leave him till later,' the inspector answered, and made his way towards the front door.

# NINE

The Reverend Nick Lawrence sat at his desk, staring through the french doors at Radetsky who was playing with a fallen leaf in the garden. To say that he was worried would have been an understatement. He was rapidly coming to the conclusion that Lakehurst housed within its apparently tranquil and unsinning walls, a vicious serial killer. Not that he could be certain that Gerrard Riddell's death was anything more than an unfortunate accident. Yet surely that would be stretching the arm of coincidence too far. The sudden murder of the Patels followed by Mrs Noakes banging on his door in an extreme state of distress to say that her employer was lying dead at the bottom of his stairs had thoroughly unnerved Nick. So much so that he found it hard to concentrate on the paperwork that was spread out before him. In fact he had just picked up a magazine and was starting to flick through the pages when there came a sudden knock at his front door. Glad to be called away from his boring task Nick went down the hall and threw it open. Dominic Tennant stood there.

'Ah, good morning, Vicar. Do you have a spare moment?'

'Certainly,' Nick answered, and followed the inspector into the living room.

'I won't keep you long. I expect you're busy.'

'Fairly. As you know I was called at the crack of dawn by Mrs Noakes shrieking that she had found Gerrard Riddell lying dead at the bottom of his staircase. It was me who rushed to your mobile headquarters. By the way, is it really necessary to have that thing parked in the High Street?'

Tennant smiled at him charmingly. 'Yes, I'm afraid it is. The incident room has been set up in Lewes. It was much easier to do that because of the computers, you see. However, a great many police personnel have been drafted into the village – which I trust you won't find inconvenient – but they must have somewhere central to report to. I hope you understand.'

Nick felt thoroughly wrong-footed. 'Yes, of course. Quite so. I wasn't implying any criticism.'

'Absolutely not,' the inspector answered, still continuing to smile. He changed the subject. 'Tell me, what did you think when Mrs Noakes came rushing in?'

'Quite honestly I thought it was murder.' Nick paused and two pairs of eyes, one like sun ripe gooseberries, the other more like the calm blue sea, locked together. 'Was it?'

'Yes, I think so.'

The vicar clasped and unclasped his hands in a hopeless gesture. 'But who can be doing it? What kind of a lunatic are we up against?'

Tennant paused, thinking, and said eventually, 'I'm going to take a risk.'

'What do you mean?'

'You do realize, Reverend Lawrence, that even a man of the cloth cannot be ruled out of our list of suspects.'

'In other words you think I might have done it.'

The inspector grinned. 'No, as a matter of fact I don't. But that is purely going on my gut instinct. Some of the old school would shoot me down in flames for what I'm about to do.'

'But you are clearly not one of them.'

'No, I'd agree with that.' From a briefcase that he had put on the floor beside his chair Tennant withdrew a piece of paper sealed in an evidence bag. 'Have a look at this, would you?'

The vicar stared at it, tentatively putting out a hand.

'It's all right. You can touch it.'

Nick scanned the words. His attention particularly drawn by the signature, 'The Acting Light of the World'. 'Where did this come from?' he said eventually.

'From the dead man's house. It was pinned on the wall on the landing.'

'Written by the murderer?'

'It would appear so, yes.'

Nick handed the paper back. 'Do you think it's the work of a religious maniac?'

'Or someone trying to give that impression.'

The vicar looked thoughtful. 'Um. I hadn't thought of that.'

'Whatever, I find it terribly sinister. It sounds to me as if he or she intends to go on killing.'

'I don't know if this will be of any interest,' Nick started, and then related the two incidents he had experienced in the church.

The inspector looked thoughtful. 'Thanks for telling me, Vicar. Keep a watchful eye out. But no have-a-go stuff.'

After he had gone Nick went to his study and copied down the words he had recently been shown. 'Second of the ten. Where next? The Acting Light of the World'. He stared at them but other than endorsing Tennant's idea that there was a serial killer on the loose, he could make nothing further of them. He was just about to put them away when there came another knock at his door. Of all the people in the world Kylie Saunters stood there, white as a sail and with panda-rings of mascara under her eyes.

'Oh Vicar, Vicar,' she wailed. 'My gran's ever so upset. They've taken Dwayne off to the police station in Lewes and we're all on our own with a murderer about.'

'Wasn't there a policewoman with Mrs Noakes?'

'Yes, but she's had to go. We've given our statements and the inspector said that he was finished with us for now. Would you come and talk to her, please.'

'Well, if you think I'll be of any help I'll come, of course.'

They started off down the street but it was like getting through an obstacle course. Everywhere groups of women huddled in tight circles of gossip, talking in subdued voices of one and the same thing. All brightened up as they saw the vicar approach.

'Good morning, Father Nick. Isn't it terrible? Poor Mr Riddell,' and so on and so forth were his constant greetings. The vicar pulled faces which he hoped were appropriate, all the time aware that poor little Kylie was pawing at his side like a nervous animal. Eventually he had run the gauntlet and found himself in Love Lane and opposite the cottage. Looking round he saw that the police had cordoned off the garden gate of Gerrard Riddell's house and that forensics were working on it. Bracing himself, Nick went inside, Kylie scurrying ahead of him.

Mrs Noakes was sitting in an armchair beside an unlit fire,

not crying now but occasionally emitting a low sob which, in a way, was almost worse.

Kylie knelt beside her. 'The vicar's 'ere to see you, Gran.'

Mrs Noakes did not look up. Nick squatted down on her other side.

'Anything I can do to help, Mrs Noakes?'

She looked at him. 'They've taken 'im away, Reverend. They've taken 'im orff for questioning.'

Nick shot an enquiring glance at Kylie, who whispered, 'He was giving 'em cheek, Vicar. That's why they took 'im. It was to give 'im a lesson, like.'

He nodded, seeing the picture quite clearly and thinking that for all his good manners it wouldn't do to mess with someone like Inspector Tennant.

'I expect he'll be back soon,' Nick said somewhat lamely.

'I'll go and get a nice cup of tea while we're waiting,' Kylie put in, making Nick think that she wasn't such a bad kid after all.

'Do you believe they're going to keep 'im in, Vicar?'

'No, I'm sure he'll be back soon. It's only routine questioning, you know. They're doing it to everybody.'

He went on burbling the same remark over and over again with variations and had never been more thankful than when Mavis Cox rang at the front door and came bustling in. At this Nick rose, made excuses about parish duties, refused the cup of tea that Kylie waved under his nose, and left the house. Walking up Love Lane he almost bumped into Sonia Tate, who made the most terrible moue at him and batted her eyelashes.

'Oh Vicar,' she said in a little-girl voice. 'I am quite frightened by what is happening. Where is it all going to end I keep wondering.'

'I wish I knew,' he answered solemnly.

She produced a small diary from her handbag. 'Now that I have you on your own, Father Nick, when can you have supper with me? I am sure that I can give you a lot of background information on the personalities of Lakehurst.'

'Including the murderer?' he said without thinking.

She flushed uncomfortably. 'I keep puzzling as to who it can be. But was Mr Riddell's death perchance an accident? Are we jumping to conclusions?'

Thinking of the note left at the scene of the crime, Nick shook his head. 'I don't think so. I believe there might well be a religious maniac on the loose.'

Sonia gave him a penetrating glance. 'What makes you say that?'

Thinking he had revealed too much, Nick answered vaguely, 'Oh, just a feeling I have.'

'Then it must be a regular churchgoer. Oh dear, oh dear.' She closed her eyes and staggered a little where she stood so that the vicar was forced to put out a reluctant arm to support her. Her eyes flew open and she gave him what might once have been a spectacular look. The eyelashes batted again. 'Now Father Nick, when can you come to dine?'

He smiled. 'I'm afraid my diary is on my desk at the vicarage. May I telephone you?'

'Oh please do.' She wagged a finger with an extremely long red nail on the end. 'Now don't forget.'

'I won't,' the vicar answered, and hurried away.

The Great House was packed that evening, everyone feeling in need of a little Dutch courage to cope with the all-pervading sense of fear that had fallen over the village of Lakehurst, to say nothing of the house-to-house enquiries that were now taking place. There was not one person present who was not discussing the murders – for though the vicar had said nothing about the note left above the place where the great Buddha had once stood – rumour was out and blood had run cold.

The vicar stood in a little group with Dr Rudniski, Giles Fielding and, for once on his feet and not sitting in his corner, Jack Boggis. He was looking taciturn and his ill-fitting false teeth were hissing slightly as he spoke.

'It's a rum business, this. Well rum.'

'I must say that I'll be quite glad to get into my car and be off to Speckled Wood at the end of the evening,' said Giles.

'Is it true,' asked Kasper of everyone in general, 'that Mr Riddell was murdered with the statue of a Buddha?'

They all looked blankly at one another, then Giles answered, 'I don't know about that but he certainly had a statue – and a bloody big one it was too – on his landing. And he used to light candles in front of it and all. I know because I delivered a sheep there one Christmas and I got a chance to look round.'

'The sheep was dead I trust?' said Kasper seriously.

Giles made a clucking sound. 'Of course it was dead. He had a lot of his gay friends coming down for Christmas and he wanted it for Christmas Day.'

'I never eat at Christmas,' put in Boggis. 'It upsets my digestion.'

'But it's a time for celebration,' protested Nick. 'We're celebrating the birthday of our Lord.'

'Lord or no Lord, all I eat is a helping of cauliflower cheese.'

'That'll make you windy,' said Giles, grinning broadly. 'They'll hear you thundering down in East Street.'

Everybody laughed but underneath the sound Nick was sure he could detect a hollow quality, an urge to escape the horror and bloodshed.

'But tell me, Giles, surely you don't seriously believe that Gerrard worshipped the Buddha? After all, he came to church.'

The craggy countenance took on a straight-faced expression. 'I'm telling you, Vicar, for all his appearances in church and his lusty singing and all, he did worship that statue. One night I called late to his place and the front door was open. I'd come for my money actually – but that's another story. Anyway I wanders into the house and into the kitchen, calling out his name like, and then I sees 'im. He was sitting cross-legged in front of the thing and he was moaning to it.'

'Moaning?'

'He was making sounds like Um and whispering prayers to it.'

Nick stared, astonished. 'Are you trying to tell me he was a Buddhist?'

'Yes. At least that's what I thought at the time.'

'Extraordinary,' Kasper said.

'Was he a patient of yours?' Jack Boggis asked in a slightly condescending manner.

'No, he went to the older doctor.'

'Wise bloke,' Boggis answered with a smile which, or so it seemed to Nick, was masking the fact that he meant every word he said.

But at this moment all further conversation ceased as a loud voice spoke from the doorway. 'I told 'em to fuck off good and proper, I did. Evening all.' Dwayne had returned from Lewes.

He strolled into the bar in what he considered to be a nonchalant manner but which actually resembled a loutish slouch, his clothes creased and mucky looking, his tee shirt with its unlovely slogan stained with an unpleasant yellowish mark. The lads playing the fruit machines tucked away round the corner hastened towards him.

'Hello, me old mucker, 'ow d'you get on then?'

'All right, Dwayne?'

And so on.

The hero of the hour said loudly, 'Bleedin' cops. I never said nuffink to 'em and they had to let me go. I just played it cool and 'ere I am.'

His voice died down as he followed his companions towards their stamping ground, kicking a bar stool on his way.

'What a creep,' said Giles, and there was a general murmur of assent.

'Another round, gentlemen?' asked the doctor, and for once everyone agreed.

It was strange, thought Nick, as there was a moment's silence while they all took a sip, how people left the pub in pairs, almost as if there were an unwritten agreement that no one should walk alone. The tension in the village was everywhere, the population was frightened.

The doors opened again and much to Nick's surprise and delight Olivia Beauchamp stood there. She was somewhat out-of-breath and decidedly flushed. She looked round, saw her group of friends and hurried to join them.

'What's been going on?' she demanded.

Jack Boggis gave a flash of his mighty false teeth. 'There's been another murder, my dear,' he said in what he considered to be a manly voice. 'But there's nothing for you to worry your pretty little head about.' And he attempted to pat Olivia's hand.

She took it away and gave it instead to the doctor, who squeezed it warmly. 'What will you have to drink, Olivia? It is my round.'

'Thanks Kasper. I think I'll have a large gin and tonic in

view of the news.' She turned to Nick as Kasper went to the bar. 'My cleaning lady told me that old Riddell was murdered last night. Is it true?'

'Aye, it's true, bumble bee,' Giles answered familiarly, rather annoying the vicar.

'But who is doing it?' asked Olivia, going from pink-cheeked to white very suddenly.

'That's the million dollar question,' Nick said grimly. 'If we knew the answer to that we'd all be a lot better off.'

'Are the police on the scene?'

'They are everywhere. They've got a mobile headquarters parked in the High Street and they're going from house-to-house making enquiries. And, Inspector Tennant would like to speak to you.'

Olivia nodded. 'I'll give him a call in the morning. I'm playing in Brighton so I'll be around for a few days.'

Nick looked anxious. 'Did you drive here?'

'Yes, of course.'

'Then I will escort you back.'

'No need for that, Vicar,' put in Giles, in his rollicking Sussex accent. 'I'll drive behind Olivia and see her into her house.'

She turned from one to the other of them. 'Are things that serious?'

Before anyone else could answer Jack Boggis piped up. 'Now then, little lady, if you're looking for someone to walk with, I'm your man. This bloody murderer doesn't scare me I can assure you.'

Kasper, who had consumed several vodkas and obviously had a touch of the fighting spirit as a result, said, 'With respect, Mr Boggis, I would have thought someone younger and fitter would have been a better protector.'

Jack burst out laughing. 'Oh, you would, would you? I could down you any time, young man. I was in the army I'll have you know.'

The vicar felt that this was the moment to intercede. 'I think it is beholden on us all to keep very calm at the present time. There is enough evil stalking this village without us adding to it.'

'Hear, hear,' said Jack loudly.

Giles spoke up. 'Well, my offer still stands, Olivia. I'll
see you home and then you must lock all your doors.'

'Thank you, Giles. I accept. I wouldn't dream of bothering the rest of you.' She downed her gin. 'Shall we go?'

Fielding drained his pint. 'Are you in the car park?'

'Yes.'

'So'm I. Goodnight one and all.'

Nick could not help but notice that Olivia squeezed
Kasper's hand as she left the building.

'A right tidy package, that,' commented Jack, watching
her departing form.

Nick agreed in a half-hearted tone, thinking to himself
that Olivia deserved far more praise than the Yorkshireman
was capable of giving. Trying to be Christian, he murmured,
'Indeed.'

The pub was emptying now, the majority of customers
leaving in twos or threes. Nick turned to Kasper. 'I locked
the church up as soon as it got dark. I didn't like the look
of that stranger I had in there recently.'

'Do you think he was the murderer?'

'I've no way of telling but he – or she – acted in a most
peculiar manner and I don't want a repeat performance.'

'Well, I'm walking home alone,' announced Jack Boggis,
attempting to look defiant, sticking out his chins.

'I'll drop you at the vicarage and then go on,' said Kasper.

Despite his bravado Boggis seemed glad of their company
and strode off with a rather sad attempt at courage when
they left him at the car park. Even though it was only a few
minutes' walk from the vicarage Nick was equally glad to
be dropped at his front door. He walked in, was greeted by
that familiar smell of times past, and listened to the silence.
Radetsky came to meet him, then his tail swelled up as
William creaked overhead.

The last person to leave the pub, mindless with alcohol and
shouting loudly about the sodding cops, was Dwayne. He
turned into one of the small alleyways that ran from the High
Street, then decided that he needed a pee. He unzipped his
jeans and was vaguely fumbling for his cock when somebody tapped him on the shoulder.

'What are you doing?' asked an unearthly voice, neither male nor female but a weird mixture of both.

Fearing the police, Dwayne spun round and looked straight into the eyes of his killer. He fell to the ground instantly and lay in an ever-growing pool of his own cascading urine.

# TEN

I t seemed to Tennant that he had been asleep all of five
minutes when the phone went off in his ear again.

'Yes?' he whispered grumpily.

'Sir.' It was Potter sounding tense.

'Oh no! Not again!' He was fully awake.

'Yes, sir. Sorry.'

Tennant sat up, pulling on a shirt. 'Who is it this time?'

'That little squirt we had down here. The one who was so
horrible to his grandma. Dwayne Saunters.'

'Oh God, it will kill the old girl. Meet me outside in ten.'

'Right, sir.'

Thank heavens for electric razors, thought the inspector,
running one perfunctorily over his chin and simultaneously
pulling on his trousers. And thank heavens for shoes that
slipped on without any bother. He ran downstairs still easing
into one just as Potter's car appeared.

'Tell me everything.'

'He was last seen leaving the pub at about eleven p.m. He
cut down one of those little alleyways where he relieved
himself and was stabbed in the neck as he did so.'

'Any witnesses?'

'Never a one.'

'Who found him?'

'A dog. Old Mrs Carteret, whose house forms part of the
alleyway, heard her pet whining at about midnight and let
him out. She didn't go with him because she was in her
nightclothes but when she heard the redoubtable Roger
worrying at something in the alley she tiptoed down in her
slippers and came across friend Dwayne. She screamed the
place down apparently.'

'Any message left?'

'Something chalked on the wall this time. The night-duty
boys have already set up a crime scene.'

'What ungodly hour is it?' asked the inspector, realizing that he had forgotten to put his watch on.

Potter glanced at his. 'Just gone four, sir.'

'God almighty. We really do earn our money, don't we.'

'We most certainly do.'

Forty-five minutes later they were in Lakehurst which seemed utterly deserted and desolate in the chill wind that had come up. But a visit to the mobile headquarters to get protective clothing proved otherwise. It was a hive of activity and, minutes later, they saw that the alleyway had been cordoned off and that there were shapes in blue standing at either end. What appeared to be a heap of clothes was lying in the pathway.

The inspector spoke to one of the constables standing at the High Street end. 'Has anyone touched the body yet?'

'No, sir. Forensics haven't arrived – and who can blame them.'

'Who indeed?'

Tennant shone his torch on to the scribbled message on the wall. It read: 'So the third one is done. Seven to go. Take great care. The Acting Light of the World.'

He moved the strong beam directly on to the corpse. With all his yobbish bravado drained away, Dwayne Saunters looked pathetic. Huddled as if he were asleep, lying in a puddle of dried-out pee, his flies undone and his penis small and somehow childlike, even the inspector – who had had no time for the youth when he was alive – felt a tiny pang of pity. He turned back to the constable.

'May as well go and have a cup of coffee. There's nothing we can do until the forensic team get here.'

'Very good, sir,' the officer answered, looking slightly jealous.

Back in the mobile unit, Tennant sat with his feet up and his eyes closed and eventually found that he was barely conscious. Then he woke with a start as the police surgeon arrived. All three of them made their way to the alleyway where Dwayne lay motionless, and bent down over him.

'Pretty clear cut,' said the doctor. 'He was stabbed in the neck whilst in the act of urinating. Poor little bugger.'

Without touching it Tennant examined the implement that

had killed the boy. It was like a paper knife, but thinner, and obviously sharp as a razor. It had penetrated the side of the neck, severing a main artery. The inspector bent closer, noticing the jewel at the top and thinking it could well have been an old-fashioned hat pin.

'Potter, look at this. At last we might have a lead to the killer.'

'I don't know about that, sir. You can pick these things up in any junk shop.'

'You reckon it's a hat pin?'

'Looks like it.'

'The murderer knew just how to use it though.'

'Yes.' The sergeant stood up and looked at the chalked message on the wall. 'So he plans on doing another seven, does he.'

'It can't happen. I've got to catch this lunatic.'

'Well the lads are working their way through the local population.'

'And Speckled Wood?'

'Speckled Wood and every outlying farmhouse. Somebody's got to know something.'

Tennant turned to Potter. 'Can you get me a detailed map of the district? And quickly. I'll want it by this afternoon at the latest.' He glanced at his watch then remembered that he had forgotten to put it on. 'Time Potter?' he said quickly.

'Coming up five, sir.'

'Where *are* forensics?'

But even as he spoke a posse of white-clad forms, some carrying suitcases, appeared walking silently towards them.

'Thank God,' said Tennant with force. 'Now we can go away and have some more coffee and let them get on with it. I suggest we return in an hour.'

Back in the mobile unit Tennant sat silently, turning over in his mind the possibility of a linking thread between the victims. Was it conceivable that Gerrard had run some sort of homosexual ring of which Dwayne had been a member? But what would that have to do with the Patels, honest hard-working folk who ordered Mr Riddell's china tea especially for him? Or could it be what Potter had believed all along?

That there was a religious maniac at work who for reasons best known to himself – or herself – was polishing off the inhabitants of the village of Lakehurst.

At eight o'clock, having investigated the corpse of Dwayne Saunters, forensics stating that they had got all they could from it, Inspector Tennant removed his protective clothing and went round, booted and suited, to see the vicar, who he caught shovelling shredded wheat into his face at great speed.

'Excuse me if I just finish my breakfast, Inspector.'

'Of course.' Tennant stared somewhat avidly at the toast.

'Would you like something?'

'Thank you very much. Yes, please.'

'Toast?' The inspector nodded. 'One or two slices?'

'Two please.'

He spread them thickly with marmalade, feeling he needed the sugar. Then turned to the vicar.

'I'm afraid I'm going to pick your brains once more.'

Nick looked up questioningly but said nothing.

'There was another message left at the scene of crime.' And Tennant handed over a piece of paper on which he had copied it down.

Nick looked at it and shook his head. 'It only confirms my suspicion that there's a religious maniac at work. Have you had a handwriting expert look at them?'

'We most certainly have but as they're all printed he can't make very much of them.'

'Not even whether it's a man or a woman?'

'Not even that, I'm sorry to say.'

Nick shook his head. 'I wish I could throw more light on it for you. But at the moment I'm stumped.'

He handed the piece of paper back to the inspector who put up his hand, barring it. 'No, you keep it, Vicar. We've got plenty of these. If you get any bright ideas don't hesitate to ring me.' And he handed the vicar a card with his mobile number as well as his land line printed on.

Nick looked apologetic. 'If I get a brainwave I'll ring straight away.'

'Thanks.' The inspector stood up. 'And thanks so much for the toast.'

'You are most welcome.'

They both stared upwards as from the room above the kitchen there came the sound of footsteps.

'I didn't know you had anybody else living here,' said Tennant, somewhat surprised.

Nick laughed. 'Oh, that's only William. He's my resident ghost.'

'Good God,' said Tennant, and looked at the vicar incredulously.

His earlier mood of extreme tiredness having vanished – probably achieved by eating holy toast, he thought – Tennant looked down the alleyway that had so recently witnessed the death of Dwayne Saunters and saw that an ambulance was parked in the High Street and that a shield had been erected round the body, from which emerged a wheeled stretcher and two attendants. On the stretcher was lying something in a zipped-up bag. The policemen formed a human cordon as the bag was transferred to the ambulance and driven away at some speed.

Tennant was immediately struck by a thought and hurried to the mobile headquarters to voice it.

'Has anyone told the grandmother yet?'

'Yes, sir. Sergeant Potter and a WPC are round there now.'

'In that case,' answered the inspector with a visible sigh of relief, 'I'll go and visit Miss Beauchamp. Can I borrow a car?'

Fifteen minutes later he reached Speckled Wood, finding the place as delightful as its name. At the top of a hill, which he climbed on the small road leading out of Lakehurst, were revealed a few houses dotted here and there. But by far the most spectacular thing was the view. Pulling up outside a rural-looking cottage, Dominic gazed for miles to a distant glimpse of the sea, surrounded by undulating hills and fields full of sheep. In the distance he could glimpse what had once been a manor house and narrowing his eyes saw a glint of azure water that told him the place was still moated. His heart leapt and the actor in him surfaced. Just for a moment he dreamed that he was spotted by a well-known director, became an overnight success in a major film and could afford to buy somewhere beautiful in Speckled Wood instead of his crummy flat in Lewes. And then, as if to add to his dream, he heard the nearby sounds of a violin played by an extremely competent pair of hands. He turned to the cottage he was standing outside and knew, even before he looked, that he had found the home of Olivia Beauchamp.

To be perfectly honest he made no move to knock at the front door until a good fifteen minutes had passed. She was playing a lesser known work by Tchaikovsky and Tennant stood enthralled, listening to her tackling the same few phrases over and over again, honing them until they sounded to Tennant's ears like drops of liquid crystal. Then she paused and he released himself from his almost trance-like state and knocked at her front door.

She took a minute or two to answer and Tennant thought she might have been in the loo because she had a towel in her hands on which she was wiping them.

'Hello,' she said.

With a mighty effort the inspector pulled himself together. 'Miss Beauchamp?' he asked, though he knew perfectly well that it was.

'Yes. Are you the police?'

Tennant showed his identity badge. 'Yes, I am. Look I know it's the most awful cheek to interrupt your practice but could I have a few minutes of your time?'

'Certainly. As a matter of fact I've been expecting you. Come in. Would you like a coffee?'

'I'd love one. I take it black, no sugar.'

She opened the door wide and the inspector walked into an idyllic little place with superb views from every window.

'Lovely cottage,' he said. 'But a bit remote.'

'Not really.' She gestured through the kitchen window at another house – as old as time in Tennant's opinion – which stood behind her property and slightly to the right. 'That's Giles Fielding's place. He farms there, you know.'

'And does he keep an eye on you?'

She grinned. 'Yes, but not in the way you're thinking.'

'How do you know what I am thinking?' was out of the inspector's mouth before he had time to control the words.

'It was the look on your face,' said Olivia, and laughed her wonderful laugh.

Tennant turned away for a moment, ostensibly to take another look at Giles's place but in fact to speak to himself severely about his behaviour and not to forget that Miss Beauchamp was a suspect in a murder enquiry. When he turned back it was with a very straight face.

'I believe that you also have a place in London, Miss Beauchamp.'

'Yes, I've got a flat in Chiswick.'

'Very nice.'

'Very nice and very expensive.'

'But you weren't there the night of the Patels' murder?'

'No, I went to the vicar's party. I left about eleven o'clock and Dr Rudniski saw me into my car and I drove back here. I saw lights on in Giles's place – he'd left Nick's about twenty minutes before I did – but I didn't go in.'

'Were you in the habit of calling in on him?'

Olivia's eyes twinkled. 'Yes, I was. As you said, Inspector, it's pretty remote up here and it's nice to have a good neighbour.'

Tennant sipped his coffee. 'But I believe you were out of the village when the other two murders took place.'

'Yes, and no. I was in Birmingham when Gerrard Riddell was killed but I had left the pub about half an hour before dear little Dwayne met his end.'

'I take it you didn't like him?'

'I detested the little bugger. But then so did everybody else. Only his cronies and his grandmother had any time for him at all.'

'That's rather vehement.'

'I meant it to be. He was a perfectly horrible little person.'

'So you weren't sorry when you heard he was dead. How did you hear, incidentally?'

'Giles phoned me. Someone from the pub had phoned him. This is a village, Inspector, where the grapevine never ceases to throb.'

'And can you tell me where you were at eleven o'clock last night?'

'Though we had separate cars Giles escorted me home. As I told you I left about ten thirty and the vicar and Kasper – the doctor – agreed that Giles would drive behind me and see me in.'

'Which he did?'

'Yes. You can ask him.'

'Don't worry, I will.'

Olivia suddenly smiled and said, 'This conversation is getting terribly serious.'

'I know and I apologize for it. But it is a serious matter. We have a serial killer on the loose and I must find him quickly and put a stop to it.' He stood up and held out his hand. 'Thank you for the coffee and also for the great pleasure of meeting you.'

'Me? Why is that?'

'Because I've been a fan for years. I really have. I've a great many of your CDs at home.'

'How very nice of you. Thank you very much.'

Tennant walked to the front door, then turned. 'I am calling a public meeting tonight with the police present. Will you come?'

'I most certainly will. And I'll bring Giles.'

The inspector nodded. 'Very wise. It won't do to walk about alone in Lakehurst after dark.'

He found Giles Fielding in the far field busily rescuing a sheep that had got its head stuck in the hedge. The animal was kicking frantically with its back legs but Giles had it round the shoulders in a firm grip and was pulling at it hard. The inspector stood silently, watching a true farmer at work, and heaved a sigh of relief as the animal was freed and went trotting off quietly to join its fellows.

'Oh there you are, sir,' said Giles pleasantly, turning round. 'I've been expecting you.'

'Have you now?'

'Yes. What with young Saunters being done in last night I knew it wouldn't be long before the police came looking for me.'

'Looking for you?'

Giles's ruggedly handsome face flushed. 'I don't mean in

that sense. I meant before you came to interview me. Anyway, Inspector, I think we should continue this conversation indoors, don't you?'

They made their way into one of the handsomest houses that the inspector had ever set foot in. It was so mellow with age that somehow the untidiness of a man living alone was dwindled to nothing. A pair of sheepdogs were sleeping under the table. They looked up as their master came into the room but then went quietly back to sleep again.

'You don't mind 'em?' asked Giles, nodding his head in the dogs' direction.

'As long as they don't bite.'

'If either of them was to attack someone I'd shoot them at once.'

'Quite right,' said Tennant, thinking of some of the cases he'd seen of children being mauled by so-called pets.

'Oh yes. I can be hard when I have to be,' Giles answered.

And looking at him, the inspector saw a completely different aspect to the man he was regarding, somebody ruthless appearing beneath Giles's wide blue eyes.

Tennant fired off the usual questions and discovered that Fielding had no real alibi for any of the murders. He had by his own admission bought a packet of cigarettes from Patel at around eleven that evening, just before the shop closed. The night of the Riddell death he said he had been in The Great House earlier in the evening but had then returned home and watched television alone. As for the time when Dwayne had been killed, what easier than to see Olivia through her front door then drive up the road, turn round, and go back to Lakehurst to catch that little menace and end his wretched existence?

Tennant was in an extremely thoughtful mood as he made his way back to his car.

'Oh by the way, I'm calling a public meeting tonight. Please try and come if you can,' he shouted.

'I'll be there inspector, never you fear,' Giles called back, looking his usual cheery self.

But, the inspector thought as he drove away, fear was very much what the farmer was feeling.

# ELEVEN

It was with the greatest regret that Tennant phoned the director of *The Corn is Green* and resigned his part as the Squire. This had happened so many times in the past that there were now serious doubts about casting him at all but one or two still had faith, though not for much longer if he continued at this rate, he thought. Nipping into The Great House before the meeting he downed a large vodka, while Potter, who was driving, consumed a St Clements.

'I don't like these things,' he said to his sergeant.

'Are you referring to the drink or the meeting, sir?'

'The meeting, of course.'

'I can't think why not,' Potter answered. 'I would have thought you'd have been in your element. Standing on the stage with dozens of people looking at you. Just your thing.'

'Well, you're wrong. It's very different. In acting you're creating somebody else's character. At this sort of meeting you're seriously warning people to look out for themselves.'

'It has to be done, sir. There's obviously a lunatic about. People must take precautions.'

'I should think they've already got the message.'

'It's our duty to reiterate it, sir.'

'Yes, I know you're right.'

Not altogether to his surprise Tennant saw that the Commemoration Hall was packed. The chairs had been taken out of their stacks and were now arranged in serried rows. He ran his eye over the gathering and saw that it contained several familiar faces. Ceinwen Carruthers was there, sitting amongst a handful of earnest ladies and one or two fey men who the inspector took to be the Pixie Poets. Sonia Tate, dolled up to the nines – as Tennant's mother used to say – was batting a pair of false eyelashes, one of which had slipped slightly. Mavis Cox, looking businesslike, was sitting near the vicar, who was handsome in a lightweight summer suit and dog collar. Next to him sat

Olivia, looking delightful – or so the inspector thought – in an emerald green dress with a scarlet sash. Sitting on her far side was Dr Rudniski, frowning seriously.

'Who's that?' Tennant whispered to Potter, nodding in the direction of a very slim woman with a mass of jet black hair.

'Cheryl Hamilton-Harty who runs the riding school. You want to watch her.'

As if she knew that someone was talking about her Miss Hamilton-Harty chose that moment to look round and wreathed her face into a daunting smile as she caught the inspector's eye.

Tennant took his place on the platform along with several uniformed officers, Potter close by his side, and was just about to stand up when the door opened at the back and several late-comers walked in. These were led by Giles Fielding, who had clearly been tanking up before the meeting began, followed by Ivy Bagshot, who had not. She was followed by that beauty of another era, Roseanna Culpepper, who was walking with a man who the inspector took to be her husband.

Tennant cleared his throat and rose, pausing a moment before he spoke.

'Ladies and gentlemen, good evening, and thank you so much for coming to this meeting which I hope will be of benefit to us all.'

Jack Boggis chose this moment to make an entrance, looking somewhat the worse for wear.

'Hello, little lady,' he called out and made a dash to sit close to Olivia but was fended off by the vicar and Dr Rudniski. Looking sour as a sloe he had to take a seat next to Mavis Cox which clearly did not please him at all.

'Now that we are all here,' said Tennant pointedly, 'I'll say what I have to as briefly as possible.'

'Hear, hear.' This from Boggis.

The inspector stared at him coolly, wondering if he could possibly be the man they were after. Jack, feeling several pairs of eyes turned in his direction, did his bluff Yorkshireman act. Nobody took any notice.

Tennant continued. 'You can all rest assured that the mobile police headquarters will remain in Lakehurst for the foreseeable future. If any of you notice anything suspicious – anything at all – or if you see someone that you know behaving in an unaccustomed manner – ' his eyes flicked on to Jack Boggis and remained there a second or two – 'it is your duty to go and report it immediately. The station will be manned night and day so you can go in at any time. Or if you just feel like a chat or are anxious in any way, they are there to help you. Please remember that. Now are there any questions?'

There was the usual silence and then a hand shot up at the back of the hall. 'Why are there so many police in Lakehurst at the moment? And how long are they going to stay here?'

'They are here for your protection. I expect you have been visited by people doing house-to-house checks but you must realize that this is an essential part of our enquiries.'

The doctor asked a question. 'Is it your intention to take a DNA sample from everyone in the village?'

Tennant paused. There had been talk of it but the odd thing was that the killer had left no traces at the various scenes of crime. It was almost as if he had been wearing protective clothing himself and quite definitely had worn disposable gloves. There had been no sperm, no sputum, nothing. The search for fingerprints and hairs had also been in vain.

'No, not at this time,' he answered.

'Why not?' Kasper persisted.

'I am afraid I cannot answer that.'

Somebody else asked, 'What would be your advice to people living on their own?'

'Simply to lock yourselves in by both day and night. And not to allow anyone into your house until you have checked their ID. While we're on that subject I notice that you have taken to walking round in pairs and I can't tell you how sensible that is. And if you would all escort the elderly to and from their homes and check their premises for them, you would be doing a great service.'

Mrs Ivy Bagshot waved a skinny arm. 'I am volunteering my services by offering a lift to all those who would like to share my car with me.'

Tennant felt he ought to murmur something about being public-spirited but just couldn't bring himself to do so. He and Potter exchanged a glance bordering on a grin.

There was an 'ooh' of gratitude from her fellow WI members and during this Potter murmured, 'Where's Mr Bagshot?'

'I think she "lawst" him,' Tennant muttered back.

'Not "lawst" but gone before,' Potter mouthed silently.

'Inspector.' Ceinwen was on her feet.

'Yes, Miss Carruthers?'

'We Pixie Poets often wander in the woods at night, communing with nature and all that. I wonder whether you think this a good idea or not?'

'Definitely not. I don't know how many of you there are but I would strongly advise you to curtail your activities for the time being.'

Ceinwen neighed a laugh. 'We usually number about six but if you advise against it we will certainly meet in one another's houses.'

Boggis chimed in. 'When are you going to catch this fella, that's what I want to know?'

There were murmurs of assent from the audience.

Tennant faced them and said, 'To be honest with you, I don't know. I can tell you that the killer has left very little evidence for us to go on. But we have one or two clues naturally.'

That was a complete lie. The murderer seemed to know as much about forensic evidence as the experts. Even the notes had been handled with gloves and the familiar red scrawl was written with a plain red biro. At the moment the police had nothing to go on and could only hope that he would make a mistake in future. Yet that thought had the most sinister implications.

'And what might they be?' asked Boggis in a truly nasty tone of voice.

'If you think, sir, that I am about to reveal them to a full public meeting then I am afraid you are extremely naive.'

'Well, if that's the best you can do I might as well go back to the pub as waste my time here,' Boggis answered, and standing up began to clatter down the row.

'One last thing, ladies and gentlemen,' said the inspector loudly, drawing all eyes back to him, 'I must impress on you that though the killer might have struck for the last time, it is possible that even at this very moment he might be some-where in Lakehurst, or even sitting in this hall, contemplating his next move. I must enjoin you all to take care. Goodnight and thank you.'

He sat down and whispered to Potter, 'How was that?'

'Very good, apart from those interruptions by that fellow Boggis. Rude old bastard.'

'I couldn't agree more.'

But further conversation was impossible as various people bore down on them. Tennant found himself overwhelmed by the exotic smell of Mitsouko. Roseanna and Richard Culpepper were approaching him, wreathed in smiles.

Tonight she was wearing a slightly more fashionable slouch hat, her hair pulled back within its depths. Studying her, Tennant was overwhelmed by the fact that she must have been as stunning as Garbo in her heyday. Great cheekbones stood out under enormous eyes that even with all the wear of time held enchantment in their depths. Long – and natural – eyelashes drooped down in a face that once must have been quite magical. He almost felt overpowered by her presence but sensed that she hung back with a shyness that surely was not natural to her.

Beside her Richard had the slightly sad air of an actor who was destined to play bit parts all his life. His handsome forehead was sprinkled with a light perspiration and his slicked back hair hung down on his collar. He was trying desperately to look like a West End success and failing wretchedly. He held out his hand.

'Good evening, sir. I don't think we've had the pleasure of meeting as yet. I'm playing a part in London which includes Sundays, I'm afraid.'

'Oh yes, Mr Culpepper. How do you do? I've already heard about your London engagement. You managed to get away this evening, though?'

'Yes, and I am so glad I did. I hadn't realized quite how horrendous things had become in Lakehurst. Roseanna tries to shield me from the grisliest facts, don't you angel?'

He gave her waist an affectionate squeeze. She smiled up at him and it occurred to the inspector that she was actually in love with this ageing matinee idol.

'So how come you are with us tonight?' Tennant asked.

'Actually the show was cancelled. The leading lady went down with tonsillitis, or some such thing.'

'And no understudy?'

'I'm afraid it's only fringe theatre,' Richard said with a sheepish grin.

'I see.'

'But it is very unlikely to happen again so please keep a special eye out for my wife, Inspector. I can't bear to think of her living alone and being frightened.'

'Could she not join you in your hotel in London?' the inspector enquired.

'Actually they are theatrical digs and not the sort of place I'd like Roseanna to have to live in.'

'Well in that case I would advise that she went to stay with friends until this situation has sorted itself out.'

Richard's expression became extremely earnest. 'Unfortunately they all live miles away. It would be totally impractical.'

He's got an answer for everything, thought Tennant. He smiled and said, 'We'll do our best to protect her, Mr Culpepper.'

'Thanks so much,' said Culpepper, and wrung Tennant's hand.

He was stopped on the way out by the woman with the tumbling mass of black hair who identified herself immediately.

'Hello, Mr Inspector. I've heard so much about you. I'm Cheryl Hamilton-Harty. I run a riding school out at Speckled Wood.'

Tennant smiled. 'Any relation to the famous musician?'

She gave him a totally blank glance and said, 'Was he in Queen?'

He ignored that and went on. 'I believe my sergeant came to interview you.'

'Yes. Very sweet. But I like dealing with the top man.' She leant on him a little and said, 'Would it be forward of me to invite you for a drink or are you still on duty?'

He wasn't actually and he was briefly tempted to say no. And then he thought of her reputation and definitely decided to accept.

'No, I'm not. Shall we go to The Great House?'

She gave him a brilliant glance. 'No, let's go to The White Hart. It doesn't get as crowded.'

She drove him down Arrow Street in a very large four by four with a dog in the back which growled at Tennant suspiciously.

'Oh shut up, Fern,' Cheryl shouted at it.

It subsided but Tennant was aware of its eyes boring into his back and felt that on the slightest provocation it would take a bite out of him.

'Good guard dog,' he remarked.

'Yeah. I've got another one at home. Mother and daughter. I call the daughter Flora. She's watching the house while I'm out.'

'Good idea.'

He was beginning to wish that he had bowed out of the arrangement but some devilish side of him had made him accept the invitation. As they walked into The White Hart somebody let out a low whistle and another hidden voice remarked, 'Chattin' up the police now, are we Cheryl?' She giggled but said nothing and marched through the bar to a small alcove at the back where she plonked herself down. Tennant was left with no alternative but to ask her what she wanted to drink.

'I'll have a G and T, thanks.'

A wary-eyed Kylie served him, looking beyond his shoulder to where Ms Hamilton-Harty sat.

'Gran's poorly, Mr Tennant,' she murmured.

'I'll look in on her tomorrow,' he said and smiled in what he hoped was a reassuring manner.

'She'd like that,' she answered, and he thought how ill the poor girl looked.

Cheryl meanwhile had arranged her admirable figure into what she thought of as a provocative pose. The inspector had to admit that she was quite attractive though much older than she would admit to and extremely lined around the eyes, which on close inspection were quite small and hard and a rather insipid shade of blue.

'Cheers,' she said, clinking her glass against his.

'Cheers,' he replied, wishing he were somewhere else.

'Well now, tell me everything,' she said, and under the table he felt one of her feet play round one of his. He sat back, removing it as he did so.

'What do you want me to say?'

'Who do you think is behind all these killings for a start.'

'I don't know and even if I did I wouldn't be able to tell you. Who do you think?'

Cheryl gave him a teasing smile and giggled relentlessly. 'I think it's old Jack Boggis.'

Tennant hid his look of surprise. 'Why?'

'He's such an oddball. He lives alone, drinks himself stupid, doesn't have a woman in his life despite his lechy behaviour, and hardly eats a thing.'

'I wouldn't have thought those were the characteristics of a typical murderer.'

'Well I think he's a dirty old man. He always stops when he drives past the riding stables and comes in for a peer round.'

'I see. And where does he go when he drives off?'

Cheryl ran her hand through her luxuriant hair and screwed her eyes up in merriment. 'How would I know? He could be going to Tunbridge Wells, Crowborough, who cares? I think he's probably snooping round the house of that stuck-up Olivia Beauchamp.'

'Surely you don't mean that he burgles it?'

'No, she's probably given him a key.'

Tennant actually stopped listening, convinced that he was hearing the ramblings of a mega bitch. But whether his eyes glazed over or his expression became vacant, Cheryl guessed the truth.

'I think you're very rude,' she said, a teasing expression on her face. She bit her lower lip, a habit that Tennant couldn't abide. 'You're not paying me any attention.'

He guessed that this was one of her lines so he simply said, 'You say that to all the boys.'

She looked fractionally put out and fortunately at that moment there was a welcome interruption. Potter panted in appearing out of breath and very slightly irritable.

'Oh here you are, sir. I've been looking for you everywhere. I got quite panicky. No one seemed to know where you were.'

'Well, sit down a minute while I finish my drink. Miss Hamilton-Harty this is Sergeant Potter.'

'Hello,' she said, looking Potter up and down and then

giving him a long, slow smile which meant she preferred him to Tennant. 'How very nice to see you again.'

The inspector recalled, somewhat late, that Potter had already interviewed her.

'Oh you two have met,' he said.

'Oh yes,' said Cheryl, giving Potter an upward glance. 'I promised to take him riding on one of his days off.'

'Yes,' answered Tennant, 'I'm quite sure you did.'

# TWELVE

Having extricated themselves from the clutches of Ms Hamilton-Harty, Potter drove swiftly up Arrow Street but drew to a stop outside The Great House.

'There are quite a lot of people inside who want to see you, sir. I do think you could pay them a courtesy call. Ceinwen Carruthers and the Pixie People are all expecting you.'

Tennant groaned. 'I feel like bed, to be perfectly honest.'

Potter muttered something inaudible.

'What?'

'I said anything to do with Cheryl, sir.'

'If I weren't so tired I'd have you on a charge of insubordination,' said Tennant, straight-faced.

Potter began to apologize, not quite certain, but the inspector cut across him. 'Now go and park the car, there's a good chap, and I'll just go in and chat briefly.'

He had been mixing his drinks, that was the trouble, and Tennant felt himself break out in a sweat as he entered that heaving mass of people, all anxious to have a word with him.

'Ha, Inspector, I was wondering if you would come in. Allow me to buy you a drink.' It was the would-be superstar, Richard Culpepper, who spoke.

'Thanks very much I'll have a glass of red wine, please.'

He knew he shouldn't drink any more but felt that if he didn't get a decent night's sleep tonight he would be totally wrecked.

Richard turned to the bar and once again the inspector beheld the gorgeous face of Roseanna. He wondered what her age was and guessed that she was about sixty and her husband some fifteen years younger. And then he had a memory flash which was gone before he could grasp it. Just for a second he knew that face and then the next second he felt he must have dreamt it. He was still shaking his head slightly when Richard came back with a large glass of red wine.

Ceinwen Carruthers sashayed up. 'Forgive me, I'm not interrupting?'

'Not at all,' said Richard, being frightfully charming.

'I just want to say, Inspector Tennant, that I thought your presentation tonight was terribly good. I mean we Pixie Poets really took it to heart.'

'Oh I'm pleased.'

He glanced round to where they stood, their numbers now down to four, the men stalwartly drinking lager and lime, the women with glasses of pineapple clutched bravely to their breasts. Richard followed Tennant's gaze and shot him a look of amusement.

'I'm so glad you enjoyed it,' Richard said.

Ceinwen looked startled, her nostrils flaring. 'I would have hardly used the word enjoy, Mr Culpepper.'

'Sorry, that was foolish of me. I was thinking theatre. Would you like a drink Miss Carruthers?'

'No thank you. I have had sufficient.'

She bowed her head to the inspector then stalked away to rejoin her group of fellow poets.

'Oh dear,' Richard said. 'I think I've put my foot in it.'

'Never mind, darling. You meant well,' Roseanna answered, and the drooping mouth swept up into a radiant smile.

'Tell me about your show,' said Tennant, very slightly jealous of someone who had made a career out of acting.

'Oh, it's a mere trifle. It's by the winner of the St Pancras award. It's called *Major No More*.'

Suddenly the inspector felt too tired and too apathetic to ask any further questions. He just wanted to get back to his flat in Lewes and have a good sleep. But Richard hadn't finished with him yet.

'I play the part of a forensics expert. It's an amusing cameo. The only light spot in the whole thing really.'

'I've yet to see it,' Roseanna said huskily. 'I shall go next week.'

'It will be a pleasure to have you there, darling.'

It occurred to Tennant, rather cruelly, that the former actress had made the money and that Richard was more or less her toy boy, and that he worked to fuel his vanity and not because he was bringing home the bacon.

He said, 'It has been a pleasure talking to you both. And now if you will forgive me . . .'

But Lakehurst still hadn't done with him. Ivy Bagshot swept up to him, teeth flashing. 'Ah, Inspector,' she exhaled, 'I just wanted to say well done for tonight. I think you have inspired a sense of community in the village, I truly do.'

She smelt of ham sandwich and Tennant recoiled slightly.

'For example, Ceinwen Carruthers accepting a lift from me.'

'Why should that surprise you?'

'Because she doesn't approve of the WI. Thinks we're a lot of dowdy old fuddy-duddies.'

Tennant manfully said nothing.

'Have you ever thought of becoming a speaker? Because if so I am sure the Lakehurst branch would be most interested in booking you.'

'I'm afraid I don't have time for that,' the inspector answered, looking round the room for Potter to rescue him, then saw him having an altercation with Jack Boggis. 'Potter,' he called, and a note in his voice must have told his junior officer that he needed rescuing.

'Yes, sir?'

'Time I went home, I think. I feel fit to drop.' He turned to Ivy Bagshot. 'If you will forgive me, madam. It's been a long day.'

'Of course. Thank you again.'

She went to rejoin her group, signalling to Ceinwen Carruthers as she did so.

'What did you say to bloody old Boggis?'

'I told him that any further interruptions at a meeting would be treated as impeding officers in their course of duty and could lead to arrest.'

'What did he say?'

'He started waffling about freedom of speech but I just turned on my heel and left him.'

'Good. I'm beginning to heartily dislike the fellow.'

'So am I,' said Potter with feeling.

Having walked home with Kasper, Nick plunged into the vicarage to hear the phone ringing. His heart sank as he heard the voice of Sonia Tate.

'Oh hello, Father Nick.' The volume dropped sexily. 'How are you? I've been thinking about you. Worrying about you.'

Nick's eyes rolled heavenwards. 'Were you at the lecture tonight?'

'Yes. I was sitting near the back. I was offered a lift home and I took it. Nick, when is this dreadful business going to stop?'

'I wish I knew, Mrs Tate.'

'Sonia, *please*.'

'Sonia,' he said reluctantly.

'Anyway I haven't rung you to discuss that.'

'No?' Nick answered feebly, certain that he knew what was coming.

He was right. 'I was ringing up about our dinner date. When are you free?'

'Sonia, I have decided to stay at home as much as possible at the moment. Obviously parish duties must continue but I feel that other than those we would all do as well to stay put.'

She tinkled a laugh at him, a sound which had him holding the receiver away from his ear.

'But I don't have any parish duties.'

'You know what I mean. I think we should all be especially careful.'

'In other words you don't want to come.'

'It's not that,' Nick lied, 'it's just that I feel we should all be listening to the police advice and not socializing at the moment.'

'No, you're right I suppose.'

She sounded bitterly disappointed and Nick felt a pang of guilt but quickly dismissed that when he thought of her reputation. He considered her age and guessed at sixty-five minimum. Not, he reprimanded himself, that there was anything wrong with that, provided that one looked like Joan Collins of course.

'I'm so sorry,' he said, 'but I think it's more sensible.'

'Yes, of course. Another time then.'

'Certainly. Another time.'

He went into the kitchen, justifying himself. It really wasn't safe to move round Lakehurst at present, not at night anyway. He wondered briefly whether Sonia Tate could be the murderer and that was why she was so confident about going out nocturnally. Then he dismissed the idea because in actual fact he hadn't a clue who it might be. All he could pray was that it was someone who lived outside the village and just roved in with killing on his or her mind.

Nick had locked the church's main doors at dusk and had had the vestry lock changed a few days previously. In fact he was due to give the new keys on Sunday to those who had claim to one. Yet he felt hesitant about doing so. Suppose it was a member of the choir who had fled past him in the darkness leaving him feeling afraid and nervous.

The vicar couldn't help smiling to himself as he thought about that idea. Half of them were elderly women with quavering voices, their leader a well-preserved seventy who boomed out so loudly that she drowned the rest. Absolutely nobody had had the courage to tell her that her voice had been shot to shreds years ago. The other half were assorted ages and sizes, two boy sopranos who, no doubt, would have the old ladies in tears at Christmas time; three very spotty schoolboys; one gay young man with bright red hair and masses of after shave. The rest were elderly men in various stages of baldery.

The only one of those who had any possibilities as the killer was the gay fellow whose name, improbably, was Broderick Crawford, presumably after some long-dead film star. The vicar wondered whether to withhold the key from him but decided that would make him feel put upon and Nick might get reported for being a homophobe. He sighed, wishing that the murderer would be caught quickly so that all the problems could be solved.

William paced a little upstairs and Nick almost welcomed the sound. At least the ghost was harmless. At that moment the telephone rang, making him jump out of his skin. He picked up the receiver and Kasper's voice said, 'Nick, are you alright?'

'Yes, why?'

'I thought I saw somebody hanging round the back of the vicarage when I drove past just now on my way to see a patient.'

'Oh good heavens. I'd better go and have a look.'

'Yes, do so. But be very careful.'

'Thanks.'

'I shall ring back in fifteen minutes,' Kasper said solemnly, and replaced the receiver.

Nick looked round for a weapon but the only thing that sprang to mind was the poker. Grabbing it, he went quietly to the garden door.

The place was full of pools of moonlight beyond which there were deep dark patches of shadow in which anyone could have been hiding.

'Hello,' called Nick uncertainly. 'Is there anybody there?'

There was no answer and no movement, then Radetsky appeared, winding his way round the vicar's legs as he came to find out what was going on.

'Go inside, cat,' Nick ordered sternly, of which command Radetsky took absolutely no notice whatsoever. Ears flat against his head he let out a low growl and proceeded into the undergrowth, deep into the darkness. A second or two later he let out a howl as if he had been kicked and Nick leapt into action, sprinting towards the sound. And then he heard the noise of running feet and actually glimpsed a cloaked figure leaping over the gate that led from the bottom of his garden to the lane outside.

Nick sped after it, throwing the gate open and caution to the winds. He hesitated momentarily on arriving in the alley, not knowing whether to turn to right or left. All seemed terribly quiet, in fact unnaturally so. He stood listening for the sound of those speeding feet and the direction they were going in, then he heard a sudden noise behind him – and darkness fell.

The vicar regained consciousness to see Kasper bending over him administering cold compresses to his head. As he tried to sit up he felt as if he had been struck by Thor's hammer, so immense was the pain. He fell back again and realized he was lying on his own sofa in the vicarage living room.

'What happened?' he asked, his voice a squeak.

'I phoned you as I said I would and got your answer-phone,' Kasper said solemnly. 'So I drove here and found you lying unconscious in the lane.'

'Do you feel up to answering questions, sir?' asked another

voice, and moving his eyes painfully round, Nick saw that a uniformed policeman was in the room, presumably called from the mobile headquarters.

'Yes,' he said.

'We think you might have some DNA on you,' said yet another voice, and Nick extended his gaze and saw a figure in white, complete with box of tricks, bearing down on him.

'But I didn't see anyone,' he protested.

'But they saw you,' she answered, and set to examining the wound on his head.

It was painful as she dug about with her tweezers but eventually she let out a little exclamation and Kasper asked, 'Got anything?'

'Just a fibre or two stuck to a small fragment of wood.'

'What was I hit with?' Nick asked.

'It appears to have been a fallen branch or something of that sort. All I can say at this stage is that it was a lump of wood.'

'And you say there are fibres?'

'Yes, but whether they come from what he or she was wearing or whether from something else it is impossible to say without further examination.'

The uniformed policeman spoke. 'Can you tell me what you saw, Vicar?'

'Not much,' Nick answered, and proceeded to describe exactly what had happened up to the moment when he had been struck.

'And that's all I can tell you,' he added.

Kasper spoke up. 'I would like to attend to my patient now, if you have no objection.'

He examined Nick's head and said, 'You're going to need a couple of stitches.'

'Can you put them in?'

'Yes, but you really ought to go to hospital.'

'Kasper, please.'

'Why don't you want to go? Are you frightened of such places?'

'Good Lord, no. It's just that I don't want the killer to have the satisfaction of knowing that he put me in A and E.'

'You just said he, sir. Why was that?' asked the policeman.

'I don't know really. Except that my assailant leapt over the gate and I swear that I saw a pair of trousers as they jumped.'

'I'm afraid that doesn't count for much these days. Many women wear trousers.'

'That's true enough,' answered the vicar. He shook his head. 'I'm afraid I only caught a glimpse of the person and it wasn't enough to identify which sex it was.'

The forensic expert said, 'I would normally ask you for your clothes, Vicar, but unfortunately the doctor will have corrupted them when he dragged you indoors.'

Nick smiled feebly and asked, 'Has anyone seen my cat?'

'Yes, it's in the kitchen looking a bit sorry for itself. I think it's been kicked.'

'As long as it's alright.'

'I'll have a look at it,' volunteered Kasper.

'I didn't know you were a vet as well.'

The doctor started to make a rude gesture then realized that this was probably not the most appropriate house to do it in and turned it into a wave instead.

An hour later and Nick, feeling rather drowsy thanks to an injection which Kasper had given him, was tucked up comfortably in bed. Radetsky purred beside him – a special treat – and all was serene except for the fact that a police constable stood outside the vicarage keeping a special watch in case the attacker should steal back and try to achieve his or her objective. Meanwhile throughout the streets of Lakehurst police personnel walked in pairs, looking in every dark place imaginable, hoping that they were drawing nearer to catching their victim but realizing only too well that they were dealing with a formidable enemy.

# THIRTEEN

Tennant had an almighty hangover and wished that he were anywhere but in the office of the superintendent receiving a dressing down over what his boss referred to as the 'Lakehurst affair'.

'What the hell's going on, Tennant? We've got every reporter in Christendom camped out in Lakehurst, let alone sixty more uniform, to say nothing of the vicar being attacked last night, and we still haven't got a result. What's going wrong?'

'I don't know, sir. I truly don't. The trouble is that the killer is wearing protective clothing of some kind or another, to say nothing of gloves. In short he doesn't leave any DNA.'

Superintendent Miller looked thoughtful. 'But how is he or she managing that?'

Tennant felt absolutely lost. 'Unless they've got some connection with forensics.'

It was a pretty lame remark and he knew it. Miller gave him a long, cool glance. 'But the vicar reported seeing a cloaked figure. Are you suggesting that they shed the cloak and have a protective suit underneath?'

'Well, possibly.'

If the superintendent had been the snorting type then he would have done so but fortunately his mind had raced on to other things. He had the notes left at the various crime scenes spread out before him on his desk. He pointed at them.

'Have you got any further with these?'

'I'm afraid not, sir. The handwriting expert confirms that they were written by the same person but that's about it.'

'Do they mean that our killer plans on doing ten murders altogether?'

'I presume so.'

'Then it's clearly a religious maniac – or is that what we're meant to think?'

Tennant sighed involuntarily and Miller shot him a penetrating glance. 'I think maybe it's time we took DNA samples
from the entire population of the village – male and female
alike. I mean the bugger is bound to leave a trace of himself
somewhere. For example the threads on the piece of wood
used to beat the vicar senseless – they're going to reveal
something or other.'

'Probably corrupted by the doctor when he dragged him
inside.'

'Never mind that. We must think positively.'

At that moment there was a knock on the door and Potter
put his head round.

'Sorry to interrupt, sir, but there's an important phone call
for Inspector Tennant. I think it's rather urgent.'

The superintendent waved his hand. 'Best go and deal
with it. But Tennant . . .'

'Yes, sir?'

'Get the DNA sample going as quickly as possible.'

'Yes, sir.'

Outside, Potter gave him a mischievous look. 'Trouble,
sir?'

'Almost.'

He picked up the receiver in his office and said, 'Tennant.'

A voice answered, 'Forensics here, sir. We've got something rather interesting to show you.'

'He's left a trace,' Tennant exclaimed loudly.

'Indeed he has.'

'I'll be right over.'

He entered the laboratory building and almost ran to the
department where he knew the sample was being tested. The
girl looked up as he approached.

'Hello, Dominic,' she greeted him. They had been in a
production of *Me and My Gal* together.

'Rosamund, my dear. What have you got for me?' he asked,
bending to kiss her on the cheek.

She looked slightly scandalized. 'I've managed to run
some tests on the fibres obtained from the vicar's wound.'

'And?'

'They're a wool mixture. Probably from a coat.'

'At long last. I didn't think our killer was human.'

'Well, he is.'

'The vicar said he caught a glimpse of a figure wearing a cloak.'

Rosamund nodded. 'Cloak or coat. Bring me the garment and you've got your man – or woman.'

Tennant looked thoughtful. 'The only snag is that half the population of that madhouse village probably go round wearing the damn things. Ceinwen Carruthers for one.'

'Can't you ask all those who own such an item to come forward voluntarily for the process of elimination?'

'I can ask,' the inspector answered, then he added, 'How did those fibres get on the wood anyway?'

'The assailant probably swung their arm back to get a better thrust and the wood would have picked up fibres from the shoulder.'

'I see.'

Rosamund said, 'I hear you've had to drop out of *The Corn is Green*.'

'Yes, pressure of work as usual. I don't know why I bother to audition actually.'

'Well, I'm glad you do.' She paused then added, 'Are you busy on Saturday? Because if you're not I wondered whether we could meet for a drink.'

'Normally you know I would say yes but this damnable case is proving such a nightmare that I'm afraid I might have to pull out at the last minute.'

'I'll bear that in mind. Will you come if you're around?'

'I'll be more than happy to,' Tennant answered with a smile.

Nick woke the next morning with a splitting headache but no other injuries that he could feel.

His doorbell was ringing loudly and non-stop. Pulling on a dressing gown Nick went downstairs and opened the front door to be greeted by a swarm of reporters. Lights flashed and his instant reaction was what would the Bishop think when he saw him standing thus, ill-shaven and with a sticking plaster on his head. He went to shut the door again fast but somebody or other had managed to wedge their foot in it.

'How are you feeling, Vicar?'

'Can you say a few words for television news, please?'

'How much did you see of your attacker?'

'I represent the *Daily Mail*. We're offering you ten K for an exclusive.'

Nick gaped at them and a bevy of lights flashed once more. Fortunately at this moment Kasper appeared in his car, jumped out and strode towards the vicarage, looking furious. All attention was turned to him and similar remarks were addressed. He whirled round.

'Gentlemen, if you please. I am going to see my patient. Would you kindly move on.' He sounded like an actor playing a character part.

'Dr Rudniski,' said the man from the *Daily Mail*, 'we'll offer you five K for an exclusive.'

'Not enough,' Kasper snorted, and rushed inside, shutting the door so hard that there was a yelp of pain from the owner of the foot.

'Thank God you're here,' said Nick. 'I couldn't think of a word to say to them.'

'The village is swarming with journalists,' Kasper answered, pronouncing the word carefully and sounding terribly foreign as a result. 'There's not a bed to be had in The Great House, the February Tea Rooms have let their only room and the villagers are making a great deal of money by taking in paying guests.'

'Perhaps I should let out the vicarage,' said Nick.

Kasper took him seriously and shook his head. 'I do not think that would be very wise.'

'I was only joking. How's the wound?'

Kasper delicately removed the plaster, dabbed some antiseptic on it and put on a new dressing.

'Very good. As you know I had to shave some hair off. You look more like a monk than a vicar.'

He laughed heartily at his own joke. Nick smiled weakly.

'Well, tomorrow is Sunday so I've got twenty-four hours to make a recovery.'

'I think you should rest for longer.'

'Sorry, Doctor. I feel my place is with my parishioners.'

'You must do what you think best. Now how am I going to get out of here?'

'Through the garden and the lower gate.'

'Can't do that. Forensic experts are working on it.'

'Then you'll have to brave the press.'

There was a babble of voices as the front door opened but Kasper refused to say a word and this time nobody put their foot in the entrance. Nick went upstairs and decided to have a bath and dress.

Half an hour later he came downstairs and cautiously took a peek out of the living room window. The mob had disappeared and this time it was Roseanna Culpepper who was walking towards the vicarage. Nick opened the door with a smile.

'Mrs Culpepper, how nice. Are you coming to see me?'

'Do you have a spare moment, Father Nick?'

'Indeed I do. Come in.'

As she walked past him he smelled that familiar scent she always wore and as she turned to look at him he was once again reminded of somebody.

'Would you like some coffee?' he asked.

'Yes, I would. Can I go into your kitchen? I always feel at home in that room.'

He did not ask whether it was his kitchen in particular or whether this was just a general remark. Following her in, Nick put the kettle on.

'You don't mind instant?'

'No, not at all.'

He sat down opposite her and studied her features, rather obviously, for she said, 'I clearly interest you.'

'Yes, you do. Very much. The fact is, Mrs Culpepper, I feel I know your face from somewhere.'

She laughed. 'Do you have Sky television?'

'Yes.'

'And do you watch TCM films?'

'Occasionally, yes.'

And then he made the connection. That was where he had seen her before. On black and white Hollywood epics – some made in early colour, he believed. Once upon a time she had been a well-known actress of enormous beauty. Yet he still could not quite place her name.

'Forgive me,' he said. 'Of course I have seen you in many

films and I simply adored you. But weren't you called some-thing else?'

'I used to be Rose Indigo. The Americans thought that was a catchy title. I started my career in rep – in Sidmouth of all places – and one of David Selznick's people was there on holiday, tracing his Devonian ancestors. To cut a long story short he signed me up and I was a big star for a while with the Selznick Studios.'

'Good lord,' Nick answered, and stared at her open-mouthed.

'They billed me as the new Greta Garbo.'

The vicar could see the likeness. The great moody eyes, the long straight nose, the drooping lips that could suddenly lift into a glorious expression. They lifted now as Roseanna smiled at him.

'Does anybody else know this?' Nick asked.

'I never talk about it but occasionally if somebody asks I put them out of their misery. And in case you're wondering, I am seventy-two.'

'You look nothing like that. I had thought you were sixty at the most.'

Roseanna appeared a little rueful. 'I suppose we must all accept the fact that we are getting older.'

'But you do it with such charm,' Nick answered, and he wasn't flattering her, he meant it quite sincerely.

'I must go,' she said, and put down her coffee cup.

'One thing before you leave.'

'Yes?'

'I hope you don't mind my asking but did you actually have an affair with James Pitman? You acted with him in so many films and you always looked genuinely close.'

Roseanna giggled. 'Actually we couldn't stand one another. He used to mutter obscenities at me. He married Jane Glynde, poor little innocent.'

'I remember her – I think.'

That spectacular smile appeared once more. 'Poor Jane, she never got any further than those kind of roles. I recall that she was madly jealous and really thought she'd backed a winner when she married James.'

'What happened?'

'They divorced, of course. Then she faded out. I don't

really know what became of her. I expect she's quite an old lady by now, like me.'

'You will never be old, Mrs Culpepper.

'Please call me Roseanna.'

'Thank you,' Nick answered solemnly, and kissed her hand.

He had had scarcely time to go through the *Guardian*, which contained a small item on what it called inexplicable killings in a small Sussex village, when there was another ring at his door. Peering cautiously through the window Nick saw that standing outside were Inspector Tennant and his faithful Potter. He hurried to answer it.

'Hello, Inspector. Do come in.'

'You're sure we're not bothering you?'

'Not at all.'

They stepped inside and Nick, thinking he might as well open a coffee shop, offered them a cup which they accepted with alacrity. He led the way into the kitchen.

Tennant sniffed the air. 'Mitsouku,' he said.

'Not mine,' said Nick with a wry smile. 'Mrs Culpepper just called.'

'An enigmatic woman that,' answered Tennant.

'Did you know that she was once a famous film star?'

'*Was* she?' exclaimed Potter, clearly astonished.

'Apparently so. She acted under the name Rose Indigo and was very big in the fifties and sixties.'

'How very interesting,' said Tennant thoughtfully. 'Potter go and google her will you.'

'Certainly, sir.'

And excusing himself to Nick, the sergeant put down his cup and made his way to the mobile headquarters. Tennant regarded his host with those magnetic green eyes of his.

'Are you quite recovered from your attack last night?'

Nick fingered his head gently. 'Kasper says I ought to take things easy for a day or two.'

'And I suppose you will ignore that completely.'

'Not completely.' Nick gave a feeble grin.

'And you're pretty certain your attacker was a man?'

'Well, they wore trousers. But as your police officer remarked last night that could apply to anyone these days.'

'Yes. But the leaping suggests somebody reasonably young and it also suggests a bloke to me.'

'I think you're quite right,' answered the vicar.

# FOURTEEN

P otter was having a ball on the one and only computer in the mobile headquarters, the rest being in the incident room in Lewes. The Internet had yielded up a mass of material on the former Rose Indigo, with even an entry in Wikipedia. He read:

'Roseanna Jane Austin (Rose Indigo) was born August 15, 1937, at Chelmsford, Essex, first daughter of Michael Austin, architect, and his wife Francesca. On the outbreak of war her father was called up and later killed at Tobruk. She moved with her mother and elder brother, Liam, to the West Country in 1941, where she attended Torquay High School until the age of eighteen. She had meanwhile joined the Torquay Players where she shone in younger roles such as Juliet and Titania. On leaving school she auditioned for the Sidmouth Repertory Company and was immediately accepted. She spent two years at Sidmouth playing leading parts in *The Constant Nymph*, *The Importance of Being Earnest* and *Hedda Gabler*, but her career in films began when Scott Levinson, a talent scout for David Selznick Studios, came to Devon and saw her act.

Her first role for Selznick was in 1958 as Chloe in *Pull Down the Stars*. Though only a minor part her luminous beauty raised her performance to the highest level and hailed as 'The New Garbo' she took the lead in twenty more films made for Selznick. Perhaps her greatest achievement was the part of Ondine in *The Water Nymph* for which she was nominated for an Academy Award. Finally, though, Rose Indigo gave up the stage and retired from films in the late 1970s. Since then she has slipped out of the public view and is now living quietly in Sussex.

Rose Indigo married three times:
1) James Crichton, a young actor she met in rep (divorced)
2) Mauritz Nagel, an American actor (divorced)
3) Richard Culpepper, a British actor.
She has one child, a son, Luis Nagel, who lives in America.'

'Good God,' said Potter and had just printed off a copy when there was a roar of activity outside the mobile unit. Tennant was trying to get in through a barrage of reporters.

'I have no statement for you at this time,' he was heard bellowing as he dived into the pantechnicon.

'I say, sir, look at this,' said Potter, thrusting the sheet of paper under his boss's nose.

Tennant took it and read it through twice, the first time speedily, the second time slowly and with concentration.

'So she had a child, did she,' he said thoughtfully.

'Apparently. Do you want me to check him out?'

'Please do. It may be clutching at straws but it's better than nothing.'

'Did you get any more out of the vicar?'

'No except that he's convinced his attacker was a man.'

'As am I. Now listen everyone,' said Tennant, to the handful of constables who had come in for refreshment. 'The superintendent wants a house-to-house DNA sample taken. Can you tell everyone that I will be briefing them in Lewes as we don't have room here. I'm going back there now as I've a mass of paperwork that needs attending to. Four o'clock. Alright?'

'Fine. At least we got through one night without a murder.'

'As far as we know,' Tennant replied grimly.

The milkman deliberately drove back up Arrow Street and stopped outside Ceinwen Carruthers's cottage where he peered over the gate to see if the third pint, delivered earlier that morning, still stood untouched by the front door. It did. With a mounting feeling of anxiety he pushed the milk float to its full capacity as to speed and eventually parked in the High Street, close to the mobile headquarters.

The pantechnicon was particularly empty, he thought, and there were very few policemen on the beat. They had obviously been called away somewhere. He looked round then went up to the sergeant who was on duty at the desk.

'Hello. Sorry to bother you but I thought you ought to know.'

'What's that, sir?'

'It's the milk. It hasn't been taken in, see.'

'Which house would you be referring to?'

'Ceinwen Carruthers's place. She's the leader of the Pixie Poets. We call 'em the Potty Poets round here.'

'Would you like to start at the beginning, sir.'

And the milkman, who gave his name as Derek Wickens, launched into a description of how he had noticed the milk bottles growing in number outside Ceinwen's house over a three-day period. The desk sergeant took it all very seriously and when a young WPC walked in, looking tired and rather flushed, he turned to her with a somewhat malicious smile.

'No time for a rest, Constable Castle. Off to Arrow Street with you. The milkman has reported a growing number of bottles outside one of the cottages.'

She had visibly turned pale. 'Which one?'

'I'd best come and show you,' Wickens had said eagerly, determined to be in at the kill, as it were.

Feeling very important he left the float in the High Street and proceeded down to Arrow Street in the wake of the fatigued constable. Arriving outside Ceinwen Carruthers's dwelling she halted him at the gate.

'I think you'd better wait here, Mr Wickens. I'd prefer it.'

'Are you sure?' She nodded. 'Oh, alright then.'

But he hovered by the gate, peering eagerly, as the young woman proceeded to the front door and gave a loud knock with a knocker shaped like a pixie. There was no reply. She slowly made her way round to the back and disappeared from his view. There was silence, so intense that you could almost hear it. But to WPC Sally Castle there was something eerie and forbidding about it.

'Miss Carruthers,' she called softly. Then again, 'Miss Carruthers.'

There was no reply and she tapped softly on the back door which swung open beneath her hand. Moving quietly, in fact almost creeping, Sally entered the kitchen of the cottage and looked round. There was a pair of cups by the sink with the remains of what looked like coffee inside one of them. The other was empty and seemed clean. Everything else appeared to be in its place, though the washing machine had not been emptied and a plant on the window sill was starting to wilt.

With a horrible lurching of her heart, Sally opened the kitchen door and stepped into the living room.

It was dark because the curtains were drawn, something she hadn't noticed when she'd tried the front door. She took two steps into the room and then gave an involuntary cry as she tripped over something and fell. She pushed herself up to her knees and looked down and straight into the glazed and fishy eye of Ceinwen Carruthers.

The poet was lying flat on her back staring sightlessly at the ceiling. Her mouth was open and full of white things. There were several late summer flies buzzing about the wound on her head, which was gashed and red with dried blood. Automatically Sally put her hand to the pulse on Ceinwen's neck but it was still and quiet. She had been dead for a couple of days at least, and there was a slight whiff of the morgue in the room.

Sally stood up, nauseated, and made her way out to the kitchen where she turned on her radio.

'WPC Castle reporting. There's a dead woman in the cottage who I believe to be the owner. Can you send back-up please.'

'Immediately. Don't leave the place, Castle. And don't let anyone inside. Forensics will be with you soon.'

Sally switched off and stumbled out of the back door where she inhaled deep breaths of fresh air to fight off the sickness rising in her throat. Then she remembered something. If this were the work of the serial killer there should be some sort of message left near the corpse. Steeling herself, she went back inside.

Entering the death room, her gaze went straight away to the body. And staring at it like that she could have sworn that Ceinwen moved, a common trick of the eye when in the presence of the dead. Forcing herself to look round, Sally saw a piece of paper stuck neatly to the wall with Sellotape. On it was written. 'Number Four. Six to go. Never on a Sunday. The Acting Light of the World.'

It didn't make much sense but it told her that the serial killer had struck once more.

'Bugger,' said Tennant out loud. He had briefed everyone on the house-to-house DNA tests that they were to start on

Monday and had been looking forward to an evening out with Rosamund Jenkins – and perhaps a night in – when Potter had come to him with a message from Lakehurst.

'There's been another one, sir.'

'Oh, Christ. Not again.'

'I'm afraid so, sir. Ceinwen Carruthers this time.'

Tennant was about to say something childish about it being Saturday and him having a date but stopped himself in time. His thoughts flew to Ceinwen, potty indeed but totally harmless, and he considered who could be cruel enough to end that silly blameless life.

He rang Rosamund on his mobile.

'Darling, I'm sorry. I've got called back to Lakehurst.'

'Oh my God, another murder?'

'I'm afraid so.'

'Who now?'

'A local poet named Ceinwen Carruthers. Rosamund . . .'

'Yes?'

'I really do regret this. Can we make it another time?'

'Certainly can. You ring me when you've got some spare hours.'

'You can be sure of it.'

In the car heading to Lakehurst he turned to Potter.

'Did our friend leave his usual cryptic message?'

'Yes, sir. According to Constable Castle, who was shaken to the core by the whole experience incidentally, it contained a sentence which said "Never on Sunday".'

'But it was signed by the Acting Light of the World, I take it?'

'As usual. What does that mean, Never on Sunday?'

'If memory serves that was an old film with Melina Mercouri – who was a Greek actress, I believe. Do you know, Potter, there might be some sort of showbiz connection with these murders.'

'It's a thread certainly.'

'Have you checked that boy yet?'

'Which boy?'

'The one on Rose Indigo's biography. Her son, Luis Nagel. What's he up to – and where?'

'He had a small entry in Wikipedia. It says he's a bit part

player in Hollywood. That's where his home is. He doesn't appear to see his mother.'

'Um. I'm not sure about that. Check him out with the California police, will you. By the way, did it say whether he was married or not?'

'It didn't state either way. What are you thinking?'

'I'm in the realms of fantasy. I wonder if he is here, in disguise, seeking revenge for his mother's . . .'

'What?'

'Early retirement from acting? Jealousy of the new husband? The fact that Olivia Beauchamp is his bastard half-sister and he's riddled with spite. I don't know, Potter, your guess is as good as mine.'

'We've got to try and keep level, sir,' Potter answered sensibly.

'I know. I know. But you must confess that these murders are so peculiar that one can be indulged for going off into the bizarre. Anyway,' Tennant added grimly, 'let's go and take a look at poor old Ceinwen.'

Duly suited in protective clothing they were driven down to Arrow Street and pushing up the police tape, went inside. The deputy police doctor was bent over the body as they walked into the living room, a pair of tweezers poised.

She looked round. 'Oh, I'm glad you two are here. I just wanted to remove the contents of her mouth and I didn't want to start without the official OK.'

'Hang on a minute,' said Tennant, kneeling beside her, 'I just want to have a quick look.'

He stared down into Ceinwen's dead face, peering at the wounds on her head, in the depths of which a maggot infestation had started.

'Time of death?' he asked.

'Two or three days ago,' answered the doctor. 'Rigor mortis has been and gone. But the blow flies eggs have hatched.'

She pointed to the squirming mass of maggots and Tennant gave them another glance then quickly looked away.

'Want to have a look, Potter?' he asked.

'No, thank you, sir. I'll take your word for it.'

'Wise chap,' said Tennant, rising to his feet. He turned to the doctor. 'Go on with what you were doing.'

She nodded and inserting the tweezers pulled out piece after piece of paper from Ceinwen's mouth.

'What the hell is this?' she asked.

'Looks as if it once had writing on it,' Tennant answered, leaning over the tweezers to have a closer view.

'I think it's probably one of her poems, sir,' said Potter. 'Yes, I'm right. There's the word Aidan, you can just make it out.'

'Do you mean to say she was choked to death on her own gift to literature?'

The doctor gave him a humorous glance. 'No, she was clubbed first. Then the murderer, with some sick sense of fun, rammed her poems down her throat.'

Tennant shot her a look from his vivid eyes. 'Well if you could now ram them into an evidence bag I'd be extremely grateful.'

Dr Hilary Priestly, who was recently divorced and feeling right off men as a consequence, gave him a smile nonetheless.

'Anything for you, Inspector.'

'I'll make a note of that in my little black book,' he answered.

And poor Potter was left to consider small flirtations in the presence of the newly dead.

# FIFTEEN

The church was fairly full on Sunday, everyone going in to pray for their deliverance, Nick supposed. News of the murder of Ceinwen Carruthers had whizzed along the village grapevine and though she had not been a churchgoer, preferring, apparently, to worship the Great Goddess and protest pagan views, Nick had been shocked to hear of it. Even Mrs Ely, the woman with the booming voice that had been past its best forty years before, stood silently putting on her choir robes. But the greatest effect was on Broderick Crawford, the gay young fellow with the bright red hair. He stood shivering, quite literally, and gazing at the floor as he donned his robes. The vicar went up to him.

'Come along, old chap, I know this is a terrible place to live at the moment but we must try to act normally. I believe that that is the only way forward.'

He realized that he was speaking in platitudes but found nothing else rising to his lips. Broderick glanced at him and Nick saw that he was white as a sheet.

'I'm sorry, Vicar,' he blurted out. 'I can't help myself, you see.'

Wondering to what particular aspect of his life he was referring, Nick gave him a feeble smile.

'No, of course you can't. All you can do is try your best.'

Further clichés, he thought.

Broderick blenched. 'I knew you'd understand, I truly did.'

'Yes, of course I understand. Now go out there and sing your best. Let's cheer the congregation up.'

'Yes, I will, Vicar. Thank you, thank you. You'll never know what this means to me.'

Wondering what on earth he was talking about Nick entered the procession forming up to make its way into church.

The subject of his sermon had to be Ceinwen Carruthers and how true Christians should mourn the loss of everyone, regardless of faith. As he ran his eyes over the congregation, staring up at him as he went on about this, he wondered if his words were getting home. He noticed the absence of Olivia, but knew that she was in Manchester. Jack Boggis and Kasper were also not present, along with Ms Hamilton-Harty, though the doctor was no doubt down the road with the Catholic brigade. Boggis, however, would be downing pints as if they were going out of fashion, and shaking with laughter over something written in the *Sunday Telegraph*. One person who was present, which cheered Nick up enormously, was Giles Fielding, singing the hymns robustly.

Afterwards he stood outside the church and shook hands with the parishioners. Last to leave and looking terribly flustered was Ivy Bagshot.

'Oh Vicar, can I speak to you?' she said, and he saw that her eyes behind their enormous, enlarging spectacles were red and puffy.

He drew her to one side. 'Of course, Mrs Bagshot.'

'It's the police. They arrived at nine o'clock just as I was eating my porridge. They asked me endless questions about poor Ceinwen. You see, I was the last person to see her alive.' Ivy made a muffled sound which vaguely resembled a sob. 'They asked me to tell them everything. Had I gone into the house with her, had I noticed anybody hanging round. That kind of thing. They just went on and on. It really brought it all back so vividly.'

'And did you go into her house?' Nick asked.

'Certainly not. I dropped her at the front door and drove home. I live in The Maze, you know.'

'No, I didn't actually.'

'Oh, it's a private estate with such polite neighbours . . .' And Ivy was off extolling the virtues of living amongst the best people. Nick gave her a somewhat forced smile and turned away to go to the vestry.

He had changed the key long since and had given the new one to very few people, namely the churchwardens – though he had kept Richard Culpepper's until the man returned from his season in London – the organist, the leader of the choir and old Reverend Mills. Other members of the choir, who had previously held keys, were now excluded. Since that precaution had been taken there had been no sign at all of the sinister kneeling figure that had so frightened Nick when he had first arrived in Lakehurst. Now, he had just peeled off his robe, when there came a polite knock at the vestry door. He went to answer it and saw Inspector Tennant standing there.

'Good afternoon, Inspector. How goes it?'

'Better than it was, Vicar. We've identified some fibres that come from a coat or cloak. They were clinging to the wood with which you were clouted and ended up in your head. But taking a punt on the fact it was definitely a cloak you saw, have you got any such things here?'

'Do you know, I'm not aware that we have. I've been here such a short time that I honestly haven't a clue.'

'Do you mind if I take a look?'

'No, carry on.'

The inspector threw open a cupboard door and gave an exclamation. 'You've got a dozen or so at least.'

Nick felt vaguely uncomfortable as if he had been withholding information from the police.

'I suppose they must be for when the choir go on outings.'

'Clearly they're not used very often,' Tennant answered, and removed two or three from the cupboard and began to search them.

Nick again felt wrong-footed.

'Can I help you?' he asked tentatively.

'Certainly. We're looking for a tear – or at least an abrasion – on the shoulder.'

There were a dozen or so cloaks hanging in the cupboard, one or two with name tags sewn in. He felt very amateurish in comparison with Tennant who was zipping through the search at a rate of knots. But, as luck would have it, it was the vicar who found what they were looking for. A rather moth-eaten looking item with the name Turner written on a grubby white label. Nick thought rapidly but could come to no conclusion as to who Turner might be.

'Is this what you're looking for?' he said to the inspector.

Tennant took the cloak from him and moved to the window to examine it.

'This could very well be it,' he said. 'Mind if I keep this.'

He was going to anyway but thought it only polite to ask. 'By the way, who is Turner?'

The vicar smiled and spread his hands. 'You'll have to blame this on my newness of arrival again but frankly I haven't got a clue. None of the choir is called that as far as I know.'

Tennant looked thoughtful. 'What would happen to the garment if a chorister left and somebody new took his or her place?'

'Well, I'm sure it would be handed on to the new chorister. Provided it fitted, of course.'

'I see. Would you mind making a few enquiries for me? Just ask Mrs Cox what the system is but don't say anything about the fact that we've found the cloak. If you could keep it casual and when you've got the answer give me a ring.' And he handed Nick a card.

'I'll do my best. Now can I ask you a question?'

'Certainly.'

'Did the murderer leave a note at the scene of Ceinwen's murder?'

'Yes, as a matter of fact I was going to call at the vicarage and ask you about it. Forensics have removed it from the wall and it's now in an evidence bag.'

'What did it say?'

'The usual thing. Number Four. Six to go. Never on Sunday. Potter and I have been somewhat mystified by this one.'

'You don't think,' asked Nick, fingering his chin, 'that it has anything to do with the fact that Ceinwen was a pagan?'

Tennant stared. 'What do you mean?'

'Just that. Never on Sunday could refer to the fact that she never attended church. She worshipped the Great Goddess of Earth – or something like that anyway.'

'Good heavens, that could throw an entirely new light on things. Perhaps all of them refer to some religious law or other that the poor sods had inadvertently broken.'

Nick looked at him. 'You don't think you could bring a copy of each saying round to the vicarage tonight after evensong?'

'What time would that be?'

Nick tut-tutted. 'I see you're not a churchgoer, Inspector.'

'I'm afraid not. Christenings, weddings and funerals, that's me.'

'In line with most of the rest of the population I fear.'

'These are hard times, Nick,' was the only thing that Tennant could think of by way of making a reply.

'They weren't so good in Christ's time either,' the vicar answered mildly.

Evensong was finished and Nick, changed into informal clothes, was preparing for a visit from Tennant when there was a knock at the vicarage door, somewhat earlier than he had anticipated. He went to answer it, quite looking forward to the challenge thrown down by those baffling clues, to see Sonia Tate standing on the doorstep.

'May I come in?' she said, and stepped inside before he had a chance to answer. Making her way to the living room, she sat down without invitation. She looked up at him and smiled seductively.

'Good evening, Father Nick,' she said, again with that slight emphasis on the word 'father'.

'How can I help you, Mrs Tate?' he answered in a clipped tone.

'Well, you could fetch your diary and make a date to come and have dinner with me for a start.'

He felt a wave of anger. Why should he be harassed in his own home by some old bag trying to get off with him? But then his Christian spirit returned and he knew that he should try to be nice.

'You may think me a wimp, Mrs Tate, but I am being extra careful since Ms Carruthers's murder. And, of course, since the recent attack on me. I don't go out at night any more. And I would advise you to be careful too. I mean you took a risk even coming to see me. It gets dark at six these days.'

She turned a face that had once been attractive towards him and batted her obvious pair of false eyelashes. 'I'm not frightened of anything or anyone, Father Nick. It's just the way I'm made, I suppose. When I was younger I had quite a hard life. And as for the line of women who hate me, they'd be enough to scare the pants off anyone – except me.' She laughed merrily.

The vicar put on his most serious expression. 'Despite your own personal feelings I still think you should be cautious, Mrs Tate.'

'I've told you before – my name is Sonia. Have you got a glass of wine handy?'

Memories of a previous visit when he had offered her nothing came back.

'Yes, of course. Or would you prefer gin and something?'

'No thank you. A glass of red would do very nicely.'

Nick fetched the bottle, corkscrew and two glasses wondering all the time how he was going to get rid of her. Then he remembered that Tennant was going to call and hoped sincerely that it would be in the next fifteen minutes.

'Thanks,' she said, as he handed her the glass. 'Do you know I've been longing to speak to you in private for ages.'

'Have you? What about?'

'About Lakehurst. Do you know, I hate the place. It's full of beastly gossips who make up stories about one out of sheer spite.'

'Is it? I can't say I've really noticed that.'

'Well, you haven't been here long enough. But I can tell you now that the rumour mill is positively working overtime about you and Olivia Beauchamp.'

Nick stared at her in blank surprise. 'Good heavens,' he said.

'Yes. You should hear them at it. They're all talking about the eternal triangle and saying that you and that Polish doctor are rivals for her hand.'

It was such a quaint way of describing the situation – if situation indeed there was – that Nick could feel a smile creeping over his face.

'I can see you grinning, Father, but you really ought to take the viciousness of these people seriously. I mean they can blacken your character without any further thought. Why I wouldn't be at all surprised if that attack on you the other night wasn't done by one of them.'

'Mrs Tate – Sonia – you must be joking. I admit that I haven't been in the village long but as far as I can see it is populated by perfectly honest, hard-working characters. If the attack on me was some sort of act of vengeance, then I'll leave the parish forthwith.'

He had no intention of doing any such thing and wondered if she was slightly potty. But she was smiling at him in a disarming way and hitching up her short skirt to reveal a great deal of leg clad in lacey tights.

'Well, Nick – may I call you that? – please don't even say those words. The majority of people like you enormously and you must just ignore the gossip and get on with your own life.'

'That is precisely what I intend to do.'

'Good.'

It was at that moment, thankfully, that the knocker sounded once more and Nick, excusing himself, went to answer the door to see both Tennant and Potter standing there.

'Thank goodness,' he murmured.

They both looked rather surprised. Dropping his voice to a conspiratorial whisper, the vicar whispered that he had a visitor who he was quite anxious to see the back of.

'Why's that?' asked the inspector.

'Well, it may sound crass but I think she's the village vamp and I am her latest victim.'

'Mrs Tate?' mouthed Potter.

'My, but you lads don't miss a trick, do you?'

'We do our best,' Tennant answered.

He walked into the living room.

'Good evening, Mrs Tate. I am so very sorry to have to disturb you but we're here on official business I'm afraid.'

'Oh, don't worry. I just called in for a social chat. I'll be on my way, Nick.'

To have judged from her voice one might not be blamed for thinking that she and the vicar were having an intimate relationship.

He made her a bow and said, 'Goodbye, Mrs Tate. Take my advice and go straight home.'

She gave him what she reckoned was a saucy grin. 'I've told you before, I fear nothing.'

Tennant chimed in. 'I think if you're suggesting that you walk round the streets of Lakehurst after it gets dark, then I would say you are being very foolish.'

'You can say whatever you so choose, Inspector. Goodnight.'

She minced out of the room with what she thought was a seductive wiggle and Nick was heard helping her into her coat. A few seconds later the front door closed with a final bang. Nick came back inside and said 'Phew!'

Tennant gave a broad grin. 'That's how I felt when I interviewed her. Do you think she eats men for breakfast?'

'Has 'em for an early morning snack, more likely,' Potter answered.

'What did you find out about her?' asked Nick.

'Apparently – and this is only according to rumour – she's slept with every man in the village, every man that's capable that is.'

'Really? No wonder Mrs Cox doesn't like her.'

Tennant looked suddenly stricken. 'Don't pass this on for God's sake.'

'Don't forget,' said Nick, with a smile, 'that you're talking about my boss. Now, where are these messages?'

Tennant produced typed copies of them and laid them out on a small table. The vicar picked them up, one by one, and stared at them with the utmost care. Eventually he said, 'Would you excuse me. I'm going to get my bible.'

'Do you think you've found something?'

'Possibly.'

He went to his study and while he was gone both Tennant and Potter heard a thump coming from upstairs. They looked at one another and said, 'William,' then they laughed.

Nick came back with a well-worn leather-bound book, clearly well thumbed. Sitting down, he turned the pages until he found what he was looking for.

'Listen to this, gentlemen. Exodus, two to seventeen.'

Tennant and Potter stared at one another blankly.

'I am the Lord your God, who brought you out of the land of Egypt, out of the house of slavery. Do not have any other gods before me. Does that remind you of anything?'

It was Potter who answered. 'The Patels?'

'Precisely, they were Muslims'

'Are these the Ten Commandments?' asked Tennant incredulously.

'They certainly are,' Nick answered. 'And I think they fit the case.'

'Go on.'

'You shall not make for yourself an idol, whether in the form of anything that is in heaven above, etc. etc.'

'The Buddha,' exclaimed Tennant. 'Gerrard Riddell! According to Giles Fielding he worshipped the damn thing. Oh my God, it's all becoming crystal clear.'

'What about Dwayne Saunters? How does he fit in?' This last from Potter.

'I think probably two,' Nick answered with a small laugh. 'You shall not make wrongful use of the Lord your God, and Honour your father and your mother, etc.'

'But he didn't have a mother and father,' objected Potter.

'The grandmother, acting in loco parentis. He certainly gave her a hell of a time.' Tennant turned to the vicar. 'Can you tell me the rest.'

'The next one that's appropriate is Remember the Sabbath day and keep it holy.'

'And there's the direct link with Ceinwen. Never on Sunday. It's almost as if the murderer is starting to give us clues. What's the next one?'

Nick glanced up and gave them both a deep look. 'You shall not murder. I wonder how The Acting Light of the World manages to equate that with their conscience.'

'Heaven knows,' Tennant answered. 'Presumably the Acting Light has special dispensation.'

'Do you want to hear the rest?'

'Yes please.'

'You shall not commit adultery.'

'Blimey, by her own admittance that puts Sonia Tate well in line.'

'It does rather. You shall not steal.'

Tennant and Potter looked at one another and shrugged their shoulders. 'Could be anybody.'

'And the last two are: You shall not bear false witness against your neighbour, and You shall not covet your neighbour's house, you shall not covet your neighbour's wife, or male or female slave, or ox, or donkey, or anything that belong to your neighbour.'

'Well,' said Tennant, 'that possibly covers the entire village of Lakehurst. Everybody has got their eye on everybody else's house – but as to the donkey, I wouldn't know about that.'

'I think, my dear Inspector,' Nick answered solemnly, 'that those owning beasts of burden should be particularly careful.'

'Indeed they should,' answered Tennant, and despite the awful occasion the three of them laughed.

# SIXTEEN

They had reached the outskirts of Lewes, a large village called Ringmer, when Tennant suddenly said to Potter, 'Do you know, I think I ought to go back.'

His sergeant gave him a brief glance. 'Do you mean to Lakehurst, sir?'

'Of course. Where else?'

'But why?'

'I've just got this funny feeling. We know this murderer strikes at night – though we can't be sure in the Carruthers case – but I'm pretty certain that somebody's coming under threat in the next twenty-four hours.'

'Any idea who, sir, in view of the vicar's revelations?'

'It was Exodus, actually,' Tennant responded drily. 'Yes, I think it's going to be Sonia Tate. And it's imperative that we stop the killer now.'

'Have you any idea who it is?'

'Presumably the cloaked figure who attacked the vicar. The owner of the cloak marked Turner.'

Potter nodded and turned right to Glynde. It was dark but the headlights picked up the sweep of the drive leading down to the Tudor house behind which the new opera house had been built. Tennant went once every year with a gang of like-minded friends while the rest of the local police force looked on aghast.

'You don't like that opera rubbish?' his superintendent had once said to him.

'As a matter of fact I do. Very much.'

'Too noisy for me. Give me Elton John any day.'

Tennant had not bothered with a reply.

Within half an hour they were back in Lakehurst and Tennant headed straight for the mobile headquarters.

'Oh, you're back, sir,' said the desk sergeant as the inspector walked in. 'Thought you'd gone home.'

'Home? What's that?' Tennant answered briefly. 'Listen,

I want you to call everyone in here – now. I want to see them. Get them here ten at a time.'

Five minutes later he started his first briefing.

'Well, folks. We've had nearly two weeks and the crimes have not been solved. Operation Titmuss is grinding to an unlooked-for halt. Tomorrow, as you know, we go house-to-house asking for a DNA sample. We're going to get refusals, we can't demand that the villagers cooperate, but I want a careful note of all those who say no and the reasons given.

'And now to tonight. I'd like the utmost vigilance kept by each and every one of you. Especially on the house of Mrs Sonia Tate who lives at Fernlea, 5, The Dell. I want that under observation all night long until ten o'clock tomorrow morning when you can go and collect the DNA sample. If anyone – and that means anyone at all – should approach the house I want he or she brought in for questioning. All right?'

'And where will you be, sir?'

'I hope that wasn't meant sarcastically.' There was a ripple of laughter. 'I mean to go on a bit of a walkabout. Potter will be here in charge of operations. Any further questions?'

Half-an-hour later Tennant had finished his briefings to the sixty or so extra policemen who had been drafted in for night duty in Lakehurst and drank a hasty cup of coffee before putting on his coat – he liked a good old-fashioned coat, none of your modern designs for him. Then he walked out of the mobile headquarters and turned right down the High Street.

It was a bitter night, a wind whipping up from the lower part of Lakehurst, past the Victorian houses and the Catholic church. It stung Tennant's eyes as he walked down that straight, long street towards The Dell. Overhead the moon and the stars had been totally blacked over by a thick layer of cloud and the inspector thought that this could well be the scene at the end of the world. He suddenly felt miserable and downhearted. To be defeated by some raving lunatic at this stage of his career was disheartening to say the least and he made himself a mental promise that he would not leave Lakehurst until the task was completed satisfactorily.

His thoughts turned to the cloaked figure who had attacked the vicar. He now knew that the cloak was a part of the chorister's uniform and that Mrs Cox had known Old Turner – as the vicar had described him – who had had to retire from the choir through sheer advancing years. That done, the poor old boy had died within six months and his ashes were happily buried in Lakehurst churchyard beside a rhododendron bush. The cloak had been left as an heirloom to one of the newer members but who it actually was, Mrs Cox had not been sure.

The offending garment had now been removed to Lewes in a large evidence bag and was currently under examination by Rosamund in the forensics lab. The thought of her made Tennant realize fully how much he needed a woman to make love to. He still hadn't had time to have that evening with her – and hopefully spend the night – and it didn't look to him as if any of that were going to materialize until the end of this investigation was well and truly in sight.

He fell to wondering about the owner of the cloak. Was it possible, he thought, that these were two entirely different people. That the person who stalked about and so obviously assaulted the vicar was someone entirely different from the savage and sadistic killer who killed his victims in such an horrific manner. Pictures of poor Ceinwen, her throat stuffed with her guileless and innocent poetry, came back to him and he stopped for a moment feeling suddenly short of breath.

A cyclist in bright white trousers, most unsuitable for the weather, was battling against the wind and went past Tennant, but other than for that person there was no one else about. Lakehurst was like a plague village, deserted and still, with nothing except the lights on in houses to tell him that there were living creatures here at all. With a feeling of trepidation, the inspector entered The Dell.

It was a truly depressing place. An enclave of ten identical houses, probably erected in the eighties, all built in a U shape, the end four facing one another so that the owners must have suffered from an appalling lack of privacy. Sonia lived in one of the bottom houses facing up the road so was somewhat better off than most of her neighbours.

As Tennant walked into The Dell he noticed a car without lights parked at the far end and thought to himself that his instructions were clearly being carried out. He tapped on the window. It was lowered and he looked into the startled face of a WPC. Beside her, fast asleep, was a fellow officer.

'Good evening, Constable Belloc.'

'Good evening, sir.'

The policeman struggled awake, shouting, 'What the hell's happening?'

'I am,' answered Tennant, 'and I'd advise you to keep your voice down. You'll have everybody in the street coming out to see what's going on.'

'Sorry, sir.'

'Is Mrs Tate in?'

'Yes, her lights are on downstairs.'

'So I see. Has anybody called on her?'

'Not since we've been here, sir. And that was an hour ago.'

'If anybody does come – and that includes the vicar and any of the doctors – you are to bring them in for questioning immediately.'

'Very good, sir.'

'I'll just have a look round. Stay here until somebody comes to relieve you.'

Tennant walked quietly past the curtained windows of The Dell and felt a definite stab of excitement. It reminded him of the past, when he had been a sergeant to a great inspector, one Grey, known amongst the junior members of the force as The Man. Grey had had an uncanny knack of solving his cases, in fact Tennant sometimes wondered if he used psychic powers. At this moment he wished that he possessed some.

Moving silently the inspector stood by the gate of number five. Very faintly he could hear the sound of the television from within. Quiet as a cat, the inspector stepped over the low iron fence and into Sonia's garden. Slinking his way round to the back, he peered in through the kitchen window. The room was in total darkness but he could vaguely make out various objects from the light filtering round the door.

It looked normal enough. And then he had a horrid vision of the death of Ceinwen, lying undiscovered in her sitting room. He went round to the front and was about to ring the door when he heard a pair of feet walking up the road and definitely towards this end of The Dell. Tennant froze back into the shadows.

He could see by the street light that it was Jack Boggis making his way, quite steadily for him. He wore an old-fashioned anorak – Tennant vaguely wondered if it was Jack who had inspired the word – and his usual grumpy expression. The inspector could not help but notice that Jack's slack jawline swung a little as he walked.

With an increase of pace, he went up the garden path and extended a digit to press the bell.

The inspector stepped forward.

'Good evening, Mr Boggis. I would like you to accompany me to headquarters, please.'

Jack spluttered so violently that his false teeth nearly came out.

'What do you mean? What for?'

'I am afraid that I am unable to reveal that except to say that we would like you to answer some further questions.'

'And what if I refuse?' Jack asked nastily.

'Then you leave me no alternative but to place you under arrest,' Tennant answered in the pleasantest voice he could muster.

'Now look 'ere . . .'

'No, Mr Boggis, you look here. I have been informed by Sergeant Potter that your attitude throughout this investigation has not been particularly cooperative. In fact, at times, downright obstructive. I am sure you have your reasons for this which we can investigate a little more closely at the station. Now, are you coming quietly, as they say, or do you wish me to place you under arrest?'

'This is intimidation.'

'No it isn't. It's normal police procedure.'

Jack began to bluster into Tennant's face, a fact that had the inspector taking a step back.

'What about civil liberties? I demand my rights. I want my solicitor present. I've a mind to sue the lot of you.

There was I, on my way to make a social call, and I'm suddenly wanted for questioning. It takes some beating, it truly does.'

Tennant didn't answer but frogmarched the man back towards the car.

'Constable Belloc, drive us to the mobile unit, would you.' He looked at the yawning policeman beside her. 'You wait here and keep your eyes peeled. A bracing walk round The Dell might be just what you need.' He turned to Boggis. 'Now, sir, get inside out of the cold.'

It was very late and Cheryl Hamilton-Harty was doing her final check on the horses before she went to bed. She was clad in her pyjamas with a thick coat on top and, as she had removed her make-up, was looking far from glamorous. For all her strange character and rampant nymphomania, she genuinely loved the horses and as she entered the stables the smell of horseflesh and the soft whinnies of greeting met her.

She was stabling twelve horses and two ponies at the moment, which was about the number she hired out at weekends. She loved Saturdays and Sundays when the merchant bankers and city whizz kids came down to the big houses they owned round and about, and thought that riding – no longer to hounds unfortunately, or so they agreed – would enhance their image. Afterwards, of course, Cheryl would invite them in for a little drink and then, as she was reasonably attractive and utterly unable to control her libido, they would have a small siesta. Now it was late on Sunday and everyone had left for their flats in London, and it was back to the routine of teaching toddlers and tinies for the intervening five days.

She stroked her own horse's flank. 'Hello, Florence. Do you want a carrot then?'

Cheryl extended one and was just feeling the soft mouth consuming it when a voice behind her said, 'Hello, my dear.'

She whirled round to see a figure holding a riding whip, the sort she used when she took out the governess car.

'Who is it?' she asked, disconcerted.

'Don't you know me?' continued the unearthly voice, neither male nor female.

'No, I don't,' she answered.

'Perhaps this will refresh your memory,' it said.

And the whip snaked out and tightened round Cheryl's neck until everything went dark and her body fell silently to the ground.

# SEVENTEEN

I t was the postman who found her when he eventually arrived in Speckled Wood shortly before twelve noon. He had a package to deliver – a package that would not fit through the front door – and when he knocked the door swung open.

'Cheryl,' he called out. 'Where are you? I've got a parcel for you.'

There was no reply and he heard his voice echoing through the silence of the big house that she shared with old Mickey, her lodger, though the exact nature of their relationship was still a subject for village gossip.

He turned away towards his van and then he heard an unaccustomed kicking from the stables. He thought this highly unusual because, say what you like about her, Cheryl was good with horses and would have turned them out to pasture by this time. Calling her name, the postman made his way in there.

It was dark inside and the kicking was coming from the horses who were knocking the walls of their loose boxes as a sign that they wanted attention. He took a couple of steps into the dimness and then he saw her, lying in a crumpled heap, with something obscene and black coiled round her neck like a snake. He took one nervous step closer, saw that it was a whip that had ended her life, saw something pinned up on the wall but did not stop to read it. He fled out and into his van, reversed in the stable yard and headed at top speed for Lakehurst.

Tennant had spent a most uncomfortable night – what there had been of it – trying to snatch a few hours sleep wedged in a chair in the mobile headquarters. He came to full consciousness at about six o'clock and forced himself to wake up completely by imbibing a great deal of black coffee. But his mind was full of Jack Boggis. To say he disliked the

man would have been an overstatement but there was something in Boggis's basic character that quite offended him.
Whether it was the tremendous conceit, whether it was his
blustering manner, or whether it was his ill-fitting false teeth
that added the final insult, Tennant could not be sure. But
the truth was that the less time he spent in his presence, the
better.

On the previous night he had questioned him closely about
being in The Dell and about his relationship with Mrs Tate.
Boggis had given a self-satisfied smile and had almost rushed
the information at him that he and Sonia were having 'a bit
of a fling'. Tennant had allowed his tiny wince to show, as
this was carefully added to Boggis's statement. Eventually,
with the statement typed out and signed, he had released
Jack to walk home through that most inclement of nights at
one o'clock in the morning.

At eight thirty a.m. the DNA teams set forth to take samples
from the entire village, and Tennant decided – having ascer-
tained that Sonia Tate was up and about – to make his weary
way back to Lewes to see his superintendent. He just had
time, he realized, to go back to his own flat and have a
shower and change his suit before going into the office. But
he made the mistake of stretching out on his bed and when
he woke up it was two and a half hours later.

Jumping to his feet, Tennant threw on his clothes and ran
down the street still knotting his tie. When he walked into
his office the clock on the wall was pointing to noon. In as
nonchalant a way as possible he went to the superintendent's
door and knocked on it.

'Come,' said Miller grandly.

Contorting his features into what he hoped was a confident smile, Tennant made his way in.

Miller glanced up and immediately looked down again.
'Any progress?' he said bluntly.

'Oh quite a bit, sir.'

And Tennant went waffling on about the cloak he had
found being the offending garment and how the DNA samples
were being taken this very day.

'And?' said Miller pointedly.

At that very moment Tennant's mobile rang and he raised

his eyebrows at the superintendent, who nodded briefly. The inspector took the call outside and retrospectively was glad that he did so.

'The postman found who?' he asked, the line having crackled at that important point.

'Miss Hamilton-Harty, sir. She's been strangled with a whip. Forensics are there now.'

'Was there anything written on the wall?'

'Oh yes, the usual type of thing, signed by the Acting Light of the World.'

'God damn the bastard to hell. I'll come straight back.'

He popped his head round Miller's door and said, 'Sorry, sir. I've been called back to Lakehurst. I think we're on the point of a breakthrough.'

Why he said that he couldn't possibly explain, even to himself. But the superintendent had to have some kind of encouragement or he might easily put somebody else on the case. And that would be too much to take.

He drove back to Lakehurst very fast and stood silently in the mobile unit while Potter gave him the bare outline. Tennant actually hissed between his teeth as he listened.

'And I thought it was Sonia Tate who was going to be the next victim,' he said, shaking his head slowly from side to side. 'What a fool.'

'You weren't to know, sir. I thought she would be the obvious person too.'

'And all the while poor Cheryl didn't have a copper in sight down at Speckled Wood when the Acting Light of the World came to call.'

'Let's get down there.'

They drove at a great rate, as if the turn of speed would relieve their feelings, and reached the farmhouse, behind which stood the stable block, about ten minutes later. The usual white clad figures were crawling all over it and something stirred in Tennant's memory as he saw them. He turned to Potter.

'Do you know I think my guess was right, the killer has got himself some protective clothing.'

'Why do you say that?'

'Because the other night when I went down to Sonia Tate's

there was a cyclist out and I noticed he had very white trousers on. I think they were protective gear.'

'But they themselves must be corrupted now if he commits murders wearing them. I mean he has to get to and from the locations somehow, even when he's walking.'

'And now I've seen a suspicious cyclist. I want every bicycle in Lakehurst examined.' Tennant lowered his voice. 'Potter, I'm determined to get this bugger, whoever he – or she – might be. I've told you all along that I don't believe the religious maniac theory. That I think someone or other is busy working out their own sadistic fantasies and trying to tie us up with some religious waffle.'

'Well, I'll not rest until I see him behind bars. He's been walking all over us long enough.'

'Come on, let's go in.'

They marched up to the stables and a young male SOCO handed them protective clothes. Duly clad they entered the stables. Poor Cheryl Hamilton-Harty, looking quite elderly without her make-up, was lying on the floor, a long whip wrapped round her neck and then knotted by means of twisting the lash round the handle. Hardly daring to raise his eyes Tennant looked up to see the message.

'Number Five. Thou shalt not commit A. Take great care. The Acting Light of the World.'

'He's actually mentioned the ten commandments, the bastard,' said Tennant.

'But if Cheryl was just enthusiastic about sex—' Potter didn't finish.

'Maybe her fellow riders –' Tennant allowed himself a hollow laugh – 'were all married men.'

'Maybe she's been married.'

'Maybe she still is.'

At that moment the police doctor arrived and began his examination, talking over his shoulder to Tennant.

'Strangled to death with the whip exerting so much force that the vertebrae were snapped. She would have died within a few minutes. Whoever did this must have used enormous pressure.'

'Could it have been a woman?'

'A strong woman in a frenzy – yes.'

Potter turned to Tennant. 'Oh my God, sir. Where does this leave us?'

'Determined,' said Tennant, standing upright as a small female member of the forensics team, at a nod from the doctor, delicately began to unpick the whip from around Cheryl's broken neck.

Peeling off his protective garments he said, 'This business has gone on long enough. Now we solve this case.'

Ten minutes later he was back at the mobile headquarters and on the phone to the vicar.

'Hello, Reverend Lawrence. I have some news for you. The cloak which once belonged to Turner – an ex-member of the choir – has been identified as the one worn by your assailant. I wonder if you would mind doing me a favour. When's the next choir practice?'

'Tonight as it happens.'

'Good. Would you ask them to stay on at the end of it, just for a short while. Then I want everyone in the vestry to identify which cloak is theirs. And, Vicar . . .'

'Yes?'

'Don't give them any warning at all of this. It's very important that we keep this utterly to ourselves.'

'I understand.'

'Good. What time do you usually finish?'

'About nine thirty.'

'Will you let me into the vestry at nine?'

'I most certainly will.'

They hung up and Tennant stepped outside to meet a barrage of cameras and reporters. They'd got wind of the fact that there had been another murder at Speckled Wood and the postman had already been bought by the *Sun*. The inspector assumed his 'everything is under control' face.

'Got a statement for us, Dominic?' asked an old hand who had met Tennant before on several cases.

'Only that we are proceeding with our enquiries,' he answered, smiling urbanely.

'Is there going to be an arrest?'

'I'm afraid I can't comment on that.'

'Does that mean you haven't a clue?' shouted some cheeky young Johnny-come-lately.

'We have several clues, thank you,' Tennant answered crisply, then he began to elbow his way through the crowd, most of whom were taking photographs right in his face. Potter, who was gallantly pushing through behind him, murmured, 'Where to, sir?'

'The White Hart,' Tennant muttered back. 'I need somewhere quiet to think.'

Ten minutes later they had reached their destination, having roared off in the opposite direction to put the press pack off the scent. Kylie, looking woebegone, served them.

'How's Gran bearing up?' asked Tennant.

Kylie paled visibly.

'She won't go out, no more. She just sits at 'ome all the time, watching telly.'

'Oh dear, that can't be very good for her. Doesn't she have any hobbies?'

'Well, she goes to the WI. With an escort.'

'What do you mean?'

'A lady with a torch comes and fetches her. But they cancelled the last meeting so now she don't go nowhere.'

'Tell her I'll pop in soon.'

'Ta, I will.'

As soon as she had left them alone together, Tennant leant forward over his pint of beer.

'What have we got, Potter?'

'A lot of loose ends, sir, as far as I can see. Do you still think the case is somehow connected with showbiz?'

'I don't know. I'm going to sit down with my computer tonight. But first of all I'm going to interview old man Mickey Mauser.'

'Are you serious? Is he really called that?'

'Yes, apparently. He's shared Cheryl's house for the last few years.'

'And her bed?'

'According to village gossip. Apparently the postman . . .'

'Not him again!'

'Peered through the window and saw something or other.'

'Talking of Speckled Wood, where's Giles Fielding got to?'

Tennant put his finger to his lips, motioning the other man to be quiet.

'Shush. He's sitting over there looking decidedly moody.'

Potter gave a discreet glance over his shoulder and sure enough there was Giles, looking very red about the eyes. Tennant got up and went to sit opposite him.

'I suppose you've heard the news?'

Giles nodded glumly. 'I was fond of her. I know she was a bit wild, like. But she had a good heart, for all that. I feel as if I've lost a friend with her going.'

Tennant made a sympathetic noise and Potter said earnestly, 'We're going to catch him, you know.'

Giles looked up. 'They came to my house and took my DNA this morning. I gave it gladly. The sooner that lunatic is caught the better.'

'Did you see Cheryl at all yesterday?' asked Tennant.

'Yes, I drove past when she was getting the horses in. I waved at her and she waved back. Then I went home. Strangely enough I didn't go out again. I stayed in and watched television.'

The inspector nodded. 'Tell me what you know about Cheryl's lodger.'

Giles chuckled. 'Old Mickey Mouse? That's not her lodger.'

'Well, who is he then?'

'Her husband.'

Tennant and Potter stared at one another.

'Her husband?'

'That's right. They've been married a half dozen years that I know of, though they kept it very secret mind.'

'Why for heaven's sake?'

Giles winked one of his red but sparkly eyes. 'I think you'd best ask him that.'

'This case gets weirder by the minute,' said Tennant, as they drove for the second time that day to Foxhall Farm in Speckled Wood.

The scene which had been bustling with activity earlier that day had now quietened down. The horses had been let out into a nearby field and the stable was still being combed by forensics, though the body had been removed. A handful of police officers were standing on duty, looking rather officious. They all straightened up as Tennant got out of the car and stood gazing around.

The farm was in one of the most spectacular settings he had ever seen. High on a hill, it was surrounded by beautiful views. Opposite the house were fields, going down to a spinney and then further, leading to a glimpse of an old house with a glint of water round it, that rare and splendid thing, a moated manor.

To the right of the farm was that spindly and slightly dangerous track, the road to Lakehurst. Had a cyclist, clad in protective clothing, cycled up this hill, panting and gasping to reach Foxhall, with an evil heart and black intent, lying in wait for Cheryl as she performed her nightly vigil amongst her beloved horses. To the left were Giles's fields and in the distance his farmhouse. It was hard to imagine, admittedly, but had the sheep farmer stalked across those fields in the dark of night and gone to the stables to await his prey?

Behind the house stretched out yet more fields with a large ominous Victorian building dominating the distant skyline. Tennant had been told that this vast house had been an orphanage, deserted now but originally a place of residence for the children of the poor, founded by a wealthy citizen who, no doubt, had received some sort of ennoblement for his kindness to the impoverished and many other charitable works. Now it stood gaunt and somehow menacing against the afternoon sky.

Potter too stood quietly, watching his boss and reading in his face his disappointment with himself that the murderer – who apparently left no clues and led a charmed and protected life – was still at large.

'Shall we go in, sir?' he asked quietly.

Tennant turned to look at him. 'Yes,' he said, 'let's go a'hunting one Mickey Mouse.'

# EIGHTEEN

A policewoman answered the door and showed Tennant and Potter into the living room without saying a word. The inspector didn't know quite what he had been expecting but certainly nothing like the man who sat stiffly in a high-backed chair staring silently into space. For this was an elegant man, a grandee, with a leonine head and a long mane of silver hair. He sat bolt upright, a hand on each arm, and hardly seemed to breathe as Tennant approached. He took the inspector in with a glance from his Arctic eyes that almost sent Tennant reeling, so vivid and clear and somehow familiar were they. But he said nothing.

The inspector cleared his throat. 'Forgive me disturbing you at a time like this, Mr Mauser, but I am afraid there are certain questions I have to ask you.'

The man made no reply but lifted one long hand as a signal that he was ready to be interrogated.

'First of all, were you at home last night?'

The blue eyes met Tennant's and held them in an unblinking stare.

'Yes, of course I was. As a matter of fact I had gone to bed early and got up at five in the morning and went for a long walk. When I returned it was to find the police here.'

'You did not notice that your wife had not come to bed?'

A humourless smile flitted across Mauser's face. 'We sleep in separate rooms.'

There was no mistaking it. There was the hint of an accent underlying his perfectly spoken English. Tennant took a guess at German.

Potter must have heard it too because he asked, 'How long have you been in this country, sir?'

Mauser's eyebrows rose slightly. 'I don't see what that has to do with the terrible death of my wife.'

'Probably nothing. But tiny fragments of information help us to build the entire picture. So how long, sir?'

'My mother and I came here in 1974. And before you ask I was thirty-five years old and I am now aged seventy.'

'So you were considerably older than your wife.'

'Cheryl is – was – forty-seven.'

The man had iron-like self control and Tennant could not help but feel a sneaking admiration for him. But yet again, just as he had sensed with Roseanna Culpepper, there had been something familiar about that handsome face and unnerving eyes.

He leant forward. 'Look Mr Mauser, I have no intention of prying –' liar, he thought to himself – 'but I think it might be helpful if you told us something of your history.'

A slightly amused expression appeared in Michael's eyes, though his face remained rigidly still.

'Really? Am I obliged to do so?'

'No, sir, you are not. But we have other methods. We shall find out one way or another.'

Mauser smiled, revealing a strong set of teeth, all his own.

'Then I suggest you use one of those.'

Potter was slightly gobsmacked, Tennant could tell, but he merely smiled back and said, 'Oh, we shall, Mr Mauser, don't you worry.'

'Now, gentlemen, is there anything relevant I can tell you further?' He stressed the word relevant.

'I presume you have no alibi for last night or your early morning stroll?'

'As a matter of fact, I have. When I went walking this morning I saw Giles Fielding. He was in the fields with one of his sheep.'

'Did he see you?'

'Yes. I waved at him and he at me. And last night, when I was in bed, Dr Rudniski came to see me.'

'And why was that, if I may ask?'

Michael steepled his long fingers and raised them to his chin. 'Because, Inspector Tennant, I am suffering with cancer.' And for the first time in the interview, he lowered his brilliant gaze to the floor.

'Jesus, I didn't see that coming,' said Potter in the car.

'He's too self-controlled to be true,' answered Tennant.

'And I regard it as highly suspicious that he wouldn't open up about his past.'

'Do you know why I think he did it? To give us more work.'

'You're probably right. Potter, ring Dr Rudniski's receptionist and ask him to pop into the unit as soon as possible.'

His sergeant reached for his mobile and Tennant could hear him talking, but he had switched his mind elsewhere. There were so many loose and disparate ends in this case and yet there must be some common denominator – which, of course, was the murderer himself or herself. His thoughts roamed on to the figure he had seen on the bicycle. Had that been the man? Or woman, come to think of it. He tried to envisage exactly what he had seen and recalled that the figure had been bent over the handlebars and that the upper part of the body had been covered in a waterproof oilskin with a hood which had been pulled up, concealing the face. So though those bright white trousers had made him think it was a man it could quite easily have been female. For no reason the inspector's train of thought turned to the delectable Olivia and he wished that he could see her again.

As soon as he got back to the mobile HQ he left instructions that he wanted every bicycle in Lakehurst – and Speckled Wood – noted and examined. There had been no tyre marks left at Foxhall Farm but anything unusual at all was to be reported to him. Then he sat down to read the reports of the DNA collection team.

Most people had given a sample gladly enough but several had objected, mostly standing by their human rights. Tennant ran his eye down the list and was interested to see that Ivy Bagshot, Mavis Cox and, of course, Jack Boggis had been amongst these. Olivia and Sonia Tate had been unavailable, as had a great many other people. Of those who had given, the inspector saw that all three doctors had cooperated, as well as the vicar. Now the results would be taken to Lewes, each carefully marked, awaiting any further evidence that Tennant might produce.

He was hoping to spend a late evening on his computer, researching all the people connected, however remotely, with show business. For some deep-seated hunch told him that somehow there was a connection. But just as he was packing up his things to go Kasper came into the unit and they were obliged to retire to a question room.

'Don't be intimidated by this,' Tennant said, gesturing at the general bareness. 'I'm afraid we're a bit limited for space.'

'Oh don't worry,' the doctor answered. 'It makes a change from visiting grumpy old patients. Now what is it you want to ask me?'

'It's about Michael Mauser. I believe he is a patient of yours.'

'Yes, that's right.'

'Did you call on him last evening?'

'Yes. It was about eight o'clock. He was in bed. I went to give him something to relieve the pain he was suffering.'

'Did you see Mrs Mauser?'

The look of sheer surprise on the doctor's face revealed that he had no idea of the relationship.

'Who?'

'I'm sorry. You obviously were not party to the secret. I mean Cheryl Hamilton-Harty. They were married.'

'Good God! I had no idea.'

'He admitted it quite freely to me.'

The doctor grinned and Tennant thought he could see why all the girls were after him. 'Well, you *are* a policeman.'

'Yes, but he clammed up about his past. He's German, isn't he?'

'I believe so. He spent quite a time in Poland though. He speaks Polish fluently.'

'Does he now? Do you know anything about his background?'

'Only what he told me. He arrived in this country in 1975 in the company of his very elderly mother.'

'Did he take British nationality, do you know?'

'I'm afraid I don't. I just presumed he had.'

'And you think he spent some time in Poland?'

'Judging by the way he spoke the language, the answer is yes.'

Tennant gave Kasper a very direct look. 'Tell me, Doctor, have you any reason to believe that Mr Mauser was impotent?'

'I'm afraid I can't discuss that with you. What passes between a doctor and his patient is strictly confidential.'

'I quite understand. But back to Mrs Mauser. Did you see her when you called last night?'

'Yes, she let me in. Then she went back to the living room. She had the television on.'

'And what time was this?'

'About eight o'clock. I know that was late to make a call but I always treat Mr Mauser as an exception. You see, I rather admire him.'

'Why is that?'

'Because I think he has had a lot to cope with in his life.'

'Such as what?'

The doctor looked vague and shrugged his shoulders and Tennant realized immediately that he was treading on tricky ground.

'Don't worry, Dr Rudniski, if you'd rather not say.' He glanced at the clock. 'Thank you so much for telling me what you have. Now, can I buy you a drink?'

The doctor looked at his wristwatch. 'Yes, I am officially off-duty.'

They walked across the road to The Great House to find that the vicar was there ahead of them talking to – lo and behold – Olivia Beauchamp. She looked a little tired but was still as beautiful as ever. The three men stood staring at her, jaws slightly dropping, and it occurred to Tennant that they must look like the Three Stooges, and wondered what she was thinking of them.

Olivia, however, didn't seem to notice their simultaneous looks of admiration and said with a worried expression on her face, 'Oh, Inspector, what a terrible time you've been having. Nick has just been telling me. We've had to postpone my recital in Lakehurst indefinitely.'

'It's been pretty grim,' he acknowledged. 'Most of all for the people of the village.'

'I haven't given my DNA yet. I'll come to the unit tomorrow morning.'

'Thank you. If you'd like to ask for me when you arrive.'

He could feel the vicar and the doctor glancing at him and, aware that he momentarily had the advantage, said, 'Can I buy you a drink, Miss Beauchamp?'

'Please call me Olivia. I feel that you're almost a resident.'

'I'm beginning to feel that myself. Now what will it be?'

As he went to the bar he saw Nick and Kasper simultaneously make a move and couldn't help grinning to himself at the stupidity of men. Then he thought about how many murders were caused by the crassness of both sexes, and his smile faded to nothing.

The four of them sat down at a table and were oblivious of everything going on around them when they were interrupted by a voice speaking in its usual husky tones.

'Hello, Inspector. I hear you've been searching for me.'

He straightened up, knowing who it was without even looking.

'Well not exactly, Mrs Tate.'

'I told you it was Sonia. Do you mind if I join you?'

And she sat down at the table, shooting Olivia a dirty look as she did so.

She's jealous, thought Tennant. Jealous as hell of youth and beauty.

'What's everybody having?' asked Sonia, peering beneath her lashes at Kasper, who shifted in his seat uncomfortably.

'No, I'm in the chair,' Tennant said reluctantly.

'Then a very dry Martini – shaken not stirred, as they say.'

She laughed in a juvenile way and tipped her head saucily at the inspector. Then she turned to Nick.

'And how's my favourite vicar?'

'I've no idea,' he answered, straight-faced. 'I don't believe I know the man.'

'Don't be a tease.' She touched him lightly on the arm. 'And how are you, Doctor?'

'I am in good health, thank you,' he answered, speaking very correctly and sitting bolt upright, clearly not open to flirtation.

Sonia fixed Olivia with a stare. 'My dear, how it must take it out of you, all this travelling around. You look quite worn out.'

This was one of the unkindest things that one woman can say to another, immediately suggesting that the person concerned looked old and haggard.

Olivia countered with a brilliant smile. 'Do you know I was thinking the same about you, Sonia. I hope you're not overdoing it.'

Nick was dying to snigger but controlled himself admirably while the doctor stared moodily at the ceiling. Tennant, returning from the counter, just heard the tail end of it and decided to let it pass. Olivia seemed more than capable of dealing with such cattiness. He passed Sonia her drink.

'If I may say so I think it is very foolhardy of you to wander about on your own during the hours of darkness.'

'Well, people did during the war, didn't they? They didn't let Hitler ruin their social lives. I mean my mother was brought up in Brixton and she kept going out and about despite the blackout.'

Nobody answered her and Tennant thought that her mother must have had her quite young because Sonia had always struck him as being well in her sixties, despite her attempts to present an image of eternal youthfulness. He looked at his watch.

'Well, I must be going. I've got a great deal to do this evening.'

'Would you like to come and stay the night? I think everywhere else is packed with journalists,' Nick said.

'That would be very kind.'

Sonia said archly, 'I've got a spare room available at any time.'

Everyone looked at her but nobody said a word, though eventually Tennant couldn't resist saying, 'Thank you, Sonia. I'll put it on the list for the WPCs.'

She was about to make some remark but the vicar spoiled it by rising to his feet.

'So sorry, everybody, but I have to go. Got to let the choir in for practice. Ladies, good night. Please go home with an escort.'

He gave his odd bow and almost ran back to the vicarage, where he quickly fed Radetsky, rushed up to the spare room and hastily put some fresh towels out, then hurried to the church to open it up for the choir.

Though it always gave him the creeps to enter the place at night, Nick immediately went to the light switch and turned them on. There was nothing and no one there and a few minutes later he heard the reassuring sound of several cars stopping outside and the tramp of feet as the choir approached.

The choirmaster, one Reginald Bridger, had arranged, during the present reign of terror, for those with cars to give lifts to others who had not and the first to enter the church followed by a flock of youngsters was Mrs Ely, the belting soprano with the terrible voice. She swept in like a mother hen with a brood of chicks, followed by several spotty boys, driven by somebody's sister. Last to arrive were Reginald Bridger and Broderick Crawford, who tonight looked sicker than ever.

The vicar, who had indeed a lot to do, decided to skip his tasks rather than walk home in the dark, and sat unobtrusively in one of the pews and listened. Tonight Mrs Ely, who had niggled on about having a sore throat, was singing quite quietly and some of the sounds that the choir were making were extremely beautiful. Nick felt almost moved to tears that some evil creature was roaming the village, terrorizing the people, and yet his humble choir could produce such an exquisite sound.

At nine o'clock on the dot he moved quietly into the vestry and opened the outer door. Tennant and Sergeant Potter were standing outside and crept softly within, the inspector raising his finger to his lips to indicate that they must keep totally silent. Nick nodded and went back into the church.

As the practice ended he got to his feet.

'Ladies and gentlemen, boys and girls, I would request you to come into the vestry for a moment. I have something to say that won't take more than five minutes.'

Mrs Ely said, 'But, Vicar, my throat . . .'

'Please, ma'am,' he answered, 'this will be very brief I assure you.'

They trooped into the vestry to find Inspector Tennant standing with an armful of cloaks. The sergeant had taken possession of the rest.

'Well now, people,' Tennant said cheerily, 'we thought that as it was a cold night you all ought to wear your cloaks. Could you come and take them from me, please.'

In the doorway Broderick made a most terrible retching sound, so much so that several children moved away, fearful of what he might do.

'Come along, sir,' said Tennant, horribly bright. 'Just take your cloak please.'

Broderick wheeled in the doorway and sprinted from the church, gagging as he ran.

'After him, Potter,' shouted Tennant, and as his sergeant sped away he threw the cloaks to the vicar and sped out into the night.

# NINETEEN

They brought him crashing to the ground just outside the church porch. Tennant had taken the precaution of stationing four policemen there and four more outside the vestry door. As he came sprinting out of church the quartet leapt on him and Broderick Crawford disappeared under a thrashing sea of blue legs. By this time both Potter and the inspector had arrived and watched until eventually Broderick surfaced, firmly handcuffed and weeping like a girl. Potter read him his rights and the wretched young man was escorted off to the mobile HQ.

An enterprising member of the paparazzi, who happened to be lurking in the street, just on the off-chance, took several shots of the arrest which he immediately sent off to his paper via his laptop. He then went to The Great House, looking smug. Meanwhile, having out of the kindness of their hearts given the snivelling Broderick a cup of tea, Tennant and Potter sat down to question him.

'Right, Mr Crawford,' the inspector began, 'we now have the evidence we want which tells us that the choir cloak belonging to you was worn on the night you attacked the vicar of Lakehurst with a piece of wood. Do you understand?'

'Yes, but I wasn't wearing it,' Broderick replied, wiping his eyes with his sleeve.

'Then who was?'

'I don't know. I just left it hanging there.'

'Come along, Broderick,' said Tennant gently. 'Are you trying to tell us that someone borrowed your cloak to assault the vicar and then put it back with a piece ripped out? I'm afraid that simply won't wash. You know damned well that you wore it that night and for some reason unknown launched an attack on Mr Lawrence, who saw you clambering over his gate.'

Broderick turned suddenly from broken reed to sullen youth. 'I know nothing about it,' he said, staring into the depths of his tea cup.

'And that is all you have to say?'

'Yes.'

Tennant stood up. 'Broderick Crawford, I am charging you with the murders of Ali and Rohini Patel, Gerrard Riddell, Dwayne Saunters, Ceinwen Carruthers and Cheryl Hamilton-Harty. You do not have to say anything—'

He was interrupted by a loud scream from Broderick. 'I didn't kill them, I swear it on the Bible.'

Tennant finished what he was saying then turned to Potter. 'Get him taken to Lewes. I don't want to look at him any more.'

Crawford was led out by a constable, shouting and kicking for all he was worth.

As soon as the door closed behind him, Potter said, 'But he didn't do it, sir. You know that perfectly well.'

'Yes, but I couldn't bear the arrogant little sod trying to tell me he didn't attack Nick Lawrence when we know that he did.'

They could hear Broderick weeping in the corridor outside and shouting, 'I want to see Inspector Tennant. I want to confess to what I *did* do.'

Potter and the inspector exchanged a weary glance and the sergeant rose to his feet and opened the door.

'Bring Mr Crawford back in please.'

He entered the room, gibbering.

'Right Crawford,' said Tennant, looking like an angry pixie. 'That didn't take too long, did it? Now, just settle down and talk us through everything.'

The boy went crimson. 'What do you want to know?'

'Are you gay or straight?' the inspector asked matter-of-factly.

Broderick muttered something.

'Speak up,' ordered Potter.

'I'm gay. But don't tell my mother, will you.'

Tennant sighed. 'Mr Crawford, what you say in this room is for our information only. But surely she's bound to find out one day.'

'Not necessarily. I'll just keep telling her that I haven't met the right person.'

There was a moment's silence and then the inspector asked,

'Was the attack the other night anything to do with your lover?'

'Yes.'

'Well?'

'You swear you won't tell anyone?'

'I've told you before,' answered Tennant impatiently, 'what you say is for this room only.'

Bright red, his face almost matching his hair, Crawford said, 'He's Mr Bridger.'

'You mean the choirmaster?'

Broderick nodded but could not bring himself to speak. Tennant caught Potter's eye and they could not help but smile at one another.

'Did you think he was at the vicarage that night?'

'Yes. I know it was stupid of me but I thought he might have a fancy for the new vicar. And I didn't know how Father Nick would feel about it. So I crept into the gardens and peered through the kitchen window but I couldn't see anything. I was just going away again when the vicar came out of the back door with that cat of his. He saw me jump over the gate and gave chase. So I hit him over the head with a piece of wood.'

'Because you thought he might be able to identify you?'

'Yes. But I swear on my mother's life – and Mr Bridger's – that I didn't commit any of those other murders. I honestly didn't.'

He looked so earnest, so vulnerable and so terribly young that Tennant, typically, felt a great deal of compassion for him. Potter, on the other hand, remained stony-faced.

'All right, Broderick. You may not be guilty of the murders – though your evidence will be examined along with that of all the other suspects – but you are certainly guilty of assault. I am afraid that you will still have to go to Lewes and will be charged accordingly.'

The young man looked at the floor and mumbled, 'Will my mother find out what I am?'

'I expect she will,' Potter answered ruthlessly. He stood up. 'Constable, drive Mr Crawford to Lewes. He has pleaded guilty to assault and is now in custody.'

When the door closed behind the deflated figure, Potter turned to Tennant.

'What a dirty old man that Bridger is.'
'At least he doesn't go for the very young kids.'
'I suppose that's something.'
'Yes, I suppose so.'

With the mobile unit going quiet for the night, Tennant took his seat in front of the computer and typed the words Rose Indigo into Google. Up came that familiar face, those luminous eyes and that full, fabulous mouth. He reread Wikipedia with interest but he had already seen Potter's printout of that. Now he turned to the other references about her and was pleased to find some of the stills from her early films. One in particular struck him, a scene from *Jekyll and Hyde*. All the actors seemed so familiar to him and he realized that as a small child he must have seen the film. There was James Pitman, looking suave and urbane and somehow dated, too clean cut and neat. And there were all the other players, frozen in time, forever caught in a moment of action from the film. Very, very faintly a distant bell rang in Tennant's mind, but when he sought for what it was it slipped away from him, as ephemeral as a faraway dream.

Out of interest the inspector typed in the names of her various husbands, starting with James Crichton, the young actor she had met in Sidmouth. The entry was relatively brief but telling.

'James Alexander Crichton, born 28th April, 1936, only son of Hubert Crichton, railway engineer, and his wife Gladys. Studied at Cricklewood County School where he showed early promise as an actor, playing Katharine of Aragon in Shakespeare's *Henry VIII*, and Juliet Capulet in *Romeo and Juliet*, in school productions. The entire family moved to Devon after James's father was invalided out of the RAF. Hubert began a career as a crime writer and had several popular books to his credit. James was acting with the local dramatic society in Torquay and was consequently signed up by the Sidmouth Repertory Company where he met his first wife – who was to become a Hollywood star during the fifties and sixties – the famous Rose Indigo. The marriage did not last and they were divorced in 1962. James subsequently married Jane Glynde, also an actress,

and later Beryl Miller, with whom he remained until her
death in 2002.

'He had a moderately successful career in the theatre, his
most famous part probably being William the Conqueror in
the Martin Steele film *1066*. James gave up acting in 1995
and started a small but profitable farm outside Exmouth from
which he produced free range eggs. He has two children,
Nathaniel and Thisbe, by his third wife, Beryl.'

There was no mention of his death so Tennant deduced
that the old man was still alive. On a whim he telephoned
a contact he had in the Devon and Cornwall constabulary
and asked him a few discreet questions. It appeared that
James Crichton was quite a well known figure in the Lower
Chudleigh public houses, where he would sit in a corner and
regale the passing population with tales of show business
and the people he had known.

'Funny old character apparently,' said the contact.

'Ever been in any trouble that you know of?'

'Never. As good as gold. His wife was a bit odd, though.'

'Oh? Which one?'

But at that moment there was an interruption at the other
end and the contact said, 'Sorry. Got to go. Ring me another
time,' and the receiver was put down.

Tennant, feeling curious, typed in the words Michael
Mauser but nothing came up except a question: Do you mean
Sieglinde Mauser? At that moment Potter came into the room
and Tennant reluctantly switched the computer off. Third
time lucky? he thought.

'I'm off, guv. Is that all right?'

'Yes, I'm staying with the vicar. Are the night duty boys
here?'

'Yes, hundreds of 'em. If there's a murder tonight . . .'

'Don't even say it,' interrupted Tennant.

'Right, sir, I won't. Goodnight.'

Five minutes later the inspector made his way to the vicarage,
where the lights were still on. Nick answered the door, smiling
a most welcoming smile.

'Come in, come in. Mrs Culpepper is here. I fetched her,'
he added in an undertone.

Tennant felt vaguely uncomfortable that he had just

been looking at her personal details on the Internet. But when he saw her face, which tonight seemed particularly beautiful, he forgot all about them and felt himself start to relax.

'Hello Roseanna,' he said. 'How nice to see you again.'

'And you my dear Inspector. It was so kind of Nick to invite me this evening. I must admit to feeling a little nervous when I'm on my own and after it gets dark. What is it about darkness that makes one afraid, I wonder.'

Tennant smiled. 'I don't know. Night terrors, I suppose.'

'I know some adults who will insist on having a night light on and others who like their rooms as dark as an Egyptian tomb,' said Nick.

Roseanna looked squarely at the inspector.

'It is like living in the village of the damned at the moment. Please, when are you going to make an arrest?'

'Well, we have arrested someone but only for the assault on the vicar. It's Broderick Crawford.'

Nick tutted but said, 'I'm not surprised about that.'

'Yes.' The inspector became deliberately vague. 'No doubt we'll learn more in time.'

There was a slight silence into which Roseanna spoke.

'Gentlemen, Richard has given me three complimentary tickets for his show and I am wondering if you would like to accompany me to London to see it.'

The vicar answered, 'Yes, very much indeed. What about you, Inspector?'

Tennant considered whether it would be possible to leave Lakehurst at such a delicate stage of the investigation. Then he thought that just one night off might give Potter a chance to take over and show what he was made of.

'Yes, I'd like that very much.'

'Oh how wonderful.'

Roseanna clasped her hands together and looked so delectable that Tennant wished he were twenty years older or she twenty years younger. Then he remembered the remarkable Joan Collins and silently came to the conclusion that age was really irrelevant.

'When are the tickets for?' asked Tennant.

'Any night we like this week. You see the show is closing on Sunday and they're anxious to fill the house.'

'Quite right,' observed the vicar. 'Well, I'll fit in with you, Inspector. You've got far more on your plate than I have.' He addressed himself to Roseanna. 'Can I refill your glass?'

'Yes please. It really is a lovely Beaujolais.'

They fell to discussing the merits of various wine growing regions, both displaying a knowledge of France which was extremely creditable. Tennant was miles away, thinking about the bicycle search and sorry that nothing had been revealed so far. He was determined, however, to identify the bike and search it thoroughly for any trace of protective clothing. It occurred to him that it might have been taken, not stolen exactly but borrowed. He turned to the other two and interrupted their conversation which had now reached the merits of the Bergerac region.

'I'm sorry, but have either of you got a bicycle?'

'Yes,' said Nick. 'It's in the garden shed.'

'Do you keep that locked?'

'Yes, I do as a matter of fact.'

'And you, Roseanna?'

'We've got two actually. One terrible old thing I used to ride – though I haven't done so for months. The other is much smarter and belongs to Richard. He cycles quite a lot when he's here. Says it helps him to keep fit.'

'And where do you keep them?'

'Again in the shed which I'm afraid is not locked.'

'I'll have a look at them in the morning if that's alright with you.'

'That will be fine,' said Roseanna, while Nick nodded his head.

The actress finished her glass of wine and stood up. 'I really must be off. I'm sorry to trouble you, Nick.'

Tennant held up an admonitory hand. 'I'll get a police car to drive you back, Roseanna, and they can search your house before you go in.'

He spoke briefly into his mobile phone and two minutes later they heard it pull up outside. Both men saw her into the vehicle and Tennant, leaning in at the door, said, 'I want you to search the house thoroughly before you drop Mrs

Culpepper inside. I'm spending the night at the vicarage but I'll be available on my mobile if I should be needed.'

'Very good, sir.'

They turned back into the warmth of the vicarage and sat down on either side of the fire.

'Tell me about Broderick now that we are alone. Was he looking for me?'

The policeman decided to be honest. 'Not really. He thought his lover was in here.'

Nick shot him a perplexed look and then after a moment or two, his face cleared.

'You don't mean Reginald Bridger do you?'

'That's the fellow.'

'Oh good Lord,' Nick answered, his face changed to thoroughly perplexed once more. 'What on earth does he see in an old boot like that.'

Tennant burst out laughing. 'Just what I was thinking.'

'Bridger's married you know. Got two children, as well. Millicent and Maurice, would you believe?'

'What's the wife like?'

'A grim-faced woman who is running to serious obesity. No wonder poor old Bridger's gone gay.'

'Poor chap. No wonder.'

Tennant held out his glass for a refill and they sat in silence, listening to the logs falling in the hearth.

'You're lucky to have this house.'

'Aren't I just. It's absolutely perfect for me. I feel totally comfortable here – and that includes old William.'

'Surely you don't believe in all that, do you?'

Nick chuckled comfortably. 'Wait and see is all I can say. By the way I take it that the kneeling figure I saw in church, who scared me half to death, was Broderick?'

'We don't know yet. We'll find out about that in the morning.'

Tennant gave a sudden yawn and said, 'Today is catching up with me. I think I'll go to bed. Would you mind showing me where I'm sleeping?'

'Of course.'

The bedroom was pleasantly warm and the inspector, after having given his teeth a brisk brush, got into bed and fell

immediately asleep. During the night, however, the temper-
ature suddenly plummeted and Tennant woke and saw
standing in the window, surrounded by moonlight, a craggy-
faced man.

'William?' he croaked.

And before the apparition vanished he saw it give him a
grin with several missing teeth.

# TWENTY

It had been very much as Tennant had thought. Traces of an unusual type of material had been found on the bicycle used by Richard Culpepper which had been removed for detailed examination to Lewes. He somehow felt that with this discovery he had drawn somewhat nearer to solving the case. For if the traces had come from protective clothing then, as sure as night follows day, something of the killer would be left on the garments. The net was beginning to tighten.

As everything in Lakehurst remained relatively quiet, he saw his way clear to going to the theatre on Tuesday night. They drove to Oakbridge Station in Tennant's car and got on an early evening train to London. The inspector could not help but notice how few people boarded and left at the station, which was the nearest to Lakehurst, out beyond Speckled Wood. It seemed that it was being regarded very much as a place not to go near. He presumed that half the Lakehurst residents – that half who were something big in the city anyway – were working from home on their computers. The rest were just busy trying to dodge the murderer as best they could.

It was observed by both Nick and Tennant that as the train began to fill up after Sevenoaks, people of all kinds shot a quick look at Roseanna, just as if she were still young and at the height of her powers. She was superbly dressed, of course, in a simple black number with shoulders heightened by a waterfall of crystal which swept down to her waist. Over this she wore a red evening coat, slightly drawn in at the bottom like a harem girl's. Her make up was subtle but clever, highlighting the glorious eyes and the curving, sulky lips. Despite her seventy-two years she looked sensational and Tennant, for one, was proud to be seen out with her.

They reached Charing Cross and took a taxi to something called Hackney People's Theatre, which turned out to be an old library converted into a strange type of community

building. Nick, who did not approve of libraries being closed
down, pulled a bit of a wry expression as he paid the taxi
off. A scruffy fellow in jeans and with a great shock of hair
which thankfully covered most of his spotty face and his
three-day growth of stubble, tore their tickets in half and
muttered something like 'Frownpairs', which indicated that
they should descend into the very depths.

The bar, to which they had apparently been directed, was
dire. Small, hot, with a lot of people talking loudly about
their theatrical experiences. There were acres of girls in jeans
and huge, unattractive jerseys with matching hair and faces,
accompanied by similar-looking men, all of whom seemed
to be involved in the arts. Then there were the slightly better
dressed aficionados discussing the St Pancras prize for all
they were worth.

'I thought Raymondo's entry was stunning, didn't you,
Nathan?'

'Utterly,' answered a youth in jeans with button at the fly,
and a shirt with ballooning sleeves. 'It couldn't have made
a statement more about the political morass in which this
country finds itself today.'

A voice soared above the rest. 'Well, d'you see, I envis-
aged this play as a kind of scena, if you take my meaning.'

'No, I don't quite,' answered a very short little woman of
interderminate age, with tiny pebble glasses which she clearly
needed desperately.

'What Marcus is trying to say, Gwendoline, is that he sees
the whole thing aerially – from above, as it were – and the
scenes enacted below represent the way in which various
people react to the news that John Major is dead.'

'But he isn't dead,' answered Gwendoline, huffily.

Marcus, clearly the author, heaved a long and pitying sigh.
'It is a pretence, Gwen dear. That is what I have created. A
pretence that Major is dead and that all is not well with the
world, d'you see.'

'No,' she said stubbornly, and kicked one shoe against the
other like a child.

At that moment they were interrupted by a short, earnest
man with a balding head. 'Excuse me, would you be Mr
Marcus Alnuff?'

'Alnough,' pronounced Marcus loftily.

'Sorry, Mr Allno. I wonder if you could spare me a few minutes of your time. I'm from the *St Pancras Commuter Echo* and we would like to do an interview with you regarding the forthcoming award.'

'Of course,' said Marcus grandly. He turned to his companions and said, 'Press' in a loud stage whisper and then turned aside.

Roseanna caught the eye of the two men and smiled broadly before saying, '*Poseur*,' in quite a carrying voice.

'Quite,' answered Tennant. 'What's everybody having to drink? I've got a feeling we're going to need it,' he added in an undertone for Nick's benefit.

He managed to get served just as the first bell rang, so changed the order to three shorts, which they all swallowed swiftly as a nasal voice announced, 'No glasses in the theatre, please.' They then started on a long trek through big empty rooms until they reached the third, the biggest of all, which had been set out with four rows of folding seats around two-thirds of its area. The space was already quite full but Roseanna, moving swiftly, managed to get three seats in the front row.

In the centre of the acting area stood a large closed coffin with a British flag draped over it and a bunch of stage flowers placed at its foot. Attached to this was a label saying, 'Always, Norma.'

Tennant was staring at it, thinking sorrowfully of Lakehurst, wondering when the action was going to begin, when suddenly it did.

A naked young man wearing a John Major mask ran across the stage, paused momentarily by the coffin and then ran off. After that appeared two women in macs both playing the part of TV commentators and both – though not at the same time – reporting on the state of the nation, shocked and stunned by the news of Major's death as it was.

Tennant closed his eyes momentarily but was brought back by a dig in the ribs from Nick as one of the women peeled off her mac to reveal that she was bare-breasted underneath.

'What's it all about?' asked the vicar, extremely puzzled.

'Search me,' Tennant whispered back.

'Oh,' said the vicar, none the wiser.

They stared in amazement as the awfulness of what they were watching dragged on but were suddenly alerted by Roseanna whispering, 'Richard is coming on now.'

Tennant gave a sharp intake of breath as what appeared to be a forensics expert came on the stage. He was dressed in the traditional white protective clothing, had mauve gloves on his hands, and his features were covered by a white disposable mask. In fact he was scarcely recognizable except for the matinee-idol eyes wildly rolling from side to side.

Roseanna's reaction was endearing. She leant forward on her seat, her hands clasped before her, her chin on her locked fingers. She looked for all the world like a little girl gazing at the Christmas tree and her very attitude made both Tennant and Nick smile.

Richard pulled the mask down and let it hang from one ear. Then he started on about Major's death being suspicious and how the police force had been called in confidentially, not a word of it leaking to the press. Enter the bare-breasted reporter – once more decently clad in the mac – who began to say through the mike she was clutching that rumours were circulating throughout the media that there might have been foul play involved and how the police were doing a secret investigation.

'Some hopes,' muttered Tennant.

The forensics man launched into a long speech about how skilled was the work he did, then everyone left the stage.

'Is that it?' asked the vicar, standing up.

'No, my dear,' answered Roseanna, 'this is only the interval.'

They staggered back to the bar, both the men feeling desperately in need of alcohol to numb the pain. Roseanna went to the Ladies and Tennant and Nick stared at one another in horror.

'This is quite the most God-awful thing I have ever seen,' said the inspector.

'What's it meant to be about? Nobody is connecting with anyone else.'

'It's a series of scenas, of course,' Tennant answered loudly, and the vicar saw that Marcus had walked into the bar surrounded by sycophants.

'Richard hasn't got much of a part, has he?' he remarked.

'Perhaps he'll do more in act two.'

But strangely enough when they took their seats again it was to find that the forensics man did not appear.

'Is Richard coming back as someone else?' the vicar asked Roseanna.

'No,' she answered, smiling. 'He's only in the first act.'

Suddenly Tennant came to life. Why had he never thought of it before? Supposing the fellow decided against taking his curtain call on certain occasions and caught the train back to Oakbridge where he might be keeping a bicycle? A short ride to Lakehurst and he could go about his grisly business unhindered. He could even borrow the protective clothing he wore in the play and next morning, arriving early, put it in the theatre washing machine.

The inspector was so gripped by his theory that he scarcely noticed the play had come to an end. The naked man wearing the Major mask ran across the stage, this time in slow motion, and everyone started to clap. They all appeared to take a bow, Richard included, and then the audience traipsed back through the empty rooms to the bar.

Marcus stood in a semicircle of admirers drinking in their compliments.

'Such meaning,' said the young man with the buttons on his fly, 'I mean it left me drained – utterly.'

'Why did that girl take her top off?' asked Gwendoline, who was turning out to be a bit of a nightmare.

'Oh, shush.'

'No, I won't shush. I mean *why* did she?'

'To show she had decent tits,' said an old bearded gentleman who was making his way out and who obviously had not enjoyed the evening at all.

'Hear, hear,' echoed the vicar unexpectedly.

But at that moment Roseanna could be seen returning and a discreet silence fell. She glanced at Nick.

'Did you enjoy it, my dear?'

'I'm afraid it was rather beyond me,' he said, looking apologetic.

'And what about you, Inspector?'

'Well, I'm a bit thick when it comes to a series of scenas,' he answered, just loudly enough for Marcus to hear.

'The last thing I would have called you was thick, my friend,' she said, and then she turned and flashed her radiant smile as Richard came up to her. Looking at him closely, Tennant wondered if he had had plastic surgery.

'Well, hello, everybody,' the actor said, putting his arm round Tennant's shoulders. 'How are we all, tonight? Did we enjoy ourselves?'

'It was a very interesting production,' said the vicar tamely.

'Hoh, hoh, hoh,' chortled Richard. 'Did you know that "interesting" is a euphemism for bloody awful in theatrical parlance.'

'No, I didn't.'

'Neither did I,' said Tennant. 'Is that a fact?'

'What can I get everyone to drink?' asked Richard, thankfully changing the subject.

'I'll have a half of light ale.'

'And so will I.'

'And I will have a vodka and tonic,' said Roseanna, before throwing her arms round her husband and giving him a look of such adoration that it plucked at Tennant's heart to see it. There could be no doubting that this marriage, regardless of the age gap, regardless of any hidden depths her husband might have – and the inspector thought that they might be deep indeed – had brought her great joy.

'You were wonderful, my darling,' she murmured. 'When you were on stage one couldn't look at anybody else.'

Considering, thought Tennant brutally, that there had only been one other person with Richard, this was not difficult to achieve.

The actor hugged Roseanna tightly to him. 'Dearest,' he said, 'you truly are so sweet.'

He could have meant it quite sincerely but he had the unfortunate habit of speaking as if every word were a piece of theatrical dialogue. But his wife either didn't – or did not want to – notice, and snuggled up as closely to him as she could possibly get.

Afterwards, going home on the train, she fell asleep on

Richard's shoulder and the actor closed his eyes, despite the fact that he had a man next to him who was eating a portion of smelly chips while prattling inanely on a mobile phone. Nick leant across to the inspector.

'Would you like a bed for the night?'

'I'd be very pleased. By the way, I saw your ghost.'

'Did you? I've never seen him. What was he like?'

Tennant laughed. 'You really believe it, don't you. Actually I had a dream and thought I saw something but in fact I must have been asleep.'

Nick laughed shortly and said, 'You policemen.' He indicated the dozing Richard with his eyes. 'What's he doing coming back with us?'

'Apparently they've got a day off tomorrow. Something to do with judging the St Pancras award.'

'Blimey. That's going to be a big deal.'

And both men roared with laughter, so much so that the man on the mobile looked annoyed and spilt his chips all over the floor.


They got back to Lakehurst at midnight and after having dropped off the Culpeppers, Tennant called in at the mobile unit before returning to the vicarage.

'Everything quiet?' he asked the desk sergeant.

'So far, so good, sir.'

'Well, fingers crossed.'

On a whim and despite the lateness of the hour Tennant sat down in front of the computer and typed in the words 'Sieglinde Mauser'. Immediately a picture came up of a somewhat frightened-looking woman standing next to – of all people – Adolf Hitler. The legend came up. 'Sieglinde Mauser, born 16th June, 1890, only surviving daughter of Fritz and Rosa Mauser. Sieglinde was an associate of Adolf Hitler and worked in the position of his secretary during the 1930s. In 1935 she met Graf Rolfe von Weisshausen, a staunch henchman of the Fuehrer, and married him a year later. (See Weisshausen, Graf Rolfe von). In 1939 their only child was born, a son, Conrad Michael. In 1946 von Weisshausen was tried at Nuremberg and subsequently executed. Sieglinde, however, escaped with her child and reverted to her maiden name in order to avoid detection. It is believed she spent some years in Poland but she eventually came to England, where she lived until her death in 1980.'

Tennant sat back in his chair, breathing hard, and typed in the words 'Rolfe von Weisshausen'. And up came the photograph of the Nazi war criminal in his high boots and his uniform, the swastika emblazoned on his arm. The inspector had never seen such a likeness between father and son. He could have been looking at the face of Michael Mauser.

# TWENTY-ONE

B roderick Crawford looked terrible after a night in the cells. His face was the colour of a slug's, his normally vivid hair hung limply down upon his grimy collar, his teeth looked as if they had been dipped in seaweed. To crown it all he had a five o'clock shadow in a shade resembling pale putty. Tennant, sitting opposite him, felt that the poor child had nothing going for him at all. To make matters worse Mrs Fothergill, his mother – she had married again after Mr Crawford had gone either to meet his maker or to the divorce court – had arrived in Lewes and was sitting in the waiting room in floods of tears, demanding to see her boy. Tennant sighed. His was not an easy life.

'Now, Mr Crawford,' he said kindly, 'can you tell me something?'

'What?' Broderick responded mulishly.

'Did you go into the church and pray when the place was empty?'

'I might have done.'

Tennant shifted in his chair. 'Did you or didn't you?'

'Sometimes, yes.'

'And was it you who bolted out past the vicar leaving him in a state of some shock.'

'I wouldn't know how he was feeling, would I?'

'So it was you,' said Potter, who was sitting beside Tennant.

'I didn't say so, did I?'

'Listen, mate,' Potter answered, losing his cool, 'stop playing silly buggers. And don't ask questions. We're doing that. Understand?'

There was silence during which Broderick cast his watery gaze to the floor and Tennant cleared his throat.

'Well?' he said.

'No comment.'

'Right,' the inspector answered, 'switch off the recording

and bring in Mrs Fothergill. We're going to have to explain to her about her son's sexual proclivities.'

Broderick jerked to life. 'No, please don't tell my mum. I'll answer your questions but don't say anything. Yes, it was me who prayed late in the church. And do you know what it was I was praying for? I was praying to sort out my life. I was praying that I could stop loving Mr Bridger and find someone my own age? It's all a total mess at the moment – and I hate it.'

He burst into passionate sobs, slumping forward on the table, shoulders heaving with grief. Tennant looked at the constable who stood by the door.

'Take Mr Crawford away, will you. And get him a cup of tea while you're at it.'

As soon as Broderick was out of the room Tennant said, 'Potter, I want to run an idea past you.'

'Right, sir.'

'It happened in the theatre last night.'

And he proceeded to tell his sergeant all that had occurred in the few hours during which they had gone their separate ways.

'What do you think?' Tennant asked at the end.

Potter grinned. 'I believe you could very well be right about Culpepper. But what a turn up about poor old Mauser. Son of a Nazi war criminal, eh!'

Tennant looked very thoughtful. 'But is it possible that he has inherited his father's killing instincts, I wonder.'

'I don't know, sir. We'd better go and have another chat with him.'

At that moment the phone rang and Potter picked it up.

'What!' he exclaimed. 'OK. We'll be with you in thirty minutes.'

He put the phone down and turned to the inspector. 'There was an attempted murder this morning in Lakehurst. Giles Fielding. He's all right because he was rescued. And you'll never guess who by.'

Tennant shook his head.

'The offspring of the Hitlerite himself.'

They did not bother with the mobile unit but went straight to Giles's farm in Speckled Wood. Two police cars were drawn up outside and there was a strong presence of uniformed officers. Tennant strode up to one.

'Has he been taken to hospital?'

'Yes. He was admitted to A and E but they have discharged him. He's got nothing more than a very sore throat.'

'What happened exactly?'

'Apparently he went out into his field because his sheep were making a noise. In the darkness somebody crept up on him, putting some wire round his neck, but he shouted out and his neighbour, who's in the habit of going for early walks, heard him and fired a pistol and the assailant ran off.'

'What time was this?' asked Potter.

'About five o'clock. It's still dark then.'

'Christ almighty,' said Tennant. 'If only I could get my hands on this lunatic, whoever he is.'

'Come on, sir. We'd best go and see poor Fielding.'

But Tennant had despair in his walk and went silently into the farmhouse, deep in gloom.

Giles was sitting in the kitchen by the range, which had been stoked up and was throwing out a considerable heat. He was wrapped in a blanket and was sipping as best he could from a mug of coffee which, the inspector thought, had a good slug of brandy in it. Sitting beside him, also drinking the brew, was the son of the war criminal.

'Well, Mr Mauser,' Tennant said slowly, 'I hear you saved the day.'

'Yes, since you put it like that. I happened to be setting out on my walk and I heard Giles shouting. So I shot at the person and they ran away.'

'Did you see who it was?'

'All I could make out in the gloom was a figure clad in white. I could not tell you whether it was male or female.'

'And you shot at him or her. Do you think you hit them?'

'I can't be certain. But I certainly scared them off.'

Tennant paused, realizing that he ought to ask Mauser about whether he had a gun licence but horribly aware that the man was dying, that he had a past that must have been almost impossible to bear. He saw Potter open his mouth but signalled to him with his hand to remain silent.

'Thank you, Mr Mauser. You did a public service in rescuing Mr Fielding.'

'I wish I'd killed the bastard,' Michael said matter-of-factly.

Tennant let that remark go, instead he asked, 'You didn't by any chance notice what direction he or she ran off in?'

'I can tell you that,' Giles croaked. 'Ran towards Lakehurst and a minute or so later I heard a car start up.'

'I too heard that sound,' said Mauser.

'Just as a matter of interest, sir, where do you go on those long walks of yours?'

Mauser drew himself up in an elegant move. 'Different directions. Sometimes I walk as far as the moated manor, sometimes to the deserted orphanage. I like to be alone with my thoughts particularly since the death of my wife.'

'We are doing everything in our power to catch the perpetrator of these crimes,' Tennant said determinedly, but even as he spoke the words a feeling of defeat came over him and he knew that if he had got no further by the end of this week he would resign from the investigation and let someone new take over the case. He looked at Giles.

'I'm going to post officers to watch your house night and day, Mr Fielding. And yours too, Mr Mauser.'

'I think I am capable of looking after myself,' the man answered proudly, staring at him, though Tennant could see that behind that handsome face and autocratic bearing, Mauser looked very grey.

'I am sure you are, sir, but it would make me happier. Speckled Wood is very remote after all.'

Mauser gave him a deep look down his long and aristocratic nose. 'Perhaps some of us prefer that,' he said.

Nick had just put the kettle on for his mid-morning coffee when there was a ring at the vicarage door. He opened it to see a small collection of villagers standing there. Jack Boggis was leading a party that consisted of Sonia Tate, Ivy Bagshot, Mavis Cox and Kylie Saunters.

'Morning, Vicar,' said Jack, who appeared to be the self-appointed spokesman. 'May we have a few minutes of your time?'

'Certainly, come in,' Nick replied, half-guessing what they had come about.

They trooped into the living room and sat down in a semicircle.

'Would you like coffee? I was just going to make myself a cup.'

'I'll get it Vicar,' said Mavis. 'Shall I use the cafetière?'

'Yes, if you would. The coffee's in the blue tin.'

She bustled out importantly and Nick took a seat in his usual armchair.

'How can I help you?' he said.

'It's about these damn murders,' said Jack, his dentures gleaming in the pale autumnal sunshine. 'We don't think that policeman's any good.'

'It seems to me he's working very hard,' Nick answered.

'But the killer is still at large,' Mrs Ivy Bagshot said, stating the obvious, 'and none of us feels safe. It truly is a ghastly situation.'

'That's right,' Kylie put in. 'Our gran is terrible. She just sits in a chair and weeps all day long. I feel like moving out but it wouldn't be fair to leave 'er.'

'So what,' said Jack importantly, 'are we going to do about it?'

'Have a cup of coffee,' Mavis called brightly as she staggered in beneath a tray laden with mugs.

'I don't mind if I do,' Jack answered. 'Have you got any of them biscuits?'

'I'll get you some,' and Mavis pattered out to the kitchen once more.

'Nick, please help us,' said Sonia Tate, fluttering her eyelashes wildly.

The vicar made an excuse of sipping his coffee before he made any answer. Then he asked, 'Do you wish me to make a formal complaint to Lewes?'

The females chorused, 'Yes,' while Jack said, 'Aye, I agree.'

'Well, I don't think I am prepared to do that. I believe that an arrest is imminent and if it is not then I suggest Mr Boggis should go to Lewes himself and tell the Chief Constable of his concerns.'

Jack eyed him over a ginger nut which he was attacking with some difficulty.

'All right by me,' he said in a muffled voice.

'But wait a few days more please,' Nick said with a great deal of calm which he did not actually feel.

'Yes, but in the meantime one of us could be murdered,' Mrs Bagshot answered him.

'I don't believe that will happen.'

'It's all very well for you, Vicar. You've got a constable hanging round your door.'

'And so have all of you, I expect.'

'Don't worry, ladies, I will take care of you,' stated Boggis expansively.

'What a good plan.' This from Nick with a smile. 'I'm sure your house is big enough to put everybody up and then you could stand guard while they sleep.'

'Well I couldn't go,' said Kylie, taking him literally. 'I've got to be at home with Gran.'

Nick remained silent, aware that Jack was glaring at him, and wondered if the murderer sat in this very room. He looked from one to the other. Miss Saunters he ruled out but Boggis, Mavis, Ivy and Sonia all had definite possibilities. He wondered what the motive could possibly be unless, of course, one of them was completely deranged. Which wouldn't be difficult, he thought uncharitably.

Jack spoke angrily. 'That might be what you women wanted – for the vicar to go – but I've a tongue in my head and I'm perfectly capable of using it, thank you very much. So I say that at the end of this week and no longer,' he added menacingly, 'if the villain hasn't been caught, I'll make an appointment with the chief constable and go and see him myself.'

'Thank you for that,' Nick answered soothingly. 'It's just that I believe the inspector is up against somebody almost impossible to find.'

'Why?' asked Sonia sharply. 'Does the murderer wear protective clothing and gloves?'

'Yes, I believe so.'

'Then clever old him, says I.'

There was a slight silence which Nick filled by saying,

'Then that's settled then. At the end of the week Mr Boggis will make a protest on your behalf.'

He stood up and the others took the hint and started to make their leave. Jack Boggis turned in the doorway.

'Don't worry, Vicar, you can rely on me to make my point.'

'I'm quite sure I can,' said Nick, as he thankfully closed the front door behind them.

On a whim Tennant drove himself down to Oakbridge Station and wandered round the car park looking for bicycles. There were several parked in a rundown shelter close to the booking office. The inspector walked in to find a strange-looking individual with what appeared to be a horn growing out of his forehead manning the ticket booth and simultaneously having an animated conversation with an extremely fat girl who had her face pressed close to the glass.

'Excuse me,' Tennant said politely.

She gave him a dirty look from heavily outlined little eyes and swung her large behind to one side.

'Police,' said Tennant abruptly. 'Would you mind coming out for a minute. I want to talk to you.'

The man grunted and reluctantly got off his stool and after a great deal of key rattling appeared in the front office.

'Yes?' he said truculently.

'I am making an enquiry about a bicycle,' the inspector said in his most authoritative voice.

The horned man glanced at the plump lump, who had now taken a seat on one of the benches, watching avidly. He seemed undecided whether to be cocky or cooperative.

'Would you prefer to come to Lewes to answer some questions?' Tennant asked.

This seemed to settle the matter. 'No, I'm very busy here, Inspector.'

As the station was utterly deserted except for the fat girl, with whom, Tennant decided, the ticket man was having an affair, he could see no sense in this, but he didn't argue.

'It's a particular bicycle I'm interested in. One that stands outside most of the time but is occasionally used late at night and returned early in the morning.'

'Trouble is that this booking office closes at nine o'clock and doesn't open again till seven.'

Tennant paused, he hadn't consciously thought of that.

The girl spoke up. 'But remember the night we . . . you . . . was here late and we saw somebody get off the train and take a bike. I can recall it because you said he was in something you'd watched on the telly.'

'That's right, Demi – *Genie in the House*, it was.'

'Go on,' said Tennant. 'This is extremely interesting.'

'Well, I was working late . . .'

Actually having shenanigans in the ticket office after hours, thought Tennant, though his face remained impassive.

'. . . about ten forty-five it was. Anyway, this bloke stood underneath the lamp while he unlocked his bicycle and I saw him clear as day. It was either that actor or his double. I'd seen him that very afternoon while I watched a bit of telly.'

'And would you be prepared to pick him out in an identity parade?'

'Yes. Why? What's he done?'

'I'm afraid I'm not at liberty to discuss that.'

'Never mind that. Is there a reward?' asked Demi, heaving to her feet and looking interested.

'No, I'm afraid not on this occasion. Now, Mr . . .? Could you give me your full name and address please?'

'Shanks. Travis Shanks. Number three, Scrag Road, Oakbridge, East Sussex. 'Ere, as this got anything to do with the lunatic killer in Lakehurst?'

'Yeah, has it?' echoed Demi.

'Possibly,' answered Tennant, giving them a crumb to please.

'Blimey,' said Travis, and winked his eye meaningfully at his girlfriend.

Tennant drove straight to Lewes and went into consultation with the superintendent.

'It's pretty flimsy,' said his boss, having heard the story.

'But, sir, it's the only lead I've got. Let's have him in for questioning at least.'

'Very well. He's either guilty or up to something immoral or illegal. Let's see if you can break him down.'

'Thank you, sir.'

Tennant reached for his mobile and gave very clear instructions to Sergeant Potter.

'I feel I can't do it after having seen him so recently. I'm afraid it's going to have to be you. And confiscate all the bicycles at Oakbridge Station and bring them carefully to the laboratory at Lewes.'

'It'll be a pleasure, sir. And it'll give the citizens of Lakehurst some peace at last.'

But that night, after it became public knowledge that Richard Culpepper had been removed from his house in police custody and the general rejoicing was at an end, there was one figure who walked home alone and late and who, in the darkness, smiled.

# TWENTY-TWO

Why was it, Tennant wondered, that actors could never be natural, could never be themselves whatever the circumstances? He sat silently for a moment trying to picture Richard Culpepper having a bath, making love, on the lavatory, and wondered what sort of person he might be in those circumstances. But though the thought both annoyed yet fascinated him, he could find no answer to it. Richard sat on the other side of the interview table exquisitely portraying a man both indignant and hurt that he should have been placed in such a position. He raised a weary eyebrow.

'Could you tell me please, Inspector, exactly with what I am charged.'

His voice was gentle, soft; the sort of voice that one would use when dealing with someone suffering from senile dementia. Tennant decided to emulate it.

'You are not charged with anything, Mr Culpepper. We are merely asking that you assist us with our enquiries. That is all.'

'And how may I do that? How may I assist you? Because you can believe you me that I will move heaven and earth to unmask the cruel creature who is stalking the village of Lakehurst at present.'

That speech, thought Tennant, was slightly overdone, said, as it was, in Henry V's ringing tones before Agincourt.

'Well, that's jolly kind of you,' he answered enthusiastically, as if he, Tennant, were sitting by the River Cam and someone had just offered him a cucumber sandwich.

'Anything I can do, and I mean that.'

'Now, Mr Culpepper, we have reason to believe that you did not always take your curtain call but sometimes caught the nine forty-five back to Oakbridge and after that got on a bicycle that you kept permanently at the station. Did you then, I wonder, go back to the village and commit murder.'

Richard literally blanched and the inspector wondered whether he had learned the trick in repertory or films. Now he turned into the deeply offended man of impeccable breeding.

'How dare you suggest such a thing? How dare you?'

Very quietly Tennant heard Potter, who was sitting beside him, give a concealed giggle.

'I dare,' said the inspector, 'because it is my duty to dare.' Is this thing catching? he thought to himself.

'Then if you don't go off to murder someone where do you go? And before you start protesting we have checked with your theatre company, Charing Cross station – who have CCTV footage – and various other relevant witnesses who have all seen you doing this on a fairly regular basis.'

Culpepper gulped and turned back into a gangling youth caught drinking or smoking or something or other, for the first time.

'How confidential is this?' he asked, going from ashen-cheeked to flame impressively fast.

Tennant sighed. 'It all depends which way the case against you goes.'

'Case? What case? You have no case.'

'Not at the moment we haven't, sir,' put in Potter, who had been dying to get a word in. 'But much depends on what you tell us now.'

'If word of this ever gets back to my wife I swear I'll put a gun to my head.'

'Oh stop being so dramatic,' said Tennant testily. 'This is 2009 not 1929. I take it from all your protestations and general mouthiness that you had another woman within cycling distance of the station, that you spent a night of wild sexual excess with her, that you got up when you felt like it and caught a train back to London. Or that is what you would like us to think. But I put it to you that the first scenario I painted could quite as easily fit the bill and until you can give us incontrovertible evidence that that was not the case, then you leave me no alternative but to regard you as our prime suspect.'

'And what about the other night?' asked Culpepper, pushing his chin out and looking like an angry schoolboy. 'What about when I came back with you and there was a murder attempt the next morning? How can you explain that?'

'Very simply. You rose early and borrowed your wife's car and went to Speckled Wood and attempted to murder Giles Fielding but somebody took a pot shot at you and you retired home, hurt.'

'My wife will prove that I remained in bed with her till eight o'clock.'

'We haven't asked her yet, but we will,' answered Potter nastily. 'And meanwhile, Mr Culpepper, you will remain in custody and not be permitted to use the telephone.'

The actor positively bristled and Tennant thought that at last they were beginning to see through all the impeccable performances.

'Would you care to give us the name and address of your mistress,' he said in a businesslike manner.

'No I would not,' Culpepper retorted.

Tennant gave a mannered sigh. 'You will eventually so why bother to spin it out? We have a certain amount of time before we have to take you in front of a magistrate and unless you give us something to go on we will press for you to remain in custody.'

'Then press, my friend, press,' said Culpepper, easily slipping into the role of gallant Englishman who would not betray the woman he loved at any price.

'You could have been written by John Buchan,' said Potter in amazement, aware that Tennant was looking at him in something like surprise.

'Damn you, sir,' Culpepper answered. 'You'll never get her name out of me.'

'Well, it's that or a murder charge,' Tennant answered. 'Constable, would you escort Mr Culpepper to the cells please. And put him on bread and water,' he added, with a sly wink in the officer's direction.

It was six o'clock and Nick was relaxing after a very strange day when there came a frantic knocking at his front door. Roseanna stood there, looking as tragic as only a Garbo lookalike could.

'Oh, Nick, Nick,' she sobbed. 'They have taken my husband away to Lewes. What shall I do?'

The vicar had already heard the news when he had gone to the post office earlier. Mavis Cox had told him, her eyes reduced to wicked little slants as she had relayed the story.

'It was him all along. Pretending to be in London in a show. Would you believe it!'

Somehow, Nick hadn't. As soon as Mavis had opened her mouth he had started to have doubts. Richard Culpepper may be many things but a murderer he was not.

Now he said, 'Come in and sit down. Let me get you a little drop of brandy and then you can tell me the story from the start.'

He ushered her into the living room and went to the sideboard where he poured her a large brandy and a smaller one for himself.

'Now tell me everything,' he said.

'Well, they came this afternoon. It was Sergeant Potter who made the arrest. He just said the words and then they drove him away to Lewes.' She cried again and then sipped her brandy which appeared to revive her a little. 'But the thing is, you see, that I know why.'

Those heavy-lidded eyes, somewhat puffy now, looked at him over the rim of the glass.

Nick stared at her. 'What do you mean?'

'I know why he kept a bicycle at Oakbridge Station.'

'Why?' asked Nick, not following the thread of the conversation in the least.

'Because of *her*.'

'Her who?'

Roseanna blew her nose, wiped her eyes, and had another deep drink of brandy.

'I'm sorry,' she said. 'I'm being a little incoherent. I'll start at the beginning. You know that my husband is twenty-two years younger than I am.' The vicar nodded. 'Well, about a year ago he was in a West End production – only a very small part, I'm afraid. Poor Richard, I'm sorry but he never made the big time and I doubt very much that he will now. Anyway, during this run he fell madly in love with the ingénue, a pretty little thing, very small and feminine with jet black hair and amazing bright blue eyes. To cut a long story short he promised her that one day they would be together but that he owed me a debt of gratitude and that he could never leave me.'

'And she believed him?'

'It was true, it was true,' Roseanna said tragically. 'I did give him a start. We met in 1969 when he was only ten. He had the part of a baker's boy in *Jekyll and Hyde*.' She laughed. 'Do you know I think he had a bit of a crush on me, even in those days. However, later on we met again and married and have been ever since, and it did his career no harm at all. I introduced him to agents, producers, everything. But I love him, Nick. And I know that he loves me. This little girl no doubt fills some place in his heart, yet I know that I will always come first.'

'So how does this fit in with keeping a bicycle at Oakbridge Station?' asked Nick, bemused.

'Because some nights he does not take his curtain call but catches a train and cycles to see her. They spend the night together and then he goes to the theatre the next day.'

Nick thought that Richard could have done this from the start but said nothing, presuming that he was under contract to take a bow, or something like that. He pulled himself together because Roseanna was asking him a question.

'So what shall I do, Nick?'

'Well, you'd better ring Tennant and tell him. Or better still go into the mobile unit and tell them. I'll go with you. How did you get here by the way?'

'Oh, I took the car. Because I know the murderer hasn't been caught and it's still dangerous on the streets.'

Nick shivered. Her voice had a deep and disturbing quality when she spoke like that.

'And for a few minutes I thought we were safe,' he said.

Strangely, or so it seemed to him, the police treated her story with a certain amount of caution. Admittedly neither Tennant nor Potter was present, both busy in Lewes he presumed, but for all that the policemen in the mobile unit had very little to say but merely took a statement from her which Roseanna duly signed. The vicar waited for her and afterwards invited her for a drink in The Great House which she, somewhat surprisingly, accepted. They went in and there was

Giles Fielding, regaling all and sundry with tales of his mirac-
ulous escape. Sitting on the edge of the group, drinking his
usual vodka and smiling at Giles's story, was Kasper.

'Good to see you,' said Nick, really meaning it.

Kasper stood as Roseanna approached and kissed her hand.
She smiled at him graciously.

'So, you two are out for an evening,' he said.

Roseanna went pale. 'Well hardly,' she answered.

Kasper was profuse in his apologies. 'Please forgive my
unfortunate use of the language. I was merely saying the
first thing that came into my head. I do beg your pardon.'

The vicar saved the situation. 'Unfortunately Mrs Culpepper
and I have just come in for a quick drink. As you know her
husband was arrested earlier today and she came to see me
for a bit of moral support.'

'He is innocent,' Roseanna said loudly. 'I have made a
statement to that effect to the police.'

She was very slightly hysterical, Nick thought, and obviously so did Kasper, for he escorted her to a seat and put a
glass of brandy in her hand.

'Perhaps you would like to tell me,' he said, in his most
soothing professional voice.

Roseanna drew breath, took a sip, and then poured out
the whole sad story – this time fortunately in an undertone
– to Kasper. Nick, sitting at the same table, listened to it
all again. But for some reason the fact that she had met
Richard when he had been only ten, encouraged by his
parents, no doubt, who had presumably sent him to stage
school – Nick could just imagine it – meeting his future
wife in a Selznick film, where they had obviously sent for
an English boy rather than sit through the agony of an
American kid trying to do an English accent, haunted him.
It was such an unlikely idea. Nick determined to try and
find a still from *Jekyll and Hyde* on the Internet when he
got home.

Kasper was speaking. 'All will be well I assure you, my
dear Roseanna. As soon as the inspector gets your statement
he will be round to see you and everything will be sorted out.'

Despite her weeping, despite the fact that her nose was
red and her eyelids swollen, Roseanna had never looked more

beautiful than when she said quietly, 'Thank you, Kasper. You are so kind.'

A familiar voice spoke behind them. 'Is this a private party or can anyone join?'

It was Sonia Tate, very slightly drunk, and not caring a damn. Nick and Kasper caught each other's eye and winced slightly.

'Well, I walked here because I believe that it is now safe to do so.' She looked at Roseanna and clapped her hand over her mouth. 'Oops, sorry. I didn't see you there.'

Nick knew perfectly well that she had and that the whole thing had been a cruel barb. He drew himself up.

'I'm sorry but I was about to take Mrs Culpepper home. The streets of Lakehurst are not safe until they are pronounced so by the police.'

'You sound very pompous.'

Nick struggled to keep his annoyance under control. 'I'm devastated if you think so. Apologies for leaving you like this, Kasper. Come and see me any time.'

But the doctor was not going to be left alone with Sonia. 'I, too, must take my leave of you, Mrs Tate. Please excuse me. Nick, I may come to the vicarage later if that would be all right?'

'Can I join you?' This from Sonia.

Together both men said, 'No.'

She looked petulant. 'Talk about not being wanted. Well, you can both bugger off. I can spy some younger and more amusing company.' And she went off, wiggling her behind horrendously.

'Let's get out of here,' murmured Nick, and taking Roseanna under the elbow he propelled her through the doors, followed closely by Kasper.

Later, after he had seen Roseanna into her house, Nick went back to the vicarage and fed Radetsky, then went into his study and sat down before the computer. This time instead of pressing Wikipedia he brought up another site which showed old photographs of her various films. He loved the titles of some of them: *The Seductress*, *The Waterfall*, *The Daring Lady*, *Purple Orchids*, *The Kiss of Passion*, to name but a few. Then there were the classics: *Anna Karenina, Mati Hari, The Woman in White* and *Dr Jekyll and Mr Hyde*. He came to the still that he sought. The one in which a grubby child, barely recognizable as Richard Culpepper, was standing offering Mr Hyde a bun. There were several other people in the photograph; a young James Pitman, playing the title role, a couple of women – clearly prostitutes – eyeing him up, and Roseanna walking along the other side of the street, unaware of what was going on.

But it was to the two young girls that Nick's attention was drawn, for one of them reminded him of someone he had seen quite recently, though for the life of him he could not recall who it was. It was just at that moment that there came a knock at the door and going to answer it he found Kasper standing in the entrance.

'Oh, what a ghastly woman,' said the doctor. 'I thought you acted quite nobly in getting rid of her.'

'Come in, come in,' Nick answered. 'I want you to look at something.' And he pointed out the picture which was still on the computer. 'Does it remind you of anyone?' he said.

'Yes, it does. Now who on earth is it?'

They both stared at it and then they turned to one another. 'It's . . .' started Nick.

But he got no further because at that moment a thunderous and repetitive knocking started at the front door.

'It's going to be one of those nights,' said the vicar, and went to answer it, leaving Kasper staring at the computer screen.

# TWENTY-THREE

L ate in the evening as it was, Tennant and Potter decided
to leave Lewes and head back for Lakehurst. The mobile
unit had faxed through a copy of Roseanna's statement
and that was enough to make them return.

Tennant felt terribly disappointed. He really thought they
had got their man at last; the fact of the late train home, the
protective clothing and the bicycle kept at the station had
really proved it to him. Yet now had come this wifely confes-
sion, that she knew all about his little love nest with yet
another young actress waiting there, that had blown the whole
theory out of the water.

'Could be a trick, sir. It won't be the first time a wife's
done that to protect her husband – and it won't be the last.'

'We must go and see the girl right away. Her name's Titania
Grove, by the way.'

'That surely was made up for the stage,' Potter exclaimed.
'Can you see an officer worker going round with a moniker
like that?'

'Anything's possible,' said Tennant. 'I once knew a girl
named Petal.'

They drove along in silence after that, Tennant wishing
that the tests carried out on the many bicycles he had delivered to the laboratory had come up with something. But the
most that any of them had provided were one or two items
of sweaty hands on the handlebars, scrapes of mud, a torn
piece of trouser leg, a sordid scrap of chewing gum. All this
from the commuters to London. The most hopeful was a
smear of white that looked like the deposit made by protective suiting. But this, strange to tell, had come from the
bicycle ridden by Jack Boggis which was so rusty that the
laboratory came out with the story that it hadn't been ridden
for five years at least, though admittedly there were traces
of new oil on it. The fibres clinging to Culpepper's other
cycle had turned out to be from a pair of white dungarees.

So, truth to tell, there had been no tangible clues other than for the warnings left by the murderer, which had been gone over with a fine tooth comb, revealing only the fact that he must have worn gloves when he wrote them. And Tennant had had nearly four weeks working on the case. Small wonder that he was determined to resign from it at the end of this one. With a mighty effort he put such negative thoughts from him and asked Potter, 'Do you think it is too late to call on Mrs Culpepper?'

His sergeant looked at his watch. 'It's ten o'clock, sir. I think perhaps we ought to make it tomorrow morning.'

'What about Titania? Her address was given on the fax.'

'Yes, let's do her. Showbiz people never go to bed early.'

'Except when their boyfriends are coming,' Tennant answered, and gave a hollow laugh.

She lived in Buckfield, another village about the size of Lakehurst, but with a far more imposing High Street of ancient houses all crowded together, and a truly grand Georgian mansion standing on its own, a short distance away from them.

'What number is it?'

'Fifty-eight, High Street.'

'Blimey! It looks good from the outside.'

'I think,' said Potter, peering at the door, 'that it is divided into flats.'

There were three bells and as Roseanna had either forgotten or not known whether it was A, B, or C, Potter was in something of a quandary.

'Aren't there any names?' asked Tennant.

Potter shone a torch. 'Yes, but there's no Grove.'

'Try 'em all,' said Tennant, a note of exasperation in his voice.

There was no answer from A and from B came a voice with an old Etonian accent. 'Hello.'

'Hello and good evening,' said Potter in exaggerated American tones. 'We are looking for a Miss Titania Grove. Would she be at your number by any chance?'

'No, try C. And kindly don't ring my bell after ten.'

'We'll ring it at midnight if necessary, sonny. Cos we're the cops, see.'

'Potter, have you gone completely off your head? He could report us.'

'Sorry, sir. But we could always say it was youths mucking about.' He tried ringing C and this time a beautifully modulated voice said, 'Yes?'

'Miss Titania Grove?'

'Yes. Who is it?'

'Sergeant Potter and DI Tennant from the Sussex Police.'

There was a sharp intake of breath and then the voice said, 'Come up,' and a buzzer pressed and the front door opened.

Despite this modern entrance the house was truly ancient. A winding circular staircase with doors leading off it would prove a challenge to all but the fittest, thought Tennant, as he puffed his way up to what would once have been the attic. The door was already open and a slight figure wearing pyjamas and a silken dressing gown, stood there.

'Come in,' she said breathlessly. 'Has there been an accident?'

The men walked into a gorgeous little flat, complete with sloping ceilings, which she had decorated with theatrical posters, which gave it a cosy and welcoming air.

The three of them stood looking at one another. Tennant thought she was just like her name, a fairy creature, utterly petite and feminine, with a divine little smile. Titania found him extremely attractive, instantly drawn to his green eyes and rather longish hair. Potter she passed over as being like a million and one other men that she knew.

'In answer to your question,' Tennant said quietly, 'I have to inform you that Richard Culpepper has been placed under arrest and is currently in Lewes.'

'Oh,' she said, and sat down rather abruptly, staring at a glass of wine which she had obviously poured out before their arrival. 'On what charge?'

'Murder,' answered Potter dramatically.

'That's not possible,' she said. 'Whatever gave you the idea that he could kill people?'

'May we sit down, please?' said Tennant, treating her gently. 'You see, his wife has provided us with an alibi for him. She says that sometimes he leaves the theatre, takes a late train home, then cycles to your flat and spends the night with you. Is this true?'

The round blue eyes turned in his direction. 'Yes, it is, perfectly. We met in a revival of Anouilh's *Ring Round the Moon*. Neither of us had very big parts so we spent a lot of time chatting and we fell in love. Truly, madly, deeply as they say. Anyway he told me all about Roseanna. How she had been a big star of the sixties and quite the most beautiful girl in the world and how he could never leave her. But that was OK with me. I didn't want to marry him, I just wanted to go to bed with him. He's awfully good at that, by the way. And if that sounds hard-hearted to you I think you'll find it is the coming thing. I personally think that marriage is going out of fashion.'

Tennant was so surprised that he burst out laughing and said, 'Well, you're wonderfully frank, Miss Grove.'

She laughed prettily and he suddenly saw that this was the image she had woven. She had been given the name Titania and she had by some miracle turned herself into a little fairy. But an extremely tough little fairy for all that.

'Would you like some wine?' she said. 'Or I have beer if you prefer?'

Potter refused, he was driving, but Tennant accepted and joined her in a glass of excellent Merlot.

'Tell me, how often did you see Culpepper?' he said.

'Oh, about twice a week. The rest of the time he felt obliged to stay and take his curtain. I just want to tell you that he is a truly sweet person and I know that he couldn't hurt a fly.'

Tennant wondered what it was about Culpepper that attracted the most beautiful women to him. Admittedly he had matinee idol looks – ageing slightly, but still there. And, of course, he was terrific in bed, according to this young woman. The inspector dourly wished he had the same pulling power.

He finished his wine and said, 'Would you be prepared to come to Lewes and make a statement regarding this?'

'Yes. If you'll give me a few minutes I'll go and get dressed and we can go straight away. I mean there's no time like the present, is there?'

While she was out of the room he said to Potter, 'There was nothing to stop Culpepper taking a third night off, was there. You must go to the theatre tomorrow and see the stage manager. They presumably have a log of when people miss the curtain call.'

'I don't know the answer to that, sir, but I can easily go and find out.'

'Please do.'

Titania came back into the room wearing a pair of shorts over bright emerald tights on the end of which were strappy shoes with six inch heels. On the top half she had a clinging white jumper cinched in by a black belt with gold studs. Now not looking quite so petite, Tennant supposed that even fairies must accept the latest fashions.

She got into the car with them and they drove to Lewes both men vastly entertained by her amusing chatter. Tennant slipped in a question or two.

'How old are you, Miss Grove?'

'Twenty-five. And Richard was twice that, but he was lovely. Besides, he might have been able to help my career along.'

'And what if he is the murderer?'

'Oh nonsense. He loves Roseanna and he loves me. What would he want to go and start murdering people for?'

As she entered the police station there was a kind of ripple of excitement. Nobody said anything but one could sense the change in atmosphere. Young constables stared, older ones looked urbane. From somewhere or other came the sound of a subdued wolf whistle. Tennant looked round but could not spot the miscreant.

They questioned her and took a written statement which she signed but there was no getting away from the fact that she swore Richard spent two or three nights a week with her. When she'd gone, driven back by an eager young officer who had a grin on his face like the proverbial Cheshire Cat, Tennant sat very quietly, then said, 'You think she's telling the truth, Potter?'

'I think we're going to have to prove it, sir. Ask the neighbours and so on. Get a few witnesses.'

'Undoubtedly. But with Roseanna backing up her story it's starting to look like a cast-iron alibi.'

'I know how you're feeling, sir. Believe me. If Richard Culpepper didn't do it – then who the hell did?'

'Yes, who?' asked Tennant, utterly miserable.

At that moment the phone went and Potter picked it up. His face changed.

'Hang on a minute,' he said. 'You'd better speak, sir. It's the Vicar. He says he's found something on the Internet which he thinks could be relevant. Apparently he's got the doctor with him and they've both seen the same thing.'

'What is it, do you know?'

'He says he'd rather not say over the phone. He wants you to see it in person.'

'Tell him we're on our way.'

Thinking that the police car must know the direction to Lakehurst almost without a driver, Tennant closed his eyes and snoozed gently letting his right-hand man take over. He felt that he couldn't exist without Potter, that the sensible young person who would have been far better off in business than in the police, for all that had qualities which made him absolutely indispensable. For a start he knew exactly how to deal with his boss, who had tendencies to be mercurial at times. Just as Tennant could achieve moments of brilliance – though not so many on this case – Potter got results by sheer plodding hard work.

As the car turned up the road, going past the Victorian houses where Dr Rudniski lived and had his surgery, Tennant sat up and started to concentrate. They pulled up on the other side of the road leading to the vicarage. It was now nearly midnight and the village was deserted, dark and very sinister. Potter knocked at the door and as he did so the security light came on, so bright that when the door opened they could not see who stood in the shadowy hallway beyond.

'Vicar?' said Tennant questioningly.

'Step inside, gentlemen,' replied the voice of Michael Mauser. 'The vicar is waiting for you within.'

# TWENTY-FOUR

Tennant stood staring for a moment then he brushed past Mauser, rather abruptly, and hastened into the vicarage's living room. The vicar and the doctor, who were sitting side-by-side in front of the computer, looked up at him in some surprise.

'Are you all right, sir?' asked Potter.

'Perfectly, thank you,' Nick answered. He let his gaze wander to Mauser and he added, 'Michael called on me unexpectedly and rather late.'

'The truth is,' said the German, 'that I had a desperate need to talk to someone about the relationship between my wife and myself so I rang Dr Rudniski's surgery but there was no reply. So I decided to call on the vicar instead.'

'Would you like to tell me about it?' asked Tennant.

'First,' said Kasper, 'I think you should take a look at this.' And he called the inspector over to the computer screen.

He and Potter stood staring in blank amazement the minute it was pointed out to them.

'What an idiot,' exclaimed Tennant, slapping his head with his hand. 'I've actually looked at this but never saw it.'

'It's very easy to miss,' Nick answered modestly.

'I don't know that I would have noticed it until it was shown to me,' Kasper added.

Tennant sat down and the vicar, without being asked, produced a drink and put it in the inspector's hand.

Potter asked. 'Do you want me to do anything about it tonight, sir?'

Tennant shook his head. 'No, it's too late. We'll go and ask questions in the morning. Being logical, this doesn't prove a thing though. But it's mighty suspicious.'

Mauser spoke. 'Do you know there is an ancient proverb which I believe in very much.'

'What is that?' said Kasper.

'It is, "The mills of God grind slowly but they grind

exceeding small." When I think of my father – who believed in Hitler as if the man were a god – how he was ground down until eventually he was no more. It has quite convinced me that evil comes back to those who perpetrate it.'

'So you think the key to these murders was revenge? That this –' Tennant waved at the computer – 'proves everything?'

Mauser shook his head. 'I think it was bloodlust on the part of a diseased mind. And, yes, this proves it to me.'

'I believe that is what the defence will plead,' said Potter practically.

'We've got to get the facts first,' Tennant answered gloomily.

'That shouldn't be too difficult now you know who to question.'

Tennant turned to Mauser. 'Changing the subject. Tell me about your late wife. I'd like to know.'

'Despite her outward appearance and despite her continual flirtatiousness, she had the kindness of a saint. We met in England after she came to care for my aged mother, who had senile dementia and was very difficult to cope with. I had taken a job as a translator you see – nobody questioned my origins – but it was very hard to look after her and work full time. So I took on an au pair. Then I fell in love with Cheryl and we married. All was well as long as I was able to satisfy her needs.' He sighed. 'Later on as I became older and less powerful – you understand me – she took lovers. Because she had need of them. I believe she was a nymphomaniac. But I forgave her because I loved her very much and understood. That is why I used to take those long walks alone, why I went away most weekends. To give her time and space for her own activities. But I do not want to devalue her goodness and kindness to me. I tell you all, gentlemen, she was a truly remarkable woman.'

Tennant thought of the giggling creature who had tried desperately to seduce him in The White Hart and found it almost impossible to equate the two sides of Cheryl Hamilton-Harty's personality. He said nothing. He was too wrapped up in the discovery that the vicar had made.

Potter spoke up, saying brightly, 'You obviously have a lot of grieving to do, sir.'

Which Tennant thought was kindness personified when

one considered that Potter's grandfather had been killed by a German in the Second World War.

There was silence for a moment or two broken by Michael Mauser.

'I suppose it would not be possible to lay a trap for this person and catch them in that way?'

'What do you mean?' said Tennant.

'Simply what I say. Even if you go round in the morning and ask questions, search the house, do whatever, there is still a strong possibility that you will find nothing. That the person concerned could flatly deny everything you say. That delays you, does it not?'

'What are you suggesting?' the inspector asked, interested despite himself.

'Lay a trap. I am perfectly willing to act as the bait. I will go with you to The Great House and make the sort of remarks that will draw the killer out. Then you can lie in waiting and pounce. It is a good idea, is it not?'

'It's worth a try, sir,' said Potter.

'Yes, I suppose you're right. It's not orthodox policing but it's worth a shot.'

Mauser looked round the room and just for a second Tennant had a glimpse of Michael's autocratic father, the Graf von Weisshausen, issuing orders to his Stormtroopers. But he put this thought on one side.

'When do you think we should do this?' he said.

'Why tomorrow, of course. I feel there is no time to waste.'

'And in that you are absolutely right.'

Next morning, under the pretext of organizing a village meeting to discuss the situation, Tennant booked the chapel in The Great House. It had once been a place for private prayer when the Elizabethan house had been occupied by a great family, the founder of which had worked in Lombard Street and gained a knighthood by so doing. But it had long since become a room for private parties and in this way the police had managed to lure certain people, who would not normally have attended a public house, into coming.

Tennant and Potter entered the room and ran their eyes over the assembled company. They saw that most people were present. Amongst others were Jack Boggis, Mavis Cox, Ivy Bagshot, Sonia Tate, Giles Fielding, looking very pale and with his throat bandaged up. Poor little Kylie sat next to the Reverend Nick Lawrence, while Dr Kasper Rudniski and the elegant Michael Mauser sat slightly apart from the rest. Roseanna Culpepper sat pointedly alone.

'Good morning, everyone, it was very good of you to attend at such short notice,' said Tennant.

'Why are we here?' demanded Jack Boggis. 'And why are you still here, that's what I want to know?'

Both Tennant and Potter ignored this but Michael Mauser, sounding very authoritarian, said, 'The police are doing an excellent job, I believe. Why, think, people; there has been no murder for several nights. The killer is obviously frightened out of their wits.'

Jack mumbled 'Nah-zee', à la Winston Churchill, but other than for that there was no comment.

Mrs Cox spoke up timidly. 'What I think Mr Boggis meant was have you charged the man you arrested?'

Roseanna went deadly still as Tennant answered, 'No.'

Ivy Bagshot put her oar in. 'Well, is there any likelihood of you doing so?'

Potter answered her. 'Not really, madam. It seems the man in question has an alibi for some of the killings but we are looking into that carefully.'

'Well, about time you did something bloody carefully.' Boggis again. 'It seems to me that your handling of this case has been a bloody shambles.'

Mauser spoke up again, looking down his long aristocratic nose at Jack as he did so. 'Well, I can't agree. What do the rest of you think? Miss Saunters, what is your opinion?'

'I think it's all 'orrible and I would like to leave this place tonight. And I would too,' she added defiantly, 'if it wasn't for our gran.'

Sonia Tate spoke up. 'Well, I agree with Mr Mauser.' She gave him a lingering smile. 'By the way, please accept my deepest sympathies on your sad loss.'

There was a buzz of agreement above which Boggis's voice rose with the single word, 'Condolences.'

'The reason why I called you all here,' said Tennant, 'is one that we have already touched on. Namely, that the man currently under arrest has not been charged until we have made further enquiries. So I warn you all to remain vigilant and be on your guard. We are far from certain that we have the right man.'

'Bloody palaver,' Boggis mouthed, going somewhat red in the face. 'Do you mean to say you ruined our morning just to tell us that?'

Once again Mauser spoke. 'As you are so upset, sir, allow me to buy you a drink.'

Boggis's face changed visibly. 'Don't mind if I do,' he said, looking decidedly more cheerful.

'Can I join you gentlemen?' Sonia Tate asked, her voice deep.

Mauser, who was in the act of standing up, rose to his full height and actually clicked his heels. 'The pleasure will be entirely mine, madam.'

'What a blooming smoothie,' Potter whispered to Tennant, who merely winked his eye by way of reply.

The rest went about their business just leaving Jack Boggis, Sonia Tate, Michael Mauser and Ivy Bagshot, who decided to stay for a brief sweet sherry. They were an ill-assorted quartet, made more embarrassing by the fact that Sonia Tate decided to make a pass – mild but for all that still a pass – at Mauser, whom she had hardly seen before.

'I do feel so sorry for you,' she said, all eyes. 'It must be terrible for you up there, all on your own.'

'I have accepted my neighbour Giles Fielding's invitation to stay with him. He was wounded, you know, by this killer but fortunately I saved him.'

'I heard about that. So it was you, was it, who rescued him? How very brave.'

'We must all be on our guard with such a dastardly murderer about.'

His rather quaint use of English made the others smile.

'I tell you,' said Boggis, gnashing his set, 'that if I caught the bugger I'd cut his bollocks off – begging your pardon, ladies – but that's what he deserves in my opinion. Will you have another sherry, Mrs Bagshot?'

'No, thank you,' she answered. 'I must be off. We've a WI meeting at two o'clock. Goodbye all.'

'I hope I didn't cause offence,' said Jack, as soon as the woman was out of earshot. 'Trouble with us Yorkshire folk is we don't mince our words.'

'That is obvious,' said Mauser.

'Happen,' said Jack, which clearly meant something to him.

They stayed talking generalities until Mauser finally glanced at his wristwatch.

'You must excuse me,' he said, rising and bowing. 'I promised Giles that I would meet him for lunch and I see that I am already ten minutes late. Farewell.'

'Not bad for a Nah-zee,' said Jack, when the door closed behind him.

'No, I think he's rather dishy.'

'Now, now, sweetheart. I hope you're not forgetting our little arrangement.'

'Quite honestly, Jack, I'm bored with it. You're such a fumbler. Do you mind if we call it a day?'

'Well, I like that! I've treated you to meals and all. I think you're heartless.'

She squeezed his hand. 'I'm so sorry, Jack. We've had some good times but now it's over.'

'Just because you fancy that bloody Jerry.'

But Sonia didn't answer. She stood up, kissed her finger and placed it on his lips, then left the pub in a whiff of perfume.

Darkness came quickly that November evening. The Lakehurst Bonfire Boys and Belles were due to march through the village shortly, joined by all the other local bonfire societies. But this year they had postponed the festivities on police advice. Besides that, many were fearful of strutting their stuff along the High Street with a killer lurking in some nearby alleyway. Regretfully they had reached a decision that unless the murderer were quickly caught there would be no bonfire celebrations this year.

As soon as they were under cover of night, Tennant began moving people about. First of all he placed a couple of plain clothes men in the homes of Michael and Giles, then took the two of them into the safety of the mobile unit. At the same time Potter escorted a woman into the custody of Nick

Lawrence and made sure that the vicarage was locked tight against marauders. Then he placed WPC Sally Castle – the one who had found Ceinwen Carruthers's body – inside the Culpepper's house and told her to wear plain clothes. He met up with Tennant again in the mobile HQ.

'All in place, sir.'

'Good, let's hope tonight sees some action. If not we're going to have to do the same thing all over again tomorrow and tomorrow . . .'

'And tomorrow, creeps in this petty pace from day to day,' answered Potter cheerfully.

'Shush. Don't go quoting the Scottish Play this night of all nights.'

'Very good, sir.' And Potter gave a smart salute.

'You're in a very good humour.'

'I feel we're drawing near and I'm panting like a greyhound in the slips.'

'Stop showing off your Shakespeare and get to work,' said Tennant, and gave his sergeant an affectionate cuff round the ear.

The Culpepper house was the very first of the Victorian houses that one came to, coming into the village from the north. Remote from the others, it stood at the end of a curving drive and was one of the few houses left in totally private ownership. Approaching it in the darkness of that cold night, Tennant wondered what Richard and Roseanna used all the space for. Standing hidden in the garden he counted at least four big rooms downstairs, plus a kitchen and a large conservatory leading off the drawing room. Upstairs there were another four rooms and up again, situated in the old servants quarters, were several more. Tennant wondered whether Roseanna had had these smaller rooms knocked into one to make a large studio, though with what purpose he had no idea, perhaps to give guests a living area to themselves. The whole place suggested enormous affluence to him and he thought that Roseanna must have made a mint in her heyday.

As he had instructed the blinds had been drawn in the conservatory but outlined against them was the shadow of a woman, sitting in one of the cane chairs and reading. There was the glow of a fire which had been switched on against the coldness of the night. It made a cosy picture and one could easily imagine the great actress, Garbo-face relaxed, beautiful eyes cast down as she immersed herself in a book. In the garden outside, Tennant shivered, and wished that he were the other side of the glass wall, sitting amongst the potted plants and having a drink with the woman within. He glanced at his watch and saw that it was shortly after nine o'clock. Well, he thought, at least it's not bloody raining.

Potter glanced at the clock on the wall of the mobile unit and saw that it was half past nine. His two guests, Michael Mauser and Giles Fielding, were sitting as comfortably as possible, conversing quietly over a cup of tea. Mauser, wisely, had brought a hip flask which he was offering to Giles, who took a deep swig.

'Thanks, me old mush.' He glanced at the sergeant. 'Any chance of sending out for some beer?'

'It's a bit awkward, Mr Fielding. I've only got uniform on duty. It'll cause quite a stir if one of them goes to the pub.'

'There's the offy, Sarg.'

'Same difference. Look, I tell you what. I'll go across myself but I've got to be quick. What is it you want?'

Mauser spoke up. 'I think the occasion calls for some good claret.' He fished in his pocket and produced a twenty pound note. 'Will this be enough?'

'More than. I'm afraid we haven't got much in the way of glasses but I'm sure you won't mind that.'

'I'll drink out of a bucket,' said Giles, and they all laughed.

'OK. I'll leave you in the capable hands of our desk sergeant. Won't be long.' And Potter ran across the road and into The Great House.

At ten o'clock Tennant was almost dying of the cold. In fact he was swinging his arms across his body to keep warm, when suddenly he stiffened. Scything through the air came the sound of a bicycle, quite distinctly. The inspector crouched low and listened, heard the cycle slow down and the rider dismount. Then he heard it being leant against the hedge as someone, walking very lightly, came in through the open gates and began to approach the house.

Potter was served quickly as there were few people in the pub that evening. Crossing the road with the bottle of claret clutched firmly in his hand he made his way back into the unit. Looking round he saw that Giles was in deep discussion with the desk sergeant but that of Michael Mauser there was no sign.

'Where's Mr Mauser?' he asked abruptly.

'Popped out to get a breath of air, sir. You must have passed him.'

'No, I didn't see him. How long ago was this?'

'About five minutes.'

Potter sped outside, plonking the wine down before he did so. The High Street was deserted and still except for one or two solitary figures making their way home.

'Christ almighty!' the sergeant exclaimed. 'Where the hell has he gone?'

Like one in a trance Tennant watched silently as a figure dressed in white protective clothing made its way across the front lawn and round the conservatory. He knew that on the far side of the glasshouse was a door leading into the back garden, a door which had been deliberately left unlocked. He watched, almost spellbound, as he saw the shadow of the seated figure rise and turn to the doorway. Only then was he released from his catalepsy and he sprinted forward towards the conservatory.

Potter stood uncertainly, swaying from foot to foot. He knew that he should not have allowed Mauser to slip through the net but he had given into their request for something stronger to drink and like a fool he had been tricked. He raced up the steps and into the mobile unit. He looked accusingly at Giles.

'Were you part of the plot?' he barked.

The man stared at him open-mouthed. 'What plot?' he said, his Sussex accent never more pronounced.

Potter dashed out again and started to run, full pelt, down the High Street.

From inside the glasshouse there came a loud scream just as Tennant threw open the door. The white-clad figure stood over Sally who had been knocked back into the chair and was fighting tooth-and-nail as she was slowly being strangled with a piece of cord. Tennant gave a huge leap across the space but even as he did so a shot rang out and he froze as the figure clutched its chest where a huge red patch was forming, stark and obscene against the whiteness of its clothing.

He turned back towards the door and saw there the tall and grand figure of Michael Mauser, who smiled at him.

'*Auf Wiedersehen*,' he said, and raised the gun to his head.

Potter had never run so fast in his life and panting for breath arrived at the door of the conservatory.

He saw the policewoman, gasping almost as much as he was, dragging the air back into her lungs. He saw Tennant, holding the dying Michael Mauser in his arms. He saw the dead body of someone clad in white lying on the floor. He steadied his breathing and knelt down beside it, removing the mask that covered the lower part of the face. Then he looked at Tennant.

There was silence in the conservatory and there was death in the conservatory, and the silence remained unbroken until policemen rushed in from every angle.

It was only then that Potter said to Tennant, 'It's Sonia Tate, sir.'

And Tennant answered, 'Amen.'

# TWENTY-FIVE

Why hadn't Roseanna recognized her, that was the question that burned in Tennant's brain as he mulled over the problem now that it was all over and the village had settled back to normal. He had asked her, of course, but she had looked at him with her great magnificent eyes and given him such an enigmatic smile that he had felt he should not press the point too hard. Richard, on the other hand, released from prison, was playing the part of the great man, rising superbly over the scurrilous barbs of the inferior police force who had brought an entirely false case against him. Titania, much to Tennant's amusement, had dumped him and taken up with the young policeman who had driven her home on that fateful night.

Tennant switched his computer on and again pulled up the images of the beautiful Rose Indigo letting his eyes linger on them for perhaps one of the final times. Eventually he came to the still from *Jekyll and Hyde*. There they all were: the English child actor, Richard Culpepper; the young attractive James Pitman; the glorious Rose Indigo; and that skulking figure in the background, Jane Glynde, also known as Sonia Tate.

The inspector stared closely. It was her alright, despite the ravages of time and the work of a great number of plastic surgeons, to say nothing of the change of hair colour. For Sonia had been a blonde in the still photograph, but as he had known her she had had raven black locks, obviously dyed and hard against her natural pallor.

Tennant thought about the drastic changes in the late Michael Jackson's looks and could accept that to someone whose eyes might be failing the matter of recognition could be hard.

He typed the words Jane Glynde into his computer and up came a smallish entry in Wikipedia.

'Susan Jane Cox (Jane Glynde) was born October 8, 1941,

at Brixton, in those days a poor quarter of London. Her father was the Rev. Horace Cox, a strict Baptist minister, and her mother Mildred (neé Harris). Susan, as the only child, was left alone a great deal and was allowed no books except The Bible and *The Pilgrim's Progress*. It is said that she grew up quoting passages from The Bible at length. However, she eventually rebelled against this and ran away from home at the age of fifteen, attaching herself to a concert party performing on the pier at Clacton-on-Sea. She later became an actress and played various small parts in films both in Hollywood and England. Jane Glynde married three times:

1) James Crichton
2) James Pitman
3) Roger Tate

All three marriages ended in divorce. There was no issue of any of the marriages.'

And that was it. A life banished in a few miserable words.

Tennant turned the computer off and sat deep in thought. So his hunch had been right all along. It hadn't been a religious maniac who left those terrible messages in the rooms of death, but rather a woman who at one time had been able to quote the Ten Commandments just as another child would lisp nursery rhymes.

But when, he wondered, had her obsession with Roseanna Culpepper started? Probably then, way back when they had first appeared in films together. One had been incomparably beautiful and had the magic carpet of success rolled out before her, the other had been less lovely and less lucky. Had Sonia started stalking Roseanna when she had married Roseanna's first husband, James Crichton? Had the obsession grown stronger when she thought she had achieved everything with her marriage to James Pitman, the big star, attractive, commanding any salary – and an alcoholic? Had the shattering of that illusion caused her to become slightly mad in her hatred of the great and successful Roseanna Culpepper.

Tennant knew that he would never find the answer to these questions but one answer had appeared. Sonia's third marriage had produced some rather strange evidence. Roger Tate, a civil servant, had lived in Jarvis Brook, a village quite close to Lakehurst. Had it been then that Sonia had discovered the whereabouts of the woman of whom she had always been pathologically jealous? Had she lost her over the years and then, by a miracle, located her once more?

Or had she been criminally insane right from the start? It certainly seemed that way when one considered the number of her victims. Michael Mauser's words came back again. Bloodlust of a diseased mind. It appeared to Dominic Tennant that Sonia had actually enjoyed the double life she led. Did she, like Dr Shipman, enjoy watching people actually die, or were these earlier vicims merely a lead up to her revenge on Roseanna Culpepper? Whatever, she was, without doubt, a cold-hearted and cruel character whose death at the hands of the Nazi's son had been a strange quirk of fate indeed.

Sunday morning service had been truly joyful. The congregation was large and had sung lustily, the notes of the organ had never sounded merrier, the peal of bells inviting people to church had rung out over Lakehurst with a chime that announced new hope. Best of all, or so it had seemed to Nick Lawrence, Olivia Beauchamp had sat in the front pew and there had been eye contact and smiling. And, to crown it all, Dominic Tennant had arrived somewhat late and panted his way in to a place at the back.

Afterwards it had taken nearly half an hour to greet the congregation and wish them a Happy Christmas. Waiting at the end of the queue and talking to one another with a great deal of animation and friendliness had been Olivia and Tennant. Nick felt a pang of something like jealousy but dismissed such emotion as unchristian and unsuitable for the time of year.

'Do come to The Great House,' said Olivia, who looked absolutely gorgeous in a purple beret with a sprig of holly adorning it.

'You must,' said Tennant. 'I've come to say goodbye to you all, quite informally of course.' So as soon as Nick had divested himself of his robes and told the choir, still conducted by a very subdued Mr Bridger but lacking Broderick Crawford these days, that he would see them at midnight mass on Christmas Eve, he made his way out by the vestry door. Behind him stood the ancient church and the rolling graveyard, as nice a place to be buried in as any he could think of, and stepping down the path and into the historic street he considered how lucky he had been to have been awarded the parish of Lakehurst.

He pushed his way through the crowd packing the pub being greeted by people, all with jolly faces, and Nick thought that a curse had been lifted from the village which at one time had seemed like the village of the damned.

He reached the table at which were seated Kasper, drinking a large vodka, his eyes sparkling, looking tremendously handsome, together with Olivia and Tennant. Giles Fielding, still wearing a scarf round his neck, had a sprig of mistletoe and was happily greeting the many young ladies who came to him for a Christmas greeting. He waved cheerfully at Nick.

'Hello, Vicar. How goes it?'

'Well, thank you, Giles. What about you?'

'I'm feeling much better. By the way did you know that Mickey Mouse's place is being taken over by Cheryl's cousin? Apparently she was found by those Heir Hunter people. Once all the legal do-da is out of the way she stands to inherit the lot.'

'Will she continue to run the business?'

'I believe she will. Good ending, isn't it?'

'It most certainly is.'

Giles lowered his voice. 'I still hear him about the place, you know.'

'Who?'

'Michael Mauser. In the early mornings when I am out with my sheep I hear someone walking along, distinct as anything, but there's nobody there when I go and look.'

'Do you miss him?'

'I miss him like hell.'

'So do I. Well, Happy Christmas.'

'And to you, Vicar.'

Nick joined his friends, knowing with a cynical smile, that all three of them fancied Olivia. All quite hopelessly, he reckoned.

'Well, Inspector, were you happy with the result?' he asked.

'Happy is not quite the right word. I particularly regretted Michael Mauser's suicide.'

Kasper spoke. 'He only had a few months to live, Inspector.

And he would have received heavy doses of morphia towards the end. Perhaps he considered it the best way out.'

Giles addressed them from his place on the bar stool. 'He shot Sonia Tate in revenge for the murder of Cheryl, let's make no mistake about it. He really loved that woman.'

'I think this conversation is getting morbid,' said Olivia, 'so I suggest we change it. What are you doing for Christmas, Kasper?'

'I am going back to Poland. I give my last surgery tomorrow then I have a week's holiday. And you, my dear?'

'I'm going to Winchester to be with my sister and her family. And you, Nick?'

'My widowed father is coming with his new lady friend, plus my brother and his entire family. It's going to be full house at the vicarage. What about you, Giles?'

'My brother's coming over for a drink or two. Should be a laugh.'

The vicar turned to Dominic. 'And what about you, Inspector Tennant?'

'I think,' the inspector answered, putting his hands behind his head and stretching his long legs out in front of him, 'that I'll just take it easy.'